Blending In: A Tale of Homegrown Terrorism

Norman Brewer

Published by Norman Brewer, 2017.

First Edition, June 15, 2017

Cover design by Ann Youm Oh

To Saul,
Best wishes
and good reading.
Norman Brown

Forthevictims

Chapter 1

Without warning the rocket-propelled grenade fell just short of the press conference getting underway near the gates of the Russian Embassy. Shrapnel ripped into the shoulder-to-shoulder reporters and cameramen and on to the two men standing at the podium. Cries rang out and shredded bodies flew. Russia's ambassador was killed instantly. The U.S. secretary of state went down with multiple wounds.

On the opposite side of 2650 Wisconsin Avenue, N.W., a wiry man in a tan trench coat had just limped down a side street, away from the heavy black gates, when the RPG struck. "Damn, I said 'Not a go!'" the spotter screamed into his phone. He quickly composed himself, taking in what he could see through the dust and debris. "Okay, one notch up. One notch left."

After the briefest pause, a zip-like flight and instantaneous explosion again pierced the air as a second grenade hit the diplomats and media. "Dead on. Fire again," ordered the spotter. Behind him, he heard a man shouting in his ear. "You son-of-a-bitch, you are part of this."

The spotter saw the third explosion, erupting through the expanding cloud of dust. "You're good. Get out of there." He turned to face the wizened man who had been approaching when he told his shooter, "Not a go."

Suddenly the old man, spittle flying in his excitement, attacked with his cane. "I'm a vet and I know when someone's calling in artillery!

Damn you! Damn you!" The spotter raised his arms to ward off the wild blows, uncertain how best to counter his feeble assailant.

The threat turned real when a Metropolitan Washington police cruiser careened onto Wisconsin just a block away. The old man kept screaming, "He did this! He did this!" as the officer spun from his car, reaching for his handgun.

The spotter's Glock was already out of his coat pocket. He coldly leveled it, firing two shots into the officer's face. With his left hand he grabbed the old man's belt buckle, pulled him forward and shoved hard, shooting him twice in the chest as he stumbled backward into shrubbery.

Walking north on Wisconsin, the spotter felt lucky that the old man hadn't knocked off his wide-brimmed fedora or the false gray beard and sunglasses protecting him from the embassy's prying security cameras. As uniformed guards stumbled from the carnage, frantically trying to spot the assailant, he broke into a brisk walk, forgetting his limp.

Alarmed residents streamed from their homes, onto the sidewalks and into the street. The spotter was willingly swallowed by the rapidly forming crowd. As approaching sirens wailed from all directions, what had been a quiet rush hour in upper Georgetown dissolved into confusion. People scurried about in search of answers, wandering into the street and further clogging traffic. Angry drivers swore, some trying to reverse direction. Police struggled to set up a perimeter, finally halting Wisconsin traffic north and south of the embassy gates. But no way could first responders control the frantic pedestrians.

The spotter easily worked his way across the intersection at Massachusetts Avenue, beyond the law's immediate reach, and walked north up Wisconsin past Washington National Cathedral. It was the highest point in the city, with the central Gloria in Excelsis tower soaring nearly three hundred feet above street level. Millions of people from around the world have sought solace and peace within its gently lit cross-shaped nave. Now the iconic landmark had an infamous chapter.

The spotter's flight nearly paralleled that of another man walking north on Thirty-eighth Street, away from the cathedral. He had a purposeful stride. Blocky but lean, he wore sunglasses and a baseball cap pulled low on his forehead. Though the winter day was chilly, he could feel a light sweat beneath his workman's clothes, perhaps from exertion, perhaps from stress. Approaching a non-descript sedan, he hit a button on his key fob, pulled a distinctive backpack from his shoulders and dropped it in the trunk.

As the spotter crossed Woodley Road a dumpster caught his eye. He resisted an urge to toss his Glock, taking a calculated risk should he be stopped. But he knew every dumpster, grate and crevice in the area was sure to be searched. He wanted to dispose of the gun and his silly but effective disguise. But properly, far from Washington. Besides, should something go horribly wrong, the gun would enable him to wreak further mayhem – or to deny authorities a live suspect. He walked on.

The gunner turned left on Macomb and, as planned, stopped the sedan just before Wisconsin. He had to double park. In short order, he saw a car approaching in his rearview mirror and knew he would be expected to drive on. But as he put the car in gear he saw the spotter, walking briskly. Within seconds they blended into traffic fleeing the chaos of the attack.

Six thousand miles away a man of mixed Asian descent stood in a Kapakahi Air ticket line at Hana Airport in Maui. He carried a small backpack and a well-traveled black suitcase with a yellow name tag. Reaching the counter he placed the suitcase on the scale. Twenty-four pounds, well over the limit for free checking. He handed cash to the uniformed ticket clerk, then stood on the scale. With his backpack, one hundred fifty-eight pounds. The clerk dutifully noted the weight, helpful for assigning the nine passenger seats in the small plane. The man went to the waiting area, the last to check in. Outside, another airline employee loaded bags into the belly of the small turbo-prop. The black bag with the yellow name tag went in third. The mixed Asian glanced at his watch as he settled into his seat. They would be leaving Maui a few minutes late.

Across the island at Kapalua Airport a skinny weathered man of about fifty had to pay the baggage fee, too. His flight was to depart shortly before six that evening, a few minutes ahead of the one from Hana. He was assigned the oversized seat at the back of the plane, which also carried a full passenger load. As the pilot went through his checklist, the bored co-pilot dutifully chanted passenger safety instructions. Reminded that cell phones must be turned off, the skinny man reached in a pants pocket, opened an old flip-style phone and pressed "end." The phone chimed and the man dropped it in his shirt pocket. On time, they ascended into a beautiful sky just as dusk began to dapple the horizon.

Ten minutes into the flight the skinny man was fidgety. Drawing the back row was a plus, to not be so obvious to other passengers, he thought. The armpits of his shirt were wet and a line of perspiration ran across the two-day growth above his lip. He glanced at his watch again and pulled his cell phone from his pocket. Out the starboard window he could see, perhaps a couple of miles away, another small plane. Wonder if that's my friend from Hana? Looking at his watch again, he moved his thumb to the phone's "8" button. He was watching the other plane when it suddenly became a bright orange flash that rained toward the Pacific in pieces – or bodies. The skinny man clenched his teeth, tightly shut his eyes and pressed "8."

... We now take you to Kahului Airport on Maui for this exclusive report from Rick Tweed...

Thanks, Mike. Two Kapakahi Air commuter planes suddenly disappeared from radar as they flew over the Pailolo Channel this evening. Each plane was fully loaded with nine passengers and pilot and co-pilot. All are feared dead, and the planes' disappearance is increasingly taking on ominous overtones. The passenger manifests have not been released. Kapakahi Air has not identified the pilots or co-pilots.

Dusk was approaching as the Honolulu-bound planes took off, one from Hana and the other from Kapalua. Just minutes ago I talked with a Kahului Airport official who has been in contact with investigators. He refused to be identified but said a sailor told investigators he saw two explosions over the channel about the time the planes disappeared from radar. The explosions appeared to be a few thousand feet high, probably a mile or so apart and nearly simultaneous, the sailor reportedly told the Coast Guard. The airport official also said the Coast Guard has found debris in two areas that are near where radar contact was lost. He said there has been no mention of bodies being recovered.

Local investigators have been joined by federal officials, including the Department of Homeland Security. So far there is no evidence that I know of that terrorism is involved. However, that is an unspoken concern, as my source at the airport acknowledged. That concern is heightened because the Transportation Security Administration does not screen passengers or bags for commuter flights from Hana or Kapalua. As you'll recall, Mike, that was a point of controversy in 2002 when security at Hawaii's airports was rolled out in the wake of 9/11. And finally, you have to wonder about the timing of this tragedy coming the day after that unbelievable attack on the Russian Embassy in Washington, D.C. Back to you, Mike.

Chapter 2

Reaction to the attack on the Embassy of the Russian Federation to the United States of America swiftly ran from shock and disbelief to fear and outrage. Wild speculation flew over whether the attack was against one or both of the countries or had been prompted by the event itself.

The press conference had been called to announce a surprising breakthrough in negotiations on extending the New START nuclear treaty of 2011. The treaty called for the U.S. and Russia to have no more than 1,550 strategic weapons deployed in February 2018 and also carried a ten-year deadline for extending the treaty. U.S. and Russian negotiators had reached agreement on the extension. As smoke from the disaster cleared, rumors quickly swirled about one country or the other changing course and being willing to go to horrendous lengths to derail the agreement.

With the first explosion, nearby Russian security and U.S. Secret Service officers had rushed to protect the principals. The second explosion was spot-on, leaving few survivors in the immediate area. A couple of would-be protectors quickly jumped into armored cars and vans parked nearby, driving them into what they perceived as the line of fire. That move, along with more security officers and aides bravely wading into the carnage, further drove up casualties when the third RPG struck.

A tense quiet, broken by the anguished cries of the maimed, followed the explosions. Those few still standing braced for yet another assault, one that didn't come. Survivors cautiously began providing succor to the injured. Embassy personnel quickly joined them. Medical teams began arriving. Even as medical helicopters and ambulances started transporting the most critically wounded to nearby hospitals, SWAT teams were deployed randomly in search of the unknown assailants. Metropolitan police left their beats to help.

The dead were taken into the embassy grounds and laid in uneven rows, covered with sheets and coats, in part to conceal sometimes hideous wounds. The body count quickly rose to thirty-nine. Another twenty-two were wounded, six in critical condition. The secretary of state and three others would die.

In less than an hour a semblance of order was restored at the embassy. But outside, gridlock and confusion reigned. Perimeters set up to reroute traffic into the city created obstacles to drivers backtracking from the horrific scene.

Snarled traffic deepened as frightened motorists abandoned their vehicles. Fear was palpable, with heart attacks and strokes fueling the chaos. Many commuters, particularly those already downtown, suffered flashbacks of 9/11. Determined to get home, their outbound flight added to traffic woes. The rail system and airports were shut down in reaction to what clearly was the worst attack on the country since 9/11. But riders were still pouring into Metro stations as they tried to close, overflowing platforms. Several people were crushed to death or accidently pushed in front of arriving trains. When Metro cars stalled in dark tunnels, some riders tried to walk out and perished on the electrified rail. Though the embassy was miles away, many downtown streets quickly became parking lots. Bridges across the Potomac River were clogged, first with vehicles, then with walkers. Sporadic looting broke out, as did isolated cases of muggings. Despite the magnitude of the chaos, it didn't rise to the level of 9/11, and officials didn't find it necessary to call in the military. Most businesses and public buildings closed and, gradually, downtown D.C. and the area near the Russian Embassy emptied. An eerie tension prevailed.

In a typical stroke of luck, President Jonathan T. Tower decided at the last minute not to make an unannounced appearance at the embassy press conference. It was luck both unfortunate and timely. Unfortunate because the sudden need to talk with his French counterpart was necessitated by yet another terrorist attack in Paris. Timely because that news reached the barely sworn in president and his national security advisor as they were making final edits to a speech on national security.

President Tower's maiden speech to Congress would allow him to repackage campaign themes as presidential priorities. It would drive home the need to tighten borders and immigration policies to keep the bad guys out. The speech barely touched on the New START treaty. After all, the extension was the work of his predecessor. And, before being sworn in, President Tower had suggested being open to expanding the U.S. nuclear arsenal and that an arms race might not be so bad, because the U.S. would win it.

Now, comfortable at his desk in the Oval Office, the president felt the need for information. "Mikey," he solemnly told his national security advisor, "when I go to the Hill next week I want to know the foreign country those embassy attackers came from and I want to know how they got in."

"Right now, I can't tell you where they came from or that it was even a foreign country."

After a long pause, President Tower said, "I'm not sure you are hearing me. And Mikey, what does New START stand for?"

Chapter 3

The gunner and the spotter made their way north and west, avoiding major thoroughfares in favor of streets and lesser traveled highways. Those roads were familiar, traveled many times for work and to prepare for this day. Given everything suddenly facing law enforcement, the men weren't overly concerned about encountering checkpoints. Highway 28 wound them into the Maryland countryside, beyond Point of Rocks to the rural acreage where Chancy Maple and Darrell Stickman had lived for years.

They were homegrown terrorists, deeply committed to waging their own private war on the United States. Several things set them apart from many other radical jihadists: One was patience. Another, that they did not wear their extremist views in public. Combined, those qualities enabled them to hone their terrorist skills without attracting the attention of neighbors, workmates or law enforcement. That anonymity, in turn, had helped them tackle riskier and riskier targets. Also, Stickman and Maple were not suicidal, weighing risk against the value of living to attack yet again. It was not lost on them that suicidal jihad usually was carried out by the young on orders from the old. Much the same was true for war not carried out in the name of religion, with politicians and generals framing the noble causes that sent the young to early graves.

Stickman, the spotter at the Russian Embassy, was by training a creative tech guy, a product of Silicon Valley. All things being equal he could have developed as a top-flight computer programmer or industry executive. As things were, he had no trouble finding well-paid jobs with computer firms that often contracted with the government. Maple was blue-collar, with a knack for quickly grasping how things work. He was proficient as electrician, plumber, mechanic, heavy equipment operator and more. He grew up in the Midwest, primarily the Detroit area. Both came from families rooted in the U.S. for generations, hybrid Caucasians of Western European descent. If pulled aside for additional screening by the TSA, racial profiling would not be an issue.

As children, they were introduced to their parents' respective Christian religions. But as Maple made the transition from child to teen, he questioned and then refused the leap of faith necessary to accept the Lutheran doctrine of the Trinity. With that gone, following his parents' faith became hollow. Stickman's fall from the Catholic Church was more dramatic, spurred by a priest's clumsy attempts to seduce him. Failing to engage the social issues of the day – particularly sex and drugs – the religious institutions of their youth became stunningly irrelevant.

As that irrelevance was dawning on Maple, his father, who owned a small dry cleaning chain, ran afoul of the Internal Revenue Service. He could not pay the several thousand dollars the IRS insisted was owed. Neither could he afford an effective attorney. Those he hired charged large up-front fees and then, it seemed to Maple, buckled to IRS pressure. The business was lost and Maple's father had to settle for jobs little better than minimum wage. Maple's college plans faded. He enrolled in a vocational school that, in truth, best fit his skills. But he had soured on the government.

Stickman had his own anti-government testimonial, one he fiercely believed but could not prove. It involved a beloved uncle, only a decade older, whose goal was career Army. As quartermaster of his unit he was held responsible when supplies went missing, later to be recovered on the black market. The uncle insisted he was the fall guy for his corrupt superior, a lieutenant. But the testimony of the black market thieves in exchange for leniency spelled jail time and the end of the uncle's career. Stickman could see only a rigged system, and perhaps he was right.

He also experienced a taste of how brutal authority could be. Driving home after a bachelor party, he was pulled over after a cop saw his car toying with the center line. A fun evening laced with too much alcohol had turned ugly. He never remembered what he said or did to royally piss off the L.A. cop. Maybe nothing. Maybe the cop's gout was inflamed. Maybe Stickman reminded him of his own ingrate son, again living at home. The cop swung his nightstick, maybe because he was simply mean. Stickman woke up in jail and, after repeatedly passing out, in a hospital. A fractured skull and severe concussion were diagnosed. He couldn't work for several months. A lawsuit went nowhere. The department's successful stonewall was infuriating, leaving Stickman with a smoldering anger.

While talented in different ways, both Maple and Stickman were uncommonly curious. Falling from their churches left voids and, if only because their respective circles of friends included Muslims, exposure to Islam sparked interest. For Maple, viewing the prophets of Islam as human, not divine, had appeal. The Islamic teaching that God is eternal – "He begetteth not, nor is He begotten," as found in the Quran – was as easy for him to accept as scientists' Big Bang explanation of creation. Stickman was attracted by the direct relationship Muslims have with God, one that removes the intermediary role of the clergy.

Both young men had grown up expecting to explore life's full range of pleasures. Maple was in his late teens, just sampling various rites of passage, and Stickman was scant years older when, independently, they were exposed to Islam. It was not the best time for a young man to adhere to tenants of a faith.

Add to that the attacks of 9/11. Maple and Stickman were as horrified as the rest of America, recoiling from the images of planes exploding into the Twin Towers. They were stunned as the death count neared three thousand fellow citizens. As it became evident that the terrorists were Muslim, they despaired. With rare exception, brothers in the mosques shared their feelings of betrayal.

But in their broader communities the reaction was starkly different. Friends fell silent and sullen. Suspicion hung in the air. They were no longer welcome in favorite haunts they had frequented for years. Former classmates quit seeking them out. They saw with dismay the hypocrisy of their parents' Christian churches, standing largely silent as bigotry and discrimination were heaped on Muslims. They, too, felt the sting of prejudice and hatred, not just from people they knew, but from some they didn't.

The worst involved Maple's older brother, who led by example as a committed elementary teacher in one of Detroit's inner-city schools. He was picking Maple up at the Muslim community center one evening when a motorist stopped at the end of the block. A man got out, raised a pistol and emptied a clip. In the spray of shots, Maple's beloved brother was killed. Investigators called the shooting a hate crime. The murderer was never caught.

Had they known each other then they would have agreed that the treatment of Muslims by fellow Americans was horrible and disappointing, nothing short of life-altering. Unjust blame, felt acutely, planted ominous seeds. As months passed, the anti-Muslim fallout of 9/11 persisted and remained deeply troubling. Perhaps overreacting, both Maple and Stickman came to view themselves as victims. Failed relationships and perceived slights were traced to bias against their fledgling religion.

The United States saw Afghanistan's Taliban government as a safe harbor for terrorists responsible for 9/11, for al-Qaeda and its leader, Osama bin Laden. When President George W. Bush declared war on the Taliban, a victorious outcome was of limited interest to Stickman, on the West Coast, or Maple, in the Upper Midwest. Later, they discovered, both had most closely followed reports of Afghan civilian casualties. The second war against Iraq spurred a similar reaction, plus growing distaste for a U.S. foreign policy that smacked of being a global bully. Stickman harkened back a decade, when he was soft and chubby and an easy target for bigger and stronger boys.

Seeking adventure and answers more than careers, they made their separate ways to Europe–Maple to London and Stickman to Brussels. Each found relative tolerance among the general populations. In both cities, they met Muslims who were already radicalized to greater or lesser extent. Their new friends encouraged the Americans to broaden their Islamic experiences, and paved their respective journeys to Afghanistan.

There, they met so-called collateral damage victims of U.S. airstrikes. They saw the physical destruction inflicted on villages believed to harbor al-Qaeda operatives. They befriended, and were befriended by, people who had little hunger for American-style democracy.

Maple and Stickman met at an al-Qaeda training camp, a remnant of the bin Laden organization that mostly had been driven into Pakistan by the U.S.-led war. They were struck by the similarities of their experiences, both in the U.S. and since venturing overseas. They found their personalities compatible – relatively quiet, willing to listen and learn from others, patient, committed to long-term goals. In conversations lasting deep into the night, they found compatibility, too, in what became hatred for their birth-home. Unlike many young men committed to Islam, they did not recoil from the permissiveness of America. That was, after all, the culture in which they grew up.

Rather, they were repulsed by the expansiveness of America, policies that imposed its will upon nations too weak to resist. Repulsed by the hypocrisy of America professing a commitment to self-determination while using its wealth to prop up corrupt regimes. While their government insisted its motives were altruistic, Stickman and Maple came to believe the underlying driver was greed. Cheap oil, cheap labor, cheap manufactured goods, cheap whatever was the motivation, depending on the country or continent. When not financial, they perceived the driving force to be gaining the political or strategic military advantage needed to impose the priorities of the world's only superpower. It really didn't matter whether a country supported or opposed Western values. The important thing was whether it would acquiesce to America's demands.

In the camp, the imam they most consulted fed a growing sense of purpose – pursuing jihad against the United States. Purpose, though, did not necessarily correlate with knowledge. Only vaguely did they appreciate that waging jihad was not restricted to war, that it also could reflect commitment to an inner struggle. Such teachings of Islam, which would have shaped a more benevolent approach to life, were of scant interest.

But exposure to the tools of terrorism became invaluable, the camp experience that shaped their priorities. Lessons in hand-to-hand combat were relished. They felt the power of firing an AK-47 in automatic mode, seeing its awful destructive capacity. They soaked up knowledge needed to wire and detonate C-4 and other explosives. Using a rocket launcher gave Maple, in particular, almost a sexual pleasure. Admittedly, that exposure was cursory. But they eagerly picked up the basics and left with a voracious appetite for mastering tools of destruction. Even more important was a growing confidence in their abilities to successfully wage violent jihad.

At the camp they prayed five times a day. But at night, in their private conversations, they confided to feeling little need to draw strength from prayer. Instead, prayer could be a casual, even infrequent, exercise, as it had been in the Christian faiths of their youth. Whispered talks revealed that, for them, many facets of Islam did not need to be seriously embraced. Neither felt a need to strictly observe Ramadan or to make the pilgrimages of true believers. While not heavy drinkers, neither cared to observe the ban on alcohol. The curiosity that propelled much of what they did faltered at the doorstep of religious dogma. Neither Stickman nor Maple steeped himself in Islam enough to know whether to practice as a Shia or a Sunni or one of the other Muslim doctrines. They settled on being non-denominational Muslims, sometimes drawing respite and strength but without the commitment typically seen in others. They were struck, pleasantly so, by how much they were in agreement. For them, Islam was a marriage of convenience. The self-radicalization borne of their experiences in America became crystalized by their experiences overseas. They did not fully understand or appreciate all the parts, but firmly grasped the bottom line, and it was radical jihad.

Chapter 4

Returning from Afghanistan, Maple and Stickman settled on the Washington area, with its multitude of high value targets, as their base. They were guarded in all they did, knowing the opportunity one of those targets would someday offer.

By design, Maple's construction jobs and Stickman's computer contracts usually lasted no more than a year, creating a natural break when they would move on. Very good at what they did, employers tried to persuade them to stay, but offers were declined with the explanation that money had been saved, travel planned. They used the Internet sparingly, totally avoiding Facebook and Twitter or any social media that could contribute to profiles. Except for basics, purchases were as rare and innocuous as possible and usually made with cash. They avoided getting to know neighbors beyond a wave or casual nod, and neighbors grew accustomed to barely seeing them.

Some suspected the reclusive men were gay, which wasn't true. But in keeping with their mission they were willing in large part to sacrifice relationships. Neither smoked or used drugs recreationally. They drank little and seldom ate out, frugal habits that helped finance travel. They avoided doing or saying anything suggesting even a passing interest in terrorist incidents that made the news. They made a conscious effort to never utter certain words, like jihad, or to let conversations carry them in certain directions, like the atrocities of the Islamic State. With two exceptions, they had no contact with other extremists. One exception was Stickman's small group of Muslim friends in California. After 9/11 the group moved to the state's rural north and surreptitiously committed extremist jihad, traveling around the country much like Maple and Stickman did. But there was a big difference in lifestyles. The Californians had families and, though living in the country, quietly put down roots in a nearby town. Stickman declined an invitation to join them, believing involvement with even a handful of families living in a remote area would exponentially increase chances of detection. He knew where to visit them, but seldom did. Although they had no clue where to find him, their mutual trust survived.

Mostly self-taught since the al-Qaeda training camp, Maple and Stickman were committed to polishing skills that could prove helpful. They enrolled in martial arts courses, though usually not together. Unless the instructor was unusually good, they seldom stayed for a second session. Articles on arms, munitions and survival techniques dominated their reading. They kept themselves in superb shape by running and using a gym set up in a spare bedroom of their rented house.

The terrorists were patient. In the years living near Point of Rocks they never carried out a mission locally. Reading The Washington Post and The New York Times helped them identify controversies in other parts of the U.S., mostly in urban areas large enough for them to blend in as tourists. They picked conflicts they could exploit, the goal being to make it appear those differences had turned violent. On some trips, a local antagonist died, often violently, sometimes mysteriously. Each time, Stickman and Maple learned valuable lessons about killing, with weapons ranging from knives to explosives. They learned how to dispose of weapons and other incriminating evidence, and honed their skills as stalkers and car thieves. They became expert at blending into a city's fabric and at avoiding law enforcement dragnets that sometimes popped up after an attack. They hardened, gaining a practiced calm and ability to improvise under pressure. Stickman had an eye for spotting opportunities to plant incriminating evidence that cast suspicion on unsuspecting antagonists. Twice, innocent people were arrested and convicted, adding to the terrorists' sense of accomplishment.

Their biggest success at entrapment came in Raleigh, where a well-regarded banker and a high-profile developer formed a partnership that soured. Stickman and Maple burglarized the elderly banker's house on a rainy evening, believing he was out. He was not, and suffered a heart attack when frightened by the intruders. While Stickman waited with the dead banker, Maple stole the developer's car, parking it near the banker's house. When the banker failed to come to work the next day, police found his body and, nearby, a promotional umbrella bearing the developer's company logo. His mechanic testified to having seen such an umbrella in the car's trunk. A jury found the developer responsible for the banker's heart attack and returned a manslaughter conviction.

Judging by press coverage, none of their crimes was labeled terrorism by authorities. Those crimes were, in fact, intended as terrorist acts, and there was frustration in not being able to publicly claim credit. But they had a long-term solution. They chronicled each mission as best they could, using time-dated video and still photography or tape recording their victims. Sometimes they got before and after shots of the crime scene. On a few missions they interviewed targets, either surreptitiously or while a victim begged for mercy. Neither of the terrorists much cared for torture, but they did mark and photograph some victims, knowing police would chronicle those same marks. Stickman and Maple stored records of their handiwork in a safe deposit box, intending to make it available to authorities – and the news media, if possible – at an appropriate time. Having grabbed the opportunity to shock the nation by attacking the Russian Embassy, that time could be fast approaching. But not, they had agreed, until they were apprehended or killed.

They made the drive from Washington National Cathedral in near silence, occasionally changing radio channels in search of new developments – or any hint of having left damaging evidence behind. As Maple turned into the driveway leading to a nondescript one-story frame house, Stickman snapped off the radio. WTOP, like all local media – and nationwide for that matter – was focused on the attack nonstop. The rising death toll now included confirmation that the secretary of state was dead.

"All in all, it went as well as I hoped," Stickman said.

"Better, except for that stupid man," answered Maple.

"I know. At least the geezer I shot may be blamed for killing the cop, for a while anyway."

"Next time I get to be the spotter. I saw damn near nothing except dust."

"It was beautifully horrible for sure. Worse than anything I saw in Afghanistan, by far."

"Good. Good."

Maple pressed the garage door opener and drove in. With the door shut, he removed the rocket launcher from the trunk, taking it in the house to a hall closet. Opening the door, he turned a clothes hook to the right and tugged. A large section of closet wall pulled away, revealing a chamber well-supplied with munitions. They stowed the rocket launcher and, for now, their handguns.

"We'll deal with the Glocks later. Let's crank up the TV and fix something to eat."

They soon learned of the five million dollar reward for information leading to the arrest and conviction of anyone responsible for the embassy attack.

Chapter 5

Chancy Maple sprawled on the living room sofa, body spent but mind replaying not just the day but events of the past several weeks. For years they had lived on what some might call the edge of terrorism, what others would simply label crime. Suddenly they commanded the nation's attention. They had successfully carried out a major act of domestic terrorism.

While watching television over lunch they had been nothing short of amazed by the public impact of their actions. To be so high profile and, at the same time, determined to remain anonymous was conflicting. What they saw as a straightforward attack against the hated government of the United States immediately took on complexities they had never considered. Sure, they knew generally what the press conference was about, but their target was not Russia. Within a few short hours the political ramifications had mushroomed, becoming equal to, perhaps greater than, the attack itself. Lacking answers, the questions were boundless. Was the target the U.S. or Russia? Was the motive terrorism or opposition to the treaty extension? How did the attack change the treaty, if at all? Will there be an impact on U.S. domestic policies, particularly immigration? What will be the impact on U.S.-Russia relations, long- and short-term? What are the broader international ramifications? And most cynically, did the U.S. or Russia mastermind the attack? The questions went on and on, as they can only in Washington.

Every politician and talking head had to weigh in, their comments and questions limited only by their imaginations. They were led, of course, by President Jonathan T. Tower. "Intelligence," he declared without specifics, has confirmed a link to a hostile Muslim country, which he did not name. With great solemnity he vowed to meet his foremost responsibility, protecting the United States and its citizens.

"You know," Stickman had said, "we have caused a lot more confusion and anxiety than I expected. That's a good thing." With that, he went to take a nap.

Maple had never seriously thought about how to handle the fallout of his actions, beyond knowing he must be ready to run. So just accept Stickman's view, that sowing confusion and anxiety is value added, he told himself. Nothing has really changed for me personally, not really. "All this political stuff is beyond my pay grade," he said aloud as he returned to marveling at what they had pulled off. They had picked a vulnerable high value target, gathered munitions, put together an effective attack and successful escape, and made plans for what might come.

He recalled their first decision: The nation's capital. There was no better target, not even New York. But where in the capital? They looked seriously at the White House and Capitol and had been discouraged by the heavy security. They thought about targeting a large crowd, like President Tower's inauguration. Again, security was formidable. Unless they could plant a bomb and wander off unnoticed, trying to flee hordes of people with an orgasmic commitment to his election invited being mob-stomped.

As they noodled options, it was Stickman who picked up on news stories about growing tension between the U.S. and Russia because of conflicts in the Ukraine and Syria. That made the Russian Embassy an appealing target. Not only would the U.S. be condemned, hostilities between the two nations could spin out of control.

The embassy compound on Wisconsin Avenue, N.W., with its high walls and heavy metal gates, was a fortress. That was obvious from what could be seen. What couldn't be was even more impressive, no doubt. But just up the street, sitting on high ground, was Washington National Cathedral. Launching an attack from there had potential.

After reviewing weapons, they settled on using a rocket-propelled grenade launcher. Internet maps put the distance from cathedral to embassy at about 700 yards, the edge of the RPG's effective range. But the cathedral's Gloria in Excelsis tower soars three hundred feet above the street, an elevation gain that easily put the embassy within reach. Taking the time to climb the stairs to fire from the tower was too risky and there was no public access to an elevator used by cathedral bell ringers. Access could be forced, of course. But using one of the public elevators in the west towers that serve the observation gallery was a better option. While giving up some height, that level still stretched the shoulder-fired RPG's range enough to target the embassy. Or so Maple and Stickman calculated.

At the al-Qaeda training camp, a sheik who had moved back to Afghanistan from New York had taken a liking to Stickman. Stickman confided their intention to wage violent jihad against the U.S., and their need for munitions. The sheik arranged for a source, identified only as "MR," to expect a call after Stickman returned to the states.

Contact was made. MR became Stickman and Maple's second exception to avoiding contact with other terrorists in the U.S. Over the next several years, Maple recalled Stickman picking up three shipments of Gen4 Glock pistols of various calibers, both Standard and Slimline, as well as semi-automatic AK-47 assault rifles. MR's prices were high, particularly for weapons discarded after being used only once in a crime. Stickman never met MR, following his firm order to come alone to the Hoboken, New Jersey area. There, Stickman was remotely directed through logistical gyrations intended to ensure security before finally meeting with underlings. It was a tedious way to do business. But it was better than buying online where sales information could be captured or from retail stores with their incriminating surveillance cameras.

Tedious or not, having a supplier to deliver a launcher and ample grenades was crucial. The Russian-made RPG-7, a portable model that had been around since the 1960s, was all they expected. But MR offered them the much newer RPG-7D3. It was equivalent to an earlier paratrooper model, which breaks into two parts that fit in a relatively inconspicuous designer backpack. Besides having sophisticated sighting features, the 7D3 could launch high explosive anti-tank warheads, making it far superior in killing power to the original RPG-7. All for a price, of course, which they could barely cover. MR supposedly was sympathetic to militant jihad against the U.S., but Maple was convinced that greed was his strongest motive.

Maple woke up with a start. Must have slept a couple of hours, he mused, noting the shadows in his living room had shifted. His nervous energy immediately returned and with it his recollection of the several visits he and Stickman made to the cathedral. They visited separately every few days, sometimes in disguise. They tried to note staff schedules and when tourists liked to visit, but found no predictable patterns. They talked of burglarizing the century-old building. But that could result in telltale signs of entry, leaving themselves vulnerable if still inside. Finally, they had to admit their reconnaissance was of little value, except for learning that cathedral security was light.

Attacking from the cathedral would require reacting swiftly to a promising opportunity at the embassy, which they could not control. That would put Maple, in particular, at more risk than ever before, prompting him to lightly weigh the proverbial promise of cavorting with scores of virgins. Oh, to be a true believer, he joked.

They could help themselves most by knowing about embassy events. To that end, American openness obliged. Maple recalled being impressed at how quickly Stickman hacked email accounts of reporters on international beats to find embassy press releases. When the press conference on the New START Treaty was announced, a reporter's hacked computer informed them the press conference would be at nine-thirty the next morning. If on time, Maple would be out of the cathedral before weekday tourists started arriving at ten. Instead of a general attack on the embassy to stir hostility between Russia and the U.S., they would target a real event, with real people.

Maple found himself sweating as he relived arriving at the lower level entrance to the administrative offices on the Episcopal cathedral's east side. "That stupid fool," he shouted to the room, then took a deep breath, willing his mind back to the morning.

He had parked his car a couple blocks north. He wore work slacks, a baseball cap, sunglasses and a padded denim jacket against the February cold. Besides the designer backpack, with a small canvas tarpaulin tied carefully to erase contours of its deadly contents, he carried a short aluminum ladder. He propped the ladder against a window sill near the door, as if being there to repair the aging casement window. Nervous, he waited for a cathedral employee to come down the sidewalk.

A small woman in her forties, walking with a slight limp, obliged. Maple glanced across the brownish lawn and only saw two men walking, half a block away. He waited until the woman was within two steps of the door before swinging off the ladder and to her side. "Don't scream," he said softly. "I have a gun and a knife."

Alarm filled her face but she was silent. Their eyes locked and Maple continued, making an effort to be very clear, "You are going to unlock the door and be my escort. You will act normal. Answer people if you need to. You can say you are showing me to my job. My gun has a silencer. One mistake and I will kill you and everyone else. Let's go."

She unlocked the door and they walked into a room divided into cubicles. Only four people were at their desks, engrossed in work. No one spoke.

"What's your name?" Maple asked as they entered a passageway leading to the lower level of the cathedral.

"Nadia."

"You're doing fine, Nadia. Just remember what I said."

They came to the long narrow gift shop where many tours end. Turning right, they started past racks and tables loaded with Washington and cathedral memorabilia.

A handful of employees were stocking mementoes and one stepped into the aisle. "Morning, Nadia. Slumming?"

"No, Doreen. The maintenance guys are out on the grounds somewhere. I drew the short straw for escorting this gentleman upstairs."

"No short straw, honey." Doreen gave Maple an appreciative look. "If you get lost, I can help."

Nadia managed an embarrassed smile. "We're fine, thanks."

Sliding past Doreen's ample form, Maple wondered fleetingly if cougars prowled the sixth largest Gothic cathedral in the world.

A flight of steps took them up to the nave, with its hundred-foot ceiling. Outside light gave brilliance to the magnificent Creation Rose and other stained glass windows, and gently massaged the Indiana limestone from the nearby main entrance to the High Altar at the far end. Though the sweep of the cathedral is a work of extraordinary architecture and art, Maple never gave it a glance.

A sign announcing "Out of Service" hung on an elevator door. Maple nodded toward the other elevator, the one he preferred anyway, serving the southwest tower and the Pilgrim Observation Gallery. Nadia pressed the call button and they waited. Finally, the elevator arrived.

"I want to stop at Level 6, Nadia."

"That's not open to the public. It's a maintenance floor."

"I know, but you're not the public."

"I don't have a key to stop on that floor. I work in our finance office."

Maple believed her, but pressed the button for six anyway. Nothing. "We'll ride to seven. You'll show me how to get back to six."

The elevator was old and slow. Maple flexed his shoulders against the pull of the backpack, though its destructive contents were quite light, the launcher weighing just fifteen pounds. Sweat ran down his backbone and he unzipped his jacket most of the way. He wondered what he would do if he couldn't get to the sixth floor. He had assumed too much about employee access throughout the building. He did know he would use the stairs going down. Cut the electricity and the elevator was a trap.

They arrived on seven. Without being told, Nadia led the way to a nearby door for employees only. She turned the handle. It was unlocked. Maple exhaled, followed her down one flight of stairs. "I want to go outside."

They walked into brilliant sunshine and arguably the city's most spectacular view. Knowing he had about fifteen minutes until the press conference, Maple stopped Nadia with a light touch to her shoulder. They were facing the Capitol on the far left. Pivoting right, down the Mall, were the Smithsonian castles, the low-lying White House, Washington, Jefferson and other monuments leading to Lincoln and then the high rises of Rosslyn across the Potomac River. Tiny rows of white headstones attested to the hallowed grounds of Arlington National Cemetery, with the Pentagon in the background.

The procession of landmarks punctuated the architecturally challenged buildings dominating Washington's downtown and, closer in, were winter browns and grays of trees mostly bare. The moment passed and Maple's sightline moved impatiently to Wisconsin Avenue.

He motioned for Nadia to walk toward the Gloria in Excelsis tower. On their right was a low parapet supported by identical though irregularly shaped vertical columns. They formed convenient openings for steadying the portable rocket launcher.

Maple glanced again to the southwest, toward his target, nudging Nadia forward to roughly the midpoint of the walkway. "Stop, and sit down against the wall." Seeing no masons or other workers in the cathedral's upper reaches, he pulled flexible cuffs from a jacket pocket and bound her wrists and ankles. He was mildly surprised that she offered no resistance, even when he gagged her. A leather dog leash looped around a column and snapped into her wrist cuffs kept her from going far.

Maple stepped away from her and, with binoculars, tracked the west side of Wisconsin, full of rush hour traffic, down the row of imposing apartment houses in their various shades of brown. He slowly swept past one with a vertical design, then more of the monotonous buildings until he came to an open space. That gap, he knew from reconnaissance outings, was the entrance to the Russian Embassy. The entrance was roughly rectangular but irregular, with gates set well back from the street. There was adequate space for a press conference. South of the entrance, which served pedestrians as well as motor vehicles, a tall, commanding brick wall paralleled Wisconsin to the end of the compound.

Maple could see activity at the entrance, but not make out distinct forms. A steady flashing light identified a parked emergency vehicle. In a sense he would be shooting blind, aiming just above traffic and just to the left of the last apartment building before the entrance. Aim too low and he would ruin a hapless motorist's commute, too high and the RPG would likely chew up the lawn or driveway of the compound, and little else. Aim too far right or left and the RPG would be largely absorbed by the corner of the apartment building or the wall. Scoring a direct hit suddenly posed a serious challenge. He had fired a rocket launcher only a handful of times. But just coming close would mean casualties and would panic the city, at the least, he told himself. This is going to happen.

Maple unslung the backpack, imagining he could see Nadia's eyes widen and fixate on him as he assembled the rocket launcher and its first deadly payload. He had just put in earplugs when his phone rang. It was Stickman.

"I'm across the street at the bus stop. How are you doing?"

"I just have to ...Have a little prep left but I'm fine."

"Okay. It looks like most everyone has shown up for work today."

"Good. You're breaking up a little."

"I'm going to move down Edmunds to look over some parked cars. ... Another van has arrived. There's a car pulling up inside. The boss men may be here. I think it's about time to go to work ...Are you hearing me now?

"I think we're good."

The armed launcher fit nicely between the short columns. Resting it against one to his left, Maple adjusted the back-up iron sight. He checked the optical sight, and picked up more motion than he had with the binoculars. Shapes, certainly of people, were more clearly defined. Through a break in the crowd he made out an upright form, probably the podium. The shot would be tight, but he was feeling more confident.

Maple withdrew the launcher and propped it against the corner of a column, then positioned three more RPGs for loading. He put his phone on speaker and laid it on the concrete base of the parapet. When Stickman had asked how he was doing, he almost said he only needed to check the rocket launcher's sights. That would not have gone over well. They had agreed on the need to use bland language, not knowing how closely security teams assigned to the press conference, U.S. or Russian, were monitoring conversations.

He thought to glance at the southwest tower and was relieved to not see any activity. Nadia sat motionless, her knees pulled up, watching him with frightened eyes.

"All right, I'm where I want to be," Stickman's voice crackled through the speaker. "How are you?"

"Fine, thanks."

A siren abruptly wailed near the cathedral in the direction of Wisconsin. Maple ignored it, moving the launcher back into position. In the scope, he framed the entrance opening between the apartment building and the wall. There was less motion now. The press conference must be about to start, or was maybe underway. With the siren belching erratically to his right, he strained to hear Stickman. "Go" came through and Maple squeezed off a rocket-propelled fragmentation round. The siren went silent as if giving center stage to the RPG. The grenade hit on the right edge of the entrance, just missing the apartment house. Debris and dust flew. Maple's instant analysis was, if not on target at least close enough to do damage.

"Damn, I said 'Not a go,'" Stickman's voice crackled. Maple swore under his breath. He had reloaded when Stickman ordered him to adjust a notch up, notch left. He quickly did, and fired again. The next order to fire came much faster than Maple could reload, and he questioned trying to hit the same spot. But he knew the vagaries of an RPG in flight probably meant hitting close by, just what they wanted for maximum impact, and he unleashed the third grenade. Debris and dust again filled his scope. "You're good. Get out of there." Maple withdrew the launcher, expecting to hear screams from the carnage he had just inflicted, but nothing but the murmur of traffic came from the direction of the embassy. He began repacking.

Nadia was on her side, arms up, trying to cover her ears. Though the launcher didn't seem all that loud, he wished he had given her ear plugs. He studied her momentarily. You'll be found soon enough, he thought as he stepped over her, stooping to take the work credential dangling from her neck.

Reentering the southwest tower he found himself alone and was tempted to press the button for the closest elevator. Instead, he took the stairs two at a time, the backpack bouncing, to the main floor. He gathered himself, then casually opened the door, and nearly walked into a security officer. The man was beefy, with a friendly open face, and just nodded before seeing Nadia's credential. Without looking down Maple knew it was showing her face.

"Hey buddy, hold on a minute. That sure doesn't look like you." A silly grin appeared, as if to say, I'm so smart, and he stepped squarely in Maple's path. Maple tried to appear calm.

"Well, you see, I've been working upstairs and found this. I'm on my way to turn it in. Can you direct me?"

"You'll have to come to the security office so I can confirm this was lost. Take it off, please."

As the officer's eyes followed Maple's left hand, slipping the credential over his head, his right hand curled around the silenced Glock in his jacket pocket. He jammed the gun into the guard's ribcage.

"Just be quiet." Reaching back, Maple found the handle of the staircase door. "Stay close to me and go through the door."

The officer obeyed. Maple didn't know what to do next. He should have brought more cuffs, he thought. I don't want to shoot him. The door closed behind them. "Now, just take a step back." Maple swung the gun in an arc ending on the officer's forehead. A second blow sent him to one knee, his eyes glassy. Believing the officer was losing consciousness, Maple turned toward the door.

"Goddamn you," the bleeding man growled as he lunged. Maple turned in time to absorb the charge. The Glock fired. Maple shoved back and this time fired purposely at point-blank range. The big man crumbled onto his back, lower legs pinned grotesquely beneath him, feet protruding. Maple stood over him, watching with difficulty as the man moaned softly, eyes blinking. Blood was turning his trousers crimson below the waist. Maple fixated on the much smaller, slowly growing chest wound. He knew the slaughter he had just inflicted at the embassy was worse, many times over, but he had seen nothing but dust.

This was personal, the first time he had killed up close. On the few road trips ending in murder, it had been at Stickman's hand. Maple knew if he moved suddenly, he would retch. He fought to hold himself together as he watched the eyes blinking slower, and then they were vacant.

He stepped back, wanting to run, forcing himself to take stock. He looked at himself. He saw only a few drops of blood on a pants leg. Were they from the pistol whipping or the first shot? The stupidity of the question snapped him back to the moment. Nadia's credentials were on the floor. He reached down unsteadily, picked them up thinking, fingerprints. He pulled out a handkerchief, taking rapid swipes at the elevator buttons and door handles as he went out, wondering if he had missed any. Leaving by the visitor's exit, he crossed the grounds toward Woodley Road, walking with purpose but not haste, his panic not showing, a workman needing a tool from his car.

"You stupid fool," he belatedly told the dead security guard.

"Whoa, bro. What's the problem?"

Maple's eyes opened at the sound of Stickman's voice. He heaved himself to the edge of the sofa, elbows on knees. "Sorry. Guess I was sort of dreaming, going over what happened at the cathedral."

"What happened is that we struck a hell of a blow against the US of A."

"I know. But I told you, I killed that security guard. I called him a 'stupid fool' on the way to the car. I'm pretty sure he was dead, but I hope he somehow heard me. He didn't have to die."

Maple sat in silence for a minute. "Oh, I forgot until I was thinking about things. What was that about a no go?"

"Another car showed up inside the gates and this guy got out in a hurry. He looked like he was somebody. I was going to wait to see if he went to the podium."

"Sorry."

"Doesn't matter. But all this angst about the guard ... What about the woman? You haven't said, but I assume you followed our plan."

"No, I didn't," Maple admitted. "I decided she was so frightened that it wasn't necessary. Several other people had seen me, too. I couldn't go back and kill them all."

"The others saw you briefly, even the cougar you told me about," Stickman said with irritation. "This Nadia had time to really look at you. She had time to count the little moles on your right cheek."

"Sorry. I just didn't think it was necessary."

Just didn't think is more like it, just lost your nerve, Stickman stewed to himself. He sat down, studying his partner. He had never seen Maple like this, never seen his nerves exposed, fraying at the ends.

"Forget about the woman. You're probably right. The guard you shot was a stupid fool. Let it go. He did it to himself. A casualty of war. I'm just hoping today sets off more attacks. Fort Hood, Newtown, San Bernardino, Boston, Charleston, even Orlando," Stickman ticked off the partial list of terrorist attacks in recent years in the U.S.

He got up, began pacing. "None of those attacks managed to focus attention of people like us on the government, not big time. The outrage against the shooters went in the wrong direction, man, calls for gun control, or it became a race thing, or it became the acts of nut cases. Even when Muslims were involved, nothing. Nothing has had legs since 9/11. And that caused fear, Americans being afraid, but not more attacks. Maybe we've changed that."

Chapter 6

The path forward was one of simple alternatives. Monitor the news and their police radio scanner for a couple of days. If there were no signs of law enforcement picking up their scent, get rid of the incriminating handguns. They had spent hours on the nearby C & O Canal and, more important, the adjacent Potomac River. They had identified spots, some now littered with guns and other evidence from previous missions, where the river ran swift and deep. Their routine had become comfortable. Maple broke the guns down into component parts small enough to slide into the cavities of concrete blocks and cement in place. Tied to a length of rope, a block looked like a rudimentary anchor for the flat bottom boat and trailer they pulled behind a battered Ford pickup. They had all the gear to dress the part of fishermen looking for dinner, though Stickman remained a novice. Their preferred time to drive to the canal for a day's end beer was dusk. Finding a deserted spot, Stickman acted as lookout while Maple slipped out of sight on a trail to the river. Within minutes he would return, sans concrete block.

But should the radio and scanner suggest danger, that the police search was moving their way, they were ready to run. They had weapons, camping equipment, food and plenty of cash and credit cards. In a week or so their appearances would noticeably change, more in line with their false IDs.

If no red flags surfaced, another scenario was to start looking for work in a few weeks. They would check jobs around Frederick, Maryland. Washington was certain to remain on high alert. There were too many ways a job application there could draw unwanted attention.

Should law enforcement suddenly, unexpectedly, show up on their doorstep, there was always the option of a fight, though they did not put much stock in martyrdom.

Chapter 7

Senior Agent Sam Nunn's morning sucked. He had barely slept in the three days since the attack. The near-continuous flow of coffee and fast food had turned his stomach sour and he had no time for the high impact exercise he depended on to manage his stressful job. Worst of all, he could not offer his superiors a solid lead from his slice of the FBI's five-prong investigation.

Nunn's team was charged with checking out surveillance cameras near the crime scene. Another team was doing interviews, including those with families and friends of the victims on the off chance the attack was extreme retaliation against a single target.

A third team was looking for – and pouring over – physical evidence. The search was ever-broadening from the Russian Embassy and National Cathedral as little of value was found. Evidence from the cathedral – the ladder propped outside the administrative offices, the flexible cuffs and leash used to secure Nadia, shell casings near the dead security officer, the ballistic report on the slugs in his body – would be valuable at trial, but probably of little value in tracking a killer. Employees who saw Nadia walk through with the workman offered conflicting descriptions. The cougar Doreen couldn't remember much about his face. A distraught Nadia was of even less help. And Cathedral visitors had arrived before law enforcement, smudging any fingerprints that might have been left.

The fourth team was conducting needle-in-a-haystack searches, throwing up random roadblocks, checking IDs in airports and bus stations, all done without a clue to what they were looking for. Already, the futile checks were winding down. The final team was chasing tips pouring in from around the country. Someone acting suspiciously, someone who might be a radical Muslim, someone who had threatened the president or someone in his administration, someone this, someone that. Most callers were sincere, some vindictive, others just plain kooks or fools. Still, there was always hope that a useful call would come in.

The investigation and manhunt centered on Washington, of course, where several thousand officers from every level and branch of law enforcement were mobilized. But around the country, thousands more officers followed up on tips in their home jurisdictions. Then there were players on the periphery: Communication specialists trying to both inform and calm a frightened populace. Techies searching the Internet, flight and railroad manifests, social media postings for any helpful lead. Law enforcement liaison officers reaching out to public officials and Congress, where some lawmakers showed leadership and others scrambled for political advantage.

Nunn was dismayed to learn that the cathedral's surveillance cameras were shut down the week of the attack, for an upgrade no less. That meant having to rely on other surveillance cameras in the area, private as well as police. There were a lot, and locating them all posed a challenge. Nunn ordered more than two dozen teams of four agents each to begin the tedious work of locating cameras within a mile of the embassy and the cathedral. Quickly contacting camera owners and operators was crucial to prevent time-sensitive images from being automatically erased. Already, images were being reviewed, but so far, nothing fruitful had appeared.

There was a knock, just barely, before Agent Mike Burk walked in to make Nunn's day: "Morning, senator."

Nunn answered with a scowl, wondering yet again when his favorite agent would tire of referencing his namesake, a former senator from Georgia. As usual, Burk's teasing came with a broad smile.

"What are you so damn happy about? Haven't I been working you hard enough?"

"We've got a partial license plate, a number one followed by a three that just might be bad news for these assholes."

"We've got thousands of license plate numbers, full and partial."

"But this one," Burk said, "comes with a guy putting a case of some sort or maybe a backpack in the trunk of a sedan parked within a couple blocks of National Cathedral. And get this, it was shot within five minutes or so of everything going down there. Unfortunately, you can't really see the guy. The surveillance camera is one of the rotating kind. It was at a construction site about half a block away and the camera caught only a piece of this guy from the left rear. We're trying to blow up the best photos, to see if it's a backpack that Nadia what's her name can identify."

"At least it's something to run with."

"The car appears to have a Maryland plate. We'll likely get the make and model soon and can start checking out cars with a plate ending with one and three. But I'll bet the plate is stolen so we've asked our Maryland brethren to run down any plates like that that were stolen in the last month."

"Good work, Mike."

"You're welcome ...Sam."

"What about the embassy's cameras? Maybe they can tell us why that old man and the cop were killed. Ballistics show they were shot by the same gun. But why?"

"I think the guy who shot them was calling in the RPGs. Somehow the old man and the cop got in the middle of that."

"He? Why not she?" Nunn flashed an exaggerated grin.

"Don't go all feminist on me, boss. Okay, he or she was spotting for the he or she firing the rocket launcher. That's why the second and third shots were better than the first. As to your first question, as usual the Ruskies aren't exactly forthcoming about what they've got, if anything. I'm sure we'll hear from them when it's in their best interest."

"The big boss is wondering if we have a line on who's responsible. He doesn't like my answer, but I can't make up suspects. Have you stumbled across anything you haven't told me?"

"Nope. As far as I know, none of the usual suspects has stepped up, not even ISIS. Usually they can't claim responsibility fast enough."

"What's your best hunch?"

Burk shook his head. "Pure speculation. My gut says it's not domestic. If I'm wrong though, I'd say disgruntled ex-military. Those were pretty tough shots. I'd guess the shooter is foreign, trained in the Mideast writ large, somehow got by immigration."

"I don't know if the shooter was good or just lucky. But even if he got help from a spotter on shots two and three, you have to give him full credit for the first shot. Anyway, none of this gets us anywhere."

"Right, boss."

"And Agent Burk, caution your colleagues to stick with facts in their reports. If speculation, particularly about foreign involvement, reaches the president, he'll tell the world as if it's gospel."

"Tweet, tweet."

Helpful reports were coming in by early afternoon. The car caught by surveillance camera near the cathedral was a 2010 Toyota Camry. Eleven of that make, year and model were currently licensed with plates ending in one and three. Local police were enlisted to find owners of the Camrys as quickly and quietly as possible. The order was to locate but not to approach or alert. As the car owners were located, federal officers, backed up by SWAT teams, were dispatched to conduct interviews. By nightfall, six of the owners were cleared. Only one had not been located, a woman on a two-week vacation in Europe–virtually as good as an alibi.

Just one set of Maryland plates ending in one and three had been stolen in the past month. Those plates were taken from a 2012 Chevy Volt, parked in a corner of the Montgomery County Public Library lot in downtown Bethesda. Burk telephoned First Eye, Inc., the library's contract surveillance company. A woman answered and confirmed the video was intact. "But just barely, honey. Two more days and you would have seen nothing but black." He got an address and said he'd be right out.

Agent Fay Welling, whose demeanor was as sour as Burk's was engaging, sullenly agreed to go with him. They were soon pulling up at the Georgia Avenue address of First Eye in the suburb of Silver Spring. "This way, honey," said the woman Burk had talked with minutes earlier. "I've got you set up in the conference room."

Burk and Welling settled into arm chairs and watched as the camera swept a portion of the library parking lot, then caught a shadowy form squatting at the back of a car. "That could be a Volt," said Burk. A white rectangular shape was at the person's feet. "Probably got the front plate first." The camera's focus moved away, leaving them to guess the thief was male but not giving them enough detail to be sure, let alone a description. Disappointment, and then just briefly, the camera caught the left front of another car – and another partial plate, barely legible in the dim street light.

"This was taken a little after one in the morning," Welling noted. "Pretty risky for a set of plates, given how well Bethesda is patrolled."

"If he's good with tools he's going to be exposed two minutes, maybe less," Burk answered. "Apparently a risk he was ready to take."

Within minutes the partial plate search had resumed. Three possibilities were soon identified. One was near Point of Rocks.

Burk was back in Nunn's office, calling him senator. Back with a big grin. Being ignored.

"So what you got?"

"Report from the Ruskies."

"And?"

"It's good. Embassy cameras got images of a guy across the street. They show him shooting the D.C. cop and the old man, and he's talking on a phone. Our lip readers say he's saying things that seem consistent with giving directions to a shooter. We don't have sound yet. There was too much traffic noise to pull specific words out, but we're working on it. I think one reason the Russians decided to play ball is they need help with the audio, with that and getting out a description.

"We think he's white, lean, average height or a little more, wearing a tan trench coat and fedora, probably a shade of gray or brown. He's wearing sunglasses and has a beard, though we're trying to get a good close up. It could be fake. There's good reason to think he's in disguise. He walked with a limp before the attack and seemed to forget about it afterward."

Nunn was pleased with the lip readers: "Damn, I said 'Not a go'." And "One notch up. One notch left." That fit where the second and third RPGs landed in relation to the first. "You're good" could mean cease fire, given no more grenades came in. It was easy to confirm the old man served in World War II, including theaters where artillery was used. One "Damn you" could be read, and that sounded like a proud vet. The meaning of his shouts, "He did this" seemed obvious.

Other cameras glimpsed the man in the trench coat as he made his way up Wisconsin through curious pedestrians rapidly filling the sidewalk. Then, a man in a trench coat and fedora is captured by the grimy lens of a camera near Macomb Street, but the man is clean-shaven. He gets in a sedan similar to one caught by the surveillance camera at the construction site north of the cathedral, where a man in work clothes and baseball cap had put a case, or maybe be a backpack, in the car's trunk.

"That, of course, could be the RPG launcher," said Burk. He shifted gears, telling Nunn about the surveillance camera capturing the license plate theft in the library parking lot.

"Just how good are these guys?" Nunn wondered. "The spotter forgets his limp and seems to have used a third-rate disguise. If they knew their way around, they wouldn't have risked getting caught stealing plates in a damn parking lot. There are easier ways."

"That exposes you to other people."

"It does ...On the other hand they're good enough to pull off a high-risk assault, not your garden variety high-risk assault but a major terrorist assault. There was plenty for two people to do in the cathedral but they're gutsy enough to split up so the shooter would have a spotter. And they're ruthless. The security guard may have put up a fight, but the old vet? He didn't have to be killed ...And then they just disappear, unless your partial plate works out."

"So Dr. Partial Plate, where are you coming down?"

"I don't know. What I'm afraid of, Burk, is that these guys are just starting to cut their teeth. No pun intended."

Chapter 8

A deputy sheriff's car stopped near the driveway a hundred yards up the road as Willie Slick rolled off his new bride and onto his side. She nestled in behind him, sliding her hand into his wet groin as Willie watched another deputy's car pull in behind the first. Two officers appeared to be in each car, though at that distance Willie couldn't be sure. He squinted against the dropping sun working easily through silver maple trees not yet in bud.

The officers sat in air-conditioned comfort for several minutes. Maybe waiting for backup, Willie thought. Backup for what? Willie didn't know the two men living at the far end of the drive, though they had been neighbors since he moved in more than two years ago. They didn't shun him. They just made it clear that a wave hello was enough. No introductions necessary, thank you.

Willie was just sliding a hand around his wife's dimpled bottom when his neighbors' door opened and a man, the wiry one, wearing a broad-brimmed hat, came out. Walking casually within shouting distance of the sheriff's deputies, hands stuffed in loose fitting trousers, he called, "May I help you?"

He stood waiting. Nothing broke the silence of the bumper-to-bumper cars. Willie watched. Another shout. Still nothing from the deputies. Willie heard the sound of a garage door opening and the wiry man turned toward the house. Willie could see a dark form in the shadows of the unlighted garage. A blast sent a streak of light that hit the rear of the front car. The gas tank ignited with a searing explosion, blowing away half of the other car and leaving them both burning furiously.

"Holy shit," hissed Willie, reaching for the phone on his bedside table.

Car nearly packed and ready, it took Maple and Stickman just a few minutes to remove the false panel and transfer cash, credit cards and remaining weapons. They drove leisurely down the lane, swerving around the burning patrol cars and onto the road. Stickman stuck a detonator out the window and pressed a red button. The house exploded, roof disappearing and board siding turning into kindling, leaving behind another inferno surrounded by small fires that dusk would soon accentuate.

"Find DNA in that, fuckers," Stickman said with a tight smile.

"Holy shit," Willie said redundantly, again reaching for his phone.

Maple took the second right, heading for Frederick on a preplanned route dominated by paved county roads. They drove slightly faster than the speed limit, soon hearing wailing sirens of first responders. Both men were grim, with no clue to how quickly law enforcement could start throwing up checkpoints. The air was alive with sirens when, finally it seemed, they pulled into a self-serve storage facility on Frederick's west side. Sirens but still no checkpoints. They pulled to one of the larger units, relieved that other renters were not dropping off or picking up.

Stickman opened the overhead door, revealing another non-descript car, a three-year-old beige Toyota Camry. But the six-cylinder engine had been replaced with a small, fuel-injection V-8. Most important, the back seat had been altered, creating a hollow large enough for the rocket launcher, an Army M2010 sniper rifle snagged on a rare foray into the gun community's black market, and enough other munitions to thoroughly arm a small gang. Though on the run, they could also go on the offensive.

Quickly switching cars, they were off on a westerly route roughly parallel to I-70, wanting to go only as far as Hagerstown. Their preference for lodging was a bed and breakfast on the theory that hotels and motels – particularly the cheap ones – within easy reach of the interstate would be checked first. Stickman found a B&B where their doctored driver's licenses were accepted without question.

The licenses identified them as neighbors living on the same street in Trenton, New Jersey. Friends, they told the B&B owner, on a fishing trip for a badly needed get-away. How well that story would hold up the next day if a roadblock loomed and they faced police questioning, who knew. But it was supported by the trunkful of camping gear, a case of beer, fishing equipment, suitcases and backpacks – though not the one used at the cathedral. Backed up, too, by handguns within easy reach and, if the situation allowed, the arsenal under the back seat.

Chapter 9

The FBI investigation yielded no helpful DNA, not from the demolished house or garage or mailbox. Pretty thorough, the forensics officer muttered, the bastards even thought to wipe down their mailbox. And he was right. With time on their hands after attacking the embassy, Stickman and Maple tried to wipe down everything they might have touched, mailbox included. And unlike the city and its environs, their neighborhood was devoid of surveillance cameras.

But there were the neighbors. Willie and his honey and perhaps a dozen others recalled having limited contact with the two men, some just recently and others over several years. Predictably, descriptions varied, sometimes dramatically.

As they came in, Special Agent Cecille Hudson started doing averages – of height and weight and body type, complexion and color of eyes and hair and how it was cut, how they dressed, and distinguishing marks. The space provided for distinguishing marks was usually empty. No known tattoos or body piercings. Two of the neighbors said the slimmer of the two may have a faint scar on his chin. A convenience store clerk thought the blockier man had a facial mole. Are these guys boring or what? Hudson wondered. But no, she reminded herself, they are very good at murder.

Late in the day, Hudson finally had her averages. Five people generally agreed on height and weight so she'd go with those numbers. More important, three of those five and another three were close on complexion, body types, hair style and color. Her artist, Aaron Wayne, would work with those six on composite sketches of the suspects.

Teams of officers were dispatched to bring the six to Wayne. Dinners were interrupted and children's performances were missed. Romance was delayed. Hudson, who could turn on "I feel your pain" as easily as she could "I don't give a shit," apologized and explained the obvious, why descriptions of the killers were needed as quickly as possible. She even gave ready Willie's right forearm a flirtatious little squeeze.

Accompanied by Aaron Wayne and his composite sketches, Hudson felt guilty about the late hour as she knocked at a two-story colonial, not far from National Cathedral. She felt much more guilt about why she was there.

A male nurse answered. "Come in. Thanks for calling ahead. Nadia hasn't been trying to sleep until I give her a sedative at midnight."

The small woman from the National Cathedral's finance office had been in an ill-defined level of shock since her quiet life had been violently upended. She no longer spoke, except for a whispered yes or no. She trembled without warning. Tears suddenly flowed, but she only cried out when asleep. She ate little and spent most of her time looking at, but not seeing, the television. The nurses always kept it tuned to comedy reruns, absolutely never the news.

Nadia's sister, also single, and her doctors had earlier allowed Aaron Wayne to visit. They monitored him at first, while he explained to Nadia why he was there. He did that on each of his handful of visits, waiting in vain for her to respond, never pressing her for a description of the man responsible for her fear. Very patient, he sat with her and tried to make small talk. She did not say one word to him.

The nurse led the way to the living room and, at Hudson's request, turned the lights up enough for Nadia to see Wayne's sketches. Calmly and gently, Hudson explained who she was and why they were there. She asked Nadia if she understood, but got no response.

Hudson said Wayne would show her drawings of four men. On the TV tray in front of her, he placed a sketch of a man irrelevant to the case. Nadia looked at it and then away.

"Have you ever seen this man or anyone resembling him?" Hudson asked softly. Nadia said nothing.

Wayne showed her a sketch of the spotter. Again, she looked away and said nothing.

Wayne placed the sketch of the shooter before her. Hudson saw her back straighten slightly and an eyebrow shoot up.

"Have you ever seen this man or anyone resembling him?" Nadia stared hard at the sketch and then away, saying nothing.

Hudson inhaled and nodded at Wayne. He placed the fourth sketch on the TV tray. The shooter wearing a dark baseball cap stared out at Nadia. Her mouth fell slack and her eyes opened wide. Frantic, she released a low scream unlike anything Hudson had ever heard and slammed the TV tray to one side, arms and legs flailing uncontrollably.

As Hudson and Wayne reached to console her she struck out at them. "Don't touch me! Don't touch me!" They backed off. The nurse stepped in, barely touching her at one elbow to guide her sobbing from the room.

Wayne, face white, began picking up the scattered sketches. They shook in his hand. "Was it worth it?" he asked, mostly to himself.

"Don't know," Hudson muttered, "but we got our answer."

Late that night sketches and descriptions of the two men were released to the public:

Suspect #1: White, light complexion; 5'11", 165 lbs.; late-30s; lean but muscular; brown hair starting to thin, combed straight back; light eyes; thin face; well-dressed, whether wearing casual clothes or coat and tie, sometimes with broad-brimmed felt hat. No facial hair. No known tattoos or body piercings, but suspect may have a faint v-shaped scar on his chin.

Suspect #2: White, medium complexion, perhaps tan from being outside; 5'9", 190 lbs.; mid-30s; stocky and muscular; dark hair, parted on left side, with lock falling to right; wears casual or blue-collar workman's clothes, often with a baseball-type cap and sunglasses. No facial hair, though often has stubble of beard. No known tattoos, body piercings or scars, but may have a mole the size of a dime below suspect's right front hairline.

Days before the descriptions went public, Maple and Stickman started altering their appearances. With help from a gel, Stickman trained his hair to comb over and grew stylishly trimmed short facial hair. Maple let his hair grow longer and a heavy beard started coming in, growing as it would. Both had worked on tans under sunlamps at home. Breaking from their previous dress, they wore plaid shirts and camouflage pants popular with fishermen. Before the attack they purchased the best quality temporary tattoos they could find. LOVE inscribed Maple's right hand knuckles and a discrete half-moon was on the left side of his neck, above his shirt collar. Stickman had a small American flag on his left wrist. Following Maple's lead, he bought a good pair of sunglasses.

Anticipating the fugitives would change their appearance, Special Agent Hudson asked artist Aaron Wayne to do a second sketch of both men, showing how they might look with beards and moustaches. In an unusual move, a third sketch of Suspect #2 was released, after simply adding a dark baseball cap.

The sketches and descriptions were immediately ubiquitous – on every television and website, in every newspaper and magazine. They were the stars of Post Offices across the country, and public buildings of allies around the globe. Businesses – from super markets to barber shops and movie theaters – found space to tack up their mugshots. Overnight, putting a face to a heinous crime – even an artist's rendering based on shaky and conflicting memories – turned a shocked and fearful populace into vigilantes with a cause.

Though not identifying them by name, the FBI declared that Stickman and Maple were Public Enemy No. 1 and raised the reward for each man to ten million dollars. The reward should be multiples of that, thought Special Agent Hudson, but if turning them in is a matter of money, ten million should still do the trick.

Chapter 10

Reports of sightings rolled in by the tens of thousands. The pair was seen in every state and territory and most countries. Many sightings came complete with car descriptions and license numbers. Hundreds of people identified motels or houses where the two had been seen or supposedly were living. Too many people, perhaps seeing dollar signs, took it upon themselves to follow their particular suspects, leading to more than a few altercations. One woman truck driver spotted two men she was sure were the terrorists and followed them to a rest stop, where she cut the tires of their car. She was arrested after the car's owner, who was not amused, called the highway patrol.

Stickman and Maple listened to coverage on the radio, plagued by static, in their room at the B&B. A hot breakfast was available, but so was continental fare for travelers wanting to get on the road. Maple filled a bag with yogurt and fruit and a cinnamon roll and they continued west, now on I-70. They opted for that busy route believing the almost-certain roadblocks would so tie up traffic that searches would be done in haste.

At the first rest stop, Maple parked in the last available space and put their handguns in the false chamber of the back seat. Stickman put his billfold in the pocket of a jacket, which he carefully arranged on the back seat. If pressed for his ID, and feeling threatened, he would plead the need to retrieve the jacket – and possibly get to a handgun or two.

The car radio gave up nothing of value. Law officers at every level continued to drown in reported sightings. And it was clear that all law enforcement resources were being applied – for roadblocks, checking out motels and campgrounds, watching airports and train and bus stations.

"Until we get down the road a piece and this panic starts wearing off," Stickman said, as much to himself as to Maple, "we just have to be smarter than the cops at the roadblocks."

They reached the National Freeway – I-68 – an all-too-short stretch of broad, delightfully open sweeping turns through Maryland and West Virginia's timbered farmlands and state forests. After little more than an hour they rejoined I-70 with regret, sticking with their judg- ment that the interstate's heavy traffic and long-haul trucks made it their best choice. That was tested shortly when a bevy of highway patrol cars flew past them and somewhere ahead found a large enough gap in traffic to block both westbound lanes. Break lights fashioned a stream of red.

Creeping along, they passed a car stopped on the shoulder, officers cautiously searching as its two male occupants looked on. "Dog probably sniffed out some drugs," Stickman said. "They need to teach those canines what righteous terrorists smell like."

"Right now, that is not funny."

Only a dozen cars separated them from a checkpoint and Stickman suddenly had a worrisome question: Would an explosives-trained canine react to ammunition?

Teams of officers made their way down the row of cars, letting all but those with two males proceed. If we get out of this, Maple thought, maybe we should pick up a hitch hiker. A squatty patrolman in starched uniform, backed up by a huge colleague, waved them to the shoulder of the interstate.

"Identification, from both of you," he said officiously, peering through cheap sunglasses with brown plastic frames.

"Yes, sir," answered Maple.

The officer squinted at the licenses. "Where are you going?"

"Tennessee."

"Why?"

"We're going bass fishing."

"Great state for bass, but there's plenty of good fishing much closer to, ah, New Jersey," the officer said, glancing at a license.

"We wanted to put some distance between us and the wives."

"What are you going to fish for?"

"Bass, mostly. It's early enough that we may want to go a little farther south." He was relieved that his voice was remaining calm.

"You, Mr. Henry," the patrolman said, peering in at Stickman. "What kind of bait do you like for bass?"

Stickman's throat went dry, trying to recall the names of bass lures from Maple's lessons. "Well, that depends ...A Mopps is an option."

"It's Mepps, dummy," Maple admonished. "I started teaching him last night, but we haven't gotten far. He's never been."

"Okay expert," the officer said, turning his attention back to Maple. "What bait do you like?"

"I've always used a Mepps or a Rapala, but a friend told me he's done well with the Little Cleo Kit. I'm going to pick one up."

"What test line are you guys going to use?"

"Depends on the weather and where we end up, but something pretty standard for dummy. I'll use my ultra-lite whenever I can."

"Good for you," the squatty patrolman said. "Not that it means anything, but I'm a Little Cleo man. Enjoy your trip."

Rejoining the stream of cars, Maple allowed, "Hey, who ever heard of fishermen being terrorists? I bet that dude has the big-ass bass boat with the captains' chairs and the depth finder and the whole nine yards."

Stickman cleared his throat. "Dummy, is it?"

Maple broke into a self-satisfied grin.

Chapter 11

Returning from a mission a few years earlier, Stickman and Maple had taken a side trip to Falling Water, the home designed by Frank Lloyd Wright southwest of Pittsburgh. On their way back to the interstate, a For Rent sign caught Maple's eye as they passed a long gravel driveway. Lined by mature oak and ash trees, it led them to a two-story farmhouse. It was at a fork, the other branch going to two mobile homes sitting farther back in the trees.

Maple had been greeted at the door by a robust couple who appeared well into their eighties. Briefly explaining their interest in fishing and hiking, he asked if they rented by the week. No, the woman said firmly, too much fuss, has to be at least month-to-month. Saying that might work in the future, Maple got their contact information and thanked them. That information was added to a carefully coded notebook of properties, businesses and other facilities that one day could prove valuable. The book, stowed in the back seat compartment, could take the fugitives back to the remote property.

"What do you think, Mr. Stick? Should we fade into the woodwork for a while? These checkpoints probably won't go away any time soon, not entirely anyway."

"You're right. And for an outdoor guy like me," he answered wryly, "streams and parks and fishing like we got around here, those things are my life."

Minutes later a sign announced Pennsylvania highway 381. "That's it, right?" asked Maple, taking the exit and heading south.

He recognized the old woman when she answered his knock. She was a little grayer and more shrunken, though that could have been an impression made fuzzy by time. Wearing a modest blue print dress, she was still erect and bright-eyed and with neither undue caution nor trust asked his business. Maple didn't bring up his earlier visit, just that he and his friend were interested in renting a trailer. Coming up behind her was a man, perhaps a bit older, using a walker.

"These gentlemen are interested in rentin'," the woman said.

"I see just one," the old man said.

"The other is in the car, Wilbur."

"Wilbur, Wilbur Banks," he said, pushing the storm door open to shake hands. "Haven't I seen you before, young man? I seldom forget a face. That's not always a blessin' when I can't remember anything about the person, just the face."

"That's impressive, sir. I dropped by a few years ago and hung on to your card, just in case we came back through."

"I see. This is Mrs. Violet Banks."

"I'm Alexander Simms," said Maple, using the name on the driver's license he had shown the patrolman. "My friend in the car is Demetri Henry. It's nice to see you both are well."

"Excellent, in fact," said Wilbur Banks. "And how is your vacuuming going?"

Violet slightly rolled her eyes. That was signal enough for Maple, who as a child sometimes sat with an uncle who older family members described as "touched." "It's going better, sir," Maple said. "Thanks for asking."

Violet gave him an appreciative nod and reached for keys on a pegboard just inside the door. "Go take a look. Both trailers are empty. If you're interested we'll go from there."

They were, particularly in the unit farthest from the house. It seemed a little newer and, more important, Stickman pointed out, only yards from woods where the heavy undergrowth was dominated by a mix of multiflora rose and gooseberry bushes. A path could be cut through the thorny brambles, one offering escape for the informed or a painful reckoning for the unsuspecting.

"That would be my pick," Wilbur said upon Maple's return to the house. "You no doubt noticed the vacuum in the hall closet. Whoever rents the other has to borrow ours."

"Yes, sir. I saw that," Maple lied.

Violet went to the door and waved Stickman in. Not seeing a choice he entered with a smile as she handed them pencils and rental applications. They required job histories and references from employers and former landlords. After checking their New Jersey licenses, and learning they were on vacation and probably would be there a month or less, she declared the job histories and references weren't needed. "Hardly seems worth the hassle of all those calls. You gotta pay for a full month, though. Long as you've got cash money for the rent and deposit, we're willin' to rent month-to-month."

Chapter 12

Maple and Stickman moved quickly–and unobtrusively–to establish a routine intended to appear normal but was more than it seemed. The electricity was turned on in Simms' name, backed up by a cash deposit. Both purchased fishing licenses, and they frequented streams and small lakes in the area. They fished from the relative safety of shore, not wanting their options limited by a slow-moving boat. They reduced the need to frequent bait shops by using artificial lures, not caring whether they caught fewer fish. If the Banks watched their comings and goings, they saw the men carrying in groceries, though it is doubtful they noticed the purchases came from many different stores. They bought hand weights and other equipment and exercised vigorously. Both, but especially Stickman, ran frequently in the rugged hills behind their rental.

Important precautions were taken. They parked their car on the side of the trailer away from the house – presumably for shade but when backed in, for privacy when accessing the back seat. They cut a path through the prickly undergrowth at the edge of the grove, then fashioned a gate from live multiflora rose that when closed was a prickly obstacle for anyone following. Several yards into the woods they stowed a small emergency cache of weapons, food and water in a water-repellent canvas bag. Stickman found two elevated locations–one on a turnout from a paved road, the other on a gravel county road–where from more than a mile away they could sweep the Banks' property with binoculars.

For a time, as an extra precaution, they took turns slipping out to sit in the chill of late winter nights and listen for tell-tale sounds of unwanted visitors. Maple enjoyed those periods of solitude, entertained by calls of night predators and the warblers' early morning songs. Not so much Stickman, who was committed to monitoring television and police radio.

The media gradually mixed more stories into what had become the drumbeat of an angry nation. Reports of checkpoints and disrupted air, rail and bus travel commanded less attention. Sightings of two callous killers continued to pepper law enforcement, but with less frequency or velocity. While coverage of the embassy attack slowly abated, the fact it basically did not change told its own story: Thousands upon thousands of law officers still were flailing aimlessly, having failed to find even a cold trail. They were stuck, unable to get beyond vague descriptions of two men who looked like everyone's neighbor or pod mate.

Chapter 13

Cecille Hudson stood to stretch, her bony frame protesting the eighteen-hour days that had piled up since the attack. The special agent was a thirty-year veteran, hitting an age where the big cases took a physical toll she wouldn't have noticed a few years earlier. And as a team lead she was in the toughest of jobs – too high to limit herself to the twelve-hour shifts of those she commanded, too low to delegate much work.

Putting together descriptions of the murderers was just the beginning of what made a week feel like a month. The RPG that had assassinated four officers and the explosion that turned a house into matchsticks had helped broaden the embassy investigation. From residents to store clerks to public employees, people remembered – at least vaguely – fleeting contacts with the two low-profile men now on the run.

The shorter man had rented the house, unfortunately from an absentee landlord whose only involvement was pocketing a monthly cashier's check. He paid with cash, as he did everything locally, from utility bills to groceries and gas. Using the name Harrison Willford, he had obtained a driver's license and licensed two cars. Neighbors readily identified the photo on the license. One neighbor also remembered seeing a plastic identification badge tucked in the man's back pocket as they waited in a checkout line, the lanyard hanging down the leg of his work pants. It took little checking for Special Agent Hudson to determine that the name Harrison Willford, though effective, was phony.

Still, she got the name added as a possible alias to his wanted poster description.

The taller man offered virtually nothing to go on. Apparently he was happy to have his partner handle their finances. But Willie Slick recalled picking up his mail one day when the taller man had stopped alongside to let a truck pass. In the back seat was a new PC in a box that barely fit through the door. Willie thought he saw an identification badge in the left breast pocket of his neighbor's shirt. And the rural mailman, running late one afternoon as the taller man pulled into the driveway, said he glanced in the slowly passing car. In a cup holder he saw an ID badge with a shirt clip and what might have been a gold seal glinting in the fading light.

Hudson wondered with irritation why no one on her team had flagged the ID badges for more attention. Because no one else had perused the seemingly endless reports to glean that clue, she answered herself with equal irritation. That was her job. But what were the ID badges clues to? Assume the shorter man was blue-collar and the taller one did something with electronics or computers. Hundreds if not thousands of building contractors, government agencies, computer firms and subcontractors of all stripe issued ID badges, to say nothing of firms providing support services. How could that search be narrowed?

She decided to seek permission to publicly release the photo of Harrison Willford and hope it jogged someone's memory, maybe someone he worked with or a former boss. He had to fill out forms for insurance, tax deductions, the job itself, using his real name or an alias. All federal jobs and many in the private sector require fingerprints. Any of those touchstones could be a lead, however slim. The work will be tedious, asking employers to look and look again at the photo, asking over and over again, "Are you sure you haven't hired anyone who resembles this man?" Investigators totaling in the hundreds, likely more, were available for the gritty work. How much time would be wasted, Hudson wondered, if these men hadn't worked for one of the targeted agencies or firms? Who cares? Maybe someone's memory will be jogged. Maybe someone will pick up the phone.

Chapter 14

Violet worried more about Wilbur with each passing week. It had been four years since his mental issues had tipped too far, since she insisted they consult their long-time doctor. The diagnosis was dementia, in all probability Alzheimer's. Violet was thankful the progression had been moderate, in some respects even slow. She was grateful that Wilbur had not grown violent and still remembered people. Even his short-term memory remained decent, usually sparing Violet from repeatedly answering the same question. Occasionally Wilbur was crabby, but it didn't last, and he still had a smile ready when she entered a room, still was pleased when Violet teased him.

Certainly, there was forgetfulness and a tendency to live in the past. A big part of Wilbur's slippage involved rewriting history, like turning his middle-level bookkeeping job into being chief financial officer for a Fortune 500 company. A TV report on a firm struggling against bankruptcy could prompt Wilbur to allow that he told the company's president only last week the steps needed to avert financial disaster.

Driving was a predictably tough problem, but Violet's insistence that he not go alone finally won out. Wilbur could still drive safely, but it was apt to be aimlessly. He got lost driving home on roads he had navigated for decades, and failed to find restaurants they had patronized for years. Ready solutions helped – like having Violet ride along to give directions – and she was pleased that he welcomed her company. She dreaded the day when, finally, she would have to take his keys. Having children would have given her allies, but she and Wilbur had belatedly acknowledged that could not happen. Violet rued their decision not to adopt.

Most recently he had experienced Sundowner's Syndrome, in Wilbur's case a level of confusion that could turn severe as afternoon wore into evening. Options for medication were limited and sometimes came with side effects worse than the hour or two it might take to work through the confusion.

"I've got to get home now. Violet will be worried if I'm not home soon."

"Wilbur, you are in your home, and I am Violet."

"No, I've got to get home. I know Violet will be worried if I'm not home soon."

"Look at me, Wilbur. You are at home. I am Violet."

"No, you are not my wife. I shouldn't even be with you."

Over and over again. And again until Violet breathed with relief when, after a long silence, Wilbur would just change the subject. Relieved, even if the change was to that infernal, "How's your vacuuming going?"

"It's goin' fine, Wilbur. How's your's?"

"Well, I do the best I can with this decrepit monster. I may have to break down and buy a new one."

Sometimes, in his mind, doing his best was incredibly good. As a young man Wilbur had a nice voice and his high school vocal teacher helped him develop as a tenor. He was good enough to be the vocalist in a swing band and, after it fell apart, he continued singing in his church choir and high school musicals. It was an era when small radio stations carried performers live, and sometimes he was invited to do a segment. As he grew older, he sang at weddings and funerals and opened ball games with the "Star Spangled Banner." For a time he sang in a barbershop quartet, but harmony was not his forte. What he enjoyed most was the applause that came from being on stage, and Wilbur competed fiercely for parts at the local playhouse. He landed parts, but never the lead. Regardless of the venue, if he was singing, he was happy.

As Wilbur's dementia worsened, he seriously amplified his past musical glories. His church choir gained regional and then national renown. As lead first tenor he attracted the attention of choirs that toured internationally. He was asked to join them as a soloist. Pavarotti somehow noticed him and more than once they sang duets at benefits for what Wilbur called "really good causes." Musical talent plus involvement in Democratic politics – he had served as county Democratic treasurer, after all – combined to put him on President Obama's radar. Wilbur reveled in having sung at the president's second inauguration.

"You know what he told me, don't you, Mother?"

"No, Wilbur," she said yet again.

"He said, 'When I watch the video of the swearing in, your soothing voice will calm me as I face the turmoil of my second term'."

"That's actually a wonderful contribution to the nation, Wilbur. I'm proud of you."

When Wilbur's stories – the tours and the inauguration and his business acumen – first began, Violet had objected.

"That just never happened," she chastised him. "Quit makin' things up."

Wilbur's jaw clamped up as he sulked, but his fantasies persisted, regardless of Violet's objections. Soon his response was to defend himself, to lash back.

"What do you know about it?" he demanded. "You aren't me, Mother." Which sounded like a half word.

Violet gradually understood there was nothing to be gained by trying to impose reality. Wilbur's reality was in his mind, not in facts or what others thought to be true. Violet, who had played navigator so they could drive to the polls to cast their losing votes for president in the last election, never tired of asking herself, "I wonder if he's related back there somewhere to Jonathan Tower?"

Wilbur's recollections grew to grandiose proportions. "You know, Obama's inauguration was the only one I enjoyed," Wilbur said one night. "The rest were all Republicans. Felt I had a duty.

"I have sung at four, as you know, startin' with Nixon in 1973. With all that controversy buzzin' around him I almost said no when Pat called. But she was such a nice woman ...I just couldn't. No wonder she drank, though. Nancy called afterwards and told me how she and her 'Ronnie' had loved listenin' to me and Pav in Vienna. I feel so lucky they happened to be going through when we were there."

"And it was a wonderful trip, Wilbur, even if the inauguration wasn't in Vienna that year."

"Sometimes you confuse me, Mother ...Now, I didn't much care for Ford after he pardoned Nixon and I didn't much care for the peanut farmer though I voted for him, so not singin' for those guys was okay with me. I understand Carter is buildin' houses now. Actually buildin' them. I saw him on the TV with a hammer, his wife, too. Shame how far some of those big guys can fall. I was disappointed that I didn't sing for Clinton. You remember how I got an answering machine so to not miss his call? Waste of money. He was so smart. You'd of thought he would have paid the cleanin' bill for that girl's dress and been done with it.

"And then there was Bush Two when he got re-elected. We still had that answerin' machine when one of his flunkies called and I almost didn't call back. I was so mad about Iraq. All those young men ...And you know I figured up the cost of Iraq to you and me personally and it was more than enough to pay for the damn answerin' machine."

"If you did the figurin' I don't doubt you were right." Being somewhat patronizing had become one of Violet's standard responses.

"Right, Mother. But then the great man called and explained that he wanted Pav for the inauguration but Pav said only if I sang with him. So you remember Mother? We were a duet."

"I remember, Wilbur. What about Bush One?"

"I can't recall the deal there. Maybe in my mind one Bush was enough."

Still, things were tolerable. Violet enjoyed his company most in the morning. There was less confusion then and every so often he would roll over against her and sometimes they would warm up. Reaching climax was becoming rare for both of them, but arousal still brought back sharp memories of the intensity they had shared for decades.

Most days Wilbur took an interest in his breakfast options before starting to fiddle with the TV remote in search of news. Deciding what to eat somehow focused his mind, and Violet found it a good time to try to talk about whatever was on her mind. Like the renters who had just moved in.

"They're very quiet, but seem like nice young men," was Violet's assessment.

Wilbur said he didn't understand being able to just take off for a month or more to fish or hike or whatever they were doing with their days. Accountants, he emphasized, got a job and stuck with it, and if they lost it, they tried to get another lined up quick.

"Near as I can tell they do even less at night. Usually, I can see the front of their car just sittin' there. You'd think they'd be out at bars or somethin'."

"You don't 'spose they're in some kinda trouble. Or maybe they're homosexuals and don't feel comfortable going out and 'bout in a rural area like this."

"Nope, homos aren't much liked around here. As long as they mind their own business and pay their rent, I don't much care who they are, Mother."

Chapter 15

A light in the next-door trailer greeted Maple and Stickman as they pulled in from a day of wandering that had brought discovery of a county road with promise as an escape route.

An older cream-colored four-door sedan hitched to a U-Haul was backed up to the trailer. "Looks like we have a neighbor," Maple said. "Think we should offer to help finish unloading?"

"I'd rather not. Fair chance we'll be hearing from our new neighbor soon enough. They'll either be too friendly or need something."

She was both. A few minutes later, Maple set down his tea to open the door to a woman of about 40, shoulder length hair still shower-wet, two cups in her hand. "Hey, I'm April," she smiled, showing a gap between her upper front teeth. "Just moved in. I have the coffee on but haven't been to the store yet. Do you have extra cream and sugar?"

"Be right back," Maple said, taking the cups.

When he returned she picked up her introduction as she thought any new neighbor should. She was an artist or trying to be. She was in a car accident a few months back, a hit and run that left her in a lower body cast for most of three months. Good thing was that she had to do something, couldn't just sit, and after reading and TV had worn dull a friend suggested they enroll in an art class. Didn't show much aptitude for oils, April rushed on, but by chance an exhibit of miniature art, capturing full scenes on small media, was in the building where they studied. Talking to one of the artists in the exhibit, one thing led to another, she continued with a giggle, making Maple wonder if she still was talking about art. Anyway, she picked up painting miniatures real fast – using oils, no less. A course later – oh yes, let me tell you, I went to a casino named Downstream and won thirty-one thousand dollars – convinced me to try making a living at it. Gambling? Maple asked. No, miniature painting. I've tried about everything else short of selling myself – waiting tables, painting houses but hated ladders, driving truck but couldn't get the backing up part, cold calling but felt like I was ripping people off and it's so frustrating getting hung up on all the time, retail sales. I've worked in cheese and bedspring factories and even a circus one summer. She shifted into a sing-song voice, "Three darts for a dollar. Pop one balloon and win a prize" ...So when I got out of the cast I scrounged up some rocks and stiff paper lids and tins and other pieces of metal to paint on and with plenty of money from the casino for paint and stuff I'm going to start painting and find out where the miniature shows are and then see what happens.

She was breathless. Maple's ears rang. He was still wondering about one thing leading to another for someone in a body cast.

"So," she said, "what's your story?"

"I'm going fishing."

Chapter 16

Special Agent Hudson was elated. After three days of bureaucratic debate she had permission to release the photo of one of the prime suspects. The description released earlier basically held up: White, medium complexion, perhaps tan from being outside; mid-30s; stocky and muscular.

But based on the driver's license he was a bit smaller, 5'8" and 175 pounds, and he had brown eyes and brown hair, perhaps short-cropped. May be dressed in casual or blue-collar workman's clothes and often wears a baseball cap. No facial hair, though often has beard stubble. No known tattoos, body piercings or scars, but may have a mole the size of a dime below suspect's right front hairline.

Best of all there was the driver's license photo of Harrison Willford, with the caution it was likely an alias. Although the head-on photo didn't show the dime-size mole beneath his right hairline, Hudson included that possibility in the description. She again added the artist's sketch of the suspect with a beard.

During the three days Hudson waited, hundreds of officers fanned out to interview public and private employers who may have hired the terrorists, particularly the one needing a face and name. The officers met dead end upon dead end until, finally, the HR director for a computer firm remembered a man with a faded v-shaped scar on his chin. "It was sexy," she said. She found the application and job file for a

Mitchell Applebaum. He was hired as the firm's internal programmer and repair technician, a job not requiring a federal background investigation. A photo ID was needed to access the company's offices in Rockville, Maryland.

"We were doing a lot of hiring so we had a photog set up for the day," the HR director remembered. "Mr. Applebaum didn't show, said he didn't remember when I took the extra step to call him. His resume looked good. I told him if he wanted the job he'd have to go to the photographer's studio. He didn't argue. Apparently he needed the job. He quit about a year later. When I tried to keep him he said something about not having a choice but maybe he'd be in touch later. That was a couple years ago and I haven't heard from him since."

Neighbors from around Point of Rocks who had given the best descriptions identified Applebaum from the photo. They were certain. No driver's license could be found. But now, instead of issuing the all-points bulletin for just one Harrison Willford, he was accompanied by one Mitchell Applebaum, described as:

White, light complexion; 5'11", 165 lbs.; late 30s; lean but muscular; brown thinning hair combed straight back; light green eyes; thin face; well-dressed, whether wearing casual clothes or coat and tie, sometimes wears a broad-brimmed felt hat. No facial hair. No known tattoos or body piercings, but suspect believed to have a faint v-shaped scar on his chin.

Again, the artist's rendition of the man known as Applebaum was attached, showing his hair combed over rather than straight back, and with a light growth of beard, neatly trimmed.

The world-wide bulletin finally gave the public names, real or not, and photos of both men leading the FBI's list of most wanted, for terrorism and first degree murder in the deadly attack on the Russian Embassy. They are armed and extremely dangerous, the posters advised. Do not approach. Contact law enforcement.

Chapter 17

Settled on the sofa with hot tea after a day of hiking, Maple and Stickman were jarred by TV images of their former selves, images still looking too familiar for comfort. "Shit, fuck," said Maple, his cup rattling as he set it on the coffee table. "Listen to this," Stickman ordered.

Maple went silent as he tried to concentrate on the well-known anchorman but the words swam past him like static. ... *wanted in the attack on the Russian Embassy that killed more than forty ... also in the deaths of four sheriff's deputies ambushed as they waited for backup near ... The pair disappeared without a trace ... heavily-armed and extremely dangerous ... whereabouts unknown, with sightings from around the globe. Authorities say privately that they believe the men have not left the U.S. by commercial transportation. They concede, however, that the two may have slipped across either border. So far the pair has not been linked to a terrorist group, domestic or international ... apparently homegrown though nothing is known about their backgrounds ... Officials also concede that the names very possibly are aliases ... have had enough time to alter their appearances ... ten million dollar reward for each ...*

Stickman was rapt as the anchor brought in three guests, two of them retired law enforcement, who offered nothing beyond speculation. "Good," Stickman said as the segment ended. He switched off the TV to think. There would be plenty to watch throughout the evening. "Two of those so-called experts were ex-feds who had high level jobs.

If the cop community had much more to go on those two would have known about it."

"Maybe they were told to keep their mouths shut."

"Maybe. But they would have wanted to leave the impression they knew things they couldn't talk about, if only to justify their consulting fees. They didn't do that."

There was a long silence and Maple felt his pulse settling. He had been hunted before, after some of their missions, but never with his face all over TV, let alone on national TV. Never with a very big number on his head. Never hunted, it felt, by everyone in the entire freaking country, whether wearing a badge or not. Remember what you are committed to, he told himself: This government is evil. Suicidal jihad is not our way, but no sacrifice is too great.

"It feels like it's time to move on." His words echoed in his ears as he fought to keep his voice calm. "As low-key as we've been, several people have seen us here. Now we've got a new neighbor. When people get up close a lot, that's the worst. Maybe I'm getting paranoid, but it's like I see them trying to remember where they know me from. I'm thinking it's time to find another place, somewhere we haven't been seen in the flesh."

Stickman looked intently at his partner.

"What?" Maple said finally.

"Several people have seen us briefly. Thousands of people will remember brief sightings of guys that sort of kind of look like us, thousands of them from across the country. Only three people have seen you up close for several minutes. Only two of them have seen me, and not for very long."

"So ...are you saying we get rid of them – or you get rid of me?" Maple asked, forcing a half smile as he shifted slightly to look Stickman in the eye.

"Neither. You're the one whose appearance has changed the most. I'm the one most likely to be spotted, particularly if someone has a chance to see me more than a few times. Besides truly being brothers, I need you more than you need me."

It was the first time either had expressed serious affection or commitment to the other. Maple was touched but did not want to show it. "I guess we're joined at the hip," he slowly said flippantly. "If we don't leave, then what?"

"As for getting rid of the old people and our new neighbor, that presents problems. The oldsters no doubt know so many people around here that they would soon be missed. We don't know anything about our neighbor, not about her habits. What if she has a boyfriend who plans to start coming around?"

"We'd have to hit the road and hope for the best."

But, continued Stickman, "What if I hit the road and you stayed here? That would reduce chances of them matching me with the photo they see on TV, and if I'm on the road I won't see anyone twice. You, on the other hand, don't look as much like your photo, given how fast your hair and beard grew. It would take some imagination to make a connection."

April Spring watched the news with entrepreneurial interest. An idea had hit her almost immediately. This search could go on quite a while, long enough for me to offer a line of miniature paintings of events going back to 9/11. A stone on the World Trade Center. One on the Pentagon, a couple on combating terrorism in Iraq and Syria. The Islamic State. It's a good thing I keep up on the news. Maybe pick out a few of the mass slayings. One on the new Trade Center as a symbol of emerging hope and then hope dashed by the attack on Russia's embassy. The deputies being ambushed and stones with faces of the terrorists. Ah, right, first have to come the faces of the terrorists. They're hot. And more pieces as they are captured and tried and executed. That's the sequence, follow them and then work backwards as I have time. But how do I sell them? Hell, I don't know anything about marketing. Hated cold calling. Maybe I can hook up with a big-time marketing firm, like in Pittsburgh. That's okay, that will come, get the faces done first. The Internet will tell me how to do marketing.

April's racing mind went back to the faces on the screen, ordinary everyman faces that reminded her of past lovers, of every thirty-something with regular features and a beard. Yes, this is apt to go on for some time.

She leaned the recliner back as Harrison Willford's photo came on for the umpteenth time. He had a drowsy look, one she liked. Perhaps it was purposeful, to dull up the driver's license photo, which the announcer noted does not show the mole beneath his hairline. Or perhaps it was natural cool, the look of a man who could arouse women or put men at ease. A young Redford. Or Brad. Her hand slipped to her inner thigh, then to the cut-off jeans, moving to the center seam. She pressed lightly and liked it. Pressed again. She wondered why she hadn't heard from Roy. It had been more than a week now, a busy time arranging the move and getting loaded and unloaded, all without his promised help. And cleaning a trailer that was supposed to be clean. I bet the damn cleaning crew is ripping off the old folks. She felt so ready, but also weary. The temptation was hard to resist, but she clicked off the table lamp, resting her hand despondently on her smooth belly.

Violet peered intently at the terrorists' photos. All evening she and Wilbur had been mesmerized by coverage that moved from the Russian Embassy to the mass killings of recent years–a military base, a school, a movie theater, a night club. Their lifetimes had allowed – forced? – them to experience and luckily survive most of the historic events of their primary century – the Crash and the Depression, World War II and the liberation of Holocaust camps and atomic bombs striking Japan. Then Korea. Coverage became more immediate with the Vietnam War, and even before that with Kennedy's assassination. They managed to keep up with the fast pace of reporting until the arrival of 24/7 coverage that in the new century seemed to intensify events – 9/11, war in the Mideast with video cameras mounted on tanks, Katrina. Now all this killing. If they weren't calling the footage from Paris "unbelievable," they were calling the footage from Brussels "amazing." Violet and Wilbur struggled to keep up, a losing battle when the screen bombarded them with three or four things at the same time.

That was particularly true of Wilbur. He dozed under the endless blare, but was repeatedly awakened, too. "Shut it off, Mother. What more are you goin' to learn tonight? It will be the same in the mornin'."

"Probably. But Wilbur, look at the second one. Doesn't he bear a 'semblance to one of the men who signed the month-to-month lease? Don't he now?"

Wilbur squinted. "I surely don't know. Couldn't rule it out but there must be a million like that. Hell, I could have looked like that once. Remember, Mother, when I was buildin' Hoover?"

Violet sighed.

"They had figured out most of the problems, but not how to make the blasting effective, so as much of the rubble as possible ended up close to where they needed it. Project that size, where that rubble ended up made a hell of a difference, both in time and in money."

"Wilbur, your main blastin' experience came in Alaska, those two summers during college," Violet said gently, wanting him back to tonight.

"True, Mother, that's what got me started. But Hoover was just an extension of what I learned in Alaska and for whatever reason they couldn't figure out what I could. I was just lucky, and they were just lucky, that I happened to be in the room – in the back I have to admit – when this problem came up. I piped up, 'Sir ...' and then had to go up to the front and give them my thoughts. It was scary, Mother, scary. But my idea worked. President Roosevelt himself said it did at the ceremony when the dam was closed on the Colorado. He was right there and he tipped his hat, so to speak, to a few people. And I was one of them."

"Yes, Wilbur. For a while I always thought you were with me that day, at the hospital, when we lost Thomas at near full-term. But now I remember."

Options had been swimming through Stickman's mind but the key building blocks remained the same. He needed to leave. Maple needed to stay. For Maple, that meant more of the same – staying low-profile. For Stickman, that meant what? He could run, perhaps with the advan- tage of the law looking for two men instead of one. He could change his appearance more, probably something he should do in any case. Make his way to other potential safe houses he and Maple had located over the years and check them out. But they were much like this mobile home, remote and appealing but operated by people he didn't know, people who would turn him in in a minute. Make his way west to his friends in Northern California. God, that was a long way, perhaps a lot of roadblocks, getting by sharp-eyed cops carrying a photo. A di- version. Yes, create a diversion, something to get his mug off TV for a while. How the hell do you divert law enforcement nation? Stickman weighed his options for a long time. Maple was in bed. As midnight ap- proached on the West Coast he finally made the call.

Chapter 18

Stickman set a course of blue highways taking him to the south of Pittsburgh, then northwest into Ohio. A slow, two-lane route, but hopefully one avoiding checkpoints. Anyway, his confederates had to drive three times as far.

The past three days had been busy and filled with unease. Every time he or Maple snapped on the TV, it seemed, they saw their old selves. Worse, Maple had several tasks that exposed him to public view. There was Stickman's short list of hardware items to buy, another of groceries and three shades of red hair dye. Stickman tried the most subtle of the three and it was red enough. He saw with relief that it looked more natural than he had dared hope. Most important was buying a car. Maple settled on a three-year old gray Toyota, dull but with a V-6 engine, being sold privately. Its owner stared hard at the cash being counted out, barely glancing at the driver's license Maple had expertly altered to look like the new Stickman. Picking a busy time at the DMV, it was easy to get the Toyota registered.

Maple then set about creating a hidden compartment beneath the back seat, smaller than in the car they drove from Point of Rocks but big enough to give Stickman an arsenal that could prove lifesaving. As he wedged the seat back into place, he was startled by a cheery "Hi there."

He turned to find his new neighbor standing at the front of the car. Good. Even if she had been there a minute, she was at the wrong angle to see into the back seat. "April, remember?" she said. "Alex." "Nice to meet you again, Alex." She offered a large hand. "April Spring."

She looked directly into his face with dark brown eyes, a well-proportioned woman about his height. Her dark hair fell on square shoulders at the top button of her denim shirt. Her jeans fit loosely. "Thanks again for the cream and sugar." He nodded.

"Did you catch any fish?"

"As a matter of fact, yes."

"New car?"

"New to Demetri," said Maple, wondering what question was next.

"Mrs. Banks told me you and Demetri are here fishing and hiking. Did your other car break down?"

"No, it's fine. It's just that ... Well, Demetri has a family emergency and I wasn't ready to go back to work yet so ..."

"I hope it's nothing too serious."

"I hope not, too. All things being equal I think he'll be back in a few days. How's your artwork going?" he asked, wanting another subject.

"I'm just about settled in. Maybe tomorrow I'll get started. I looked around some today and from the top of that hill," she said, pointing, "there's a scenic view where red-tailed hawks like to hunt. I haven't tried to capture that much space in a miniature before. It would be a challenge."

"How big would that painting be?"

"I have a nice, flat oval stone that's maybe two inches on the long side. Or if I can't make that work I have a couple of sardine tins. I think if I went any bigger, I couldn't call it a miniature ... What kind of work do you guys do?"

"It's more what don't we do. Demetri is an all-round computer guy. I can do a lot of the trades."

"I'll remember that, Alex, whenever something breaks. You must have pretty nice employers to take off like Mrs. Banks said."

"I suppose. Well, I need to excuse myself, April. Good luck with your art."

"'Til next time, Alex. And if I can repay your kindness just let me know."

Hearing about April's visit, Stickman had asked if there was any way she could have seen into the back seat. Not satisfied, he asked for a word-by-word recounting of the full conversation. Maple was mildly irritated but went through it in detail. In the end, Stickman grudgingly accepted that April posed no threat.

Chapter 19

She seems a bit too neighborly, Stickman was thinking as he drove through an intersection where a car marked "Sheriff's Deputy" was parked nearby. He smiled at the rearview mirror when the deputy didn't follow. Glancing back seconds later he saw his optimism was premature. Less than an hour on the road and he was in trouble. Stickman located the latch of the console between the seats, to know he could find it easily.

The deputy held his distance several car lengths back. As minutes passed, Stickman became hopeful, which again proved to be false optimism. The deputy's rooftop lights began flashing, a siren squealed briefly. Stickman swore under his breath and pulled to the shoulder of the paved county road. On impulse he pulled off the ball cap, thinking the change of hair style and color may hold more advantage than a cap that kept the focus on his face.

He watched in his side mirror as the deputy got out and strolled toward him, bright rosy cheeks glowing beneath his Ray-Bans, right hand resting casually on his Glock. He stooped at the window and Stickman saw his identification badge – Dumfries. After checking Stickman's license and registration, he asked why someone from New Jersey was driving a remote county road.

"I stopped at Falling Water, sir," Stickman answered, trying to establish a subservient demeanor to give Deputy Dumfries more feeling of control. "I'd had enough of interstates and decided to take my time for a while."

"This car was just purchased."

"That's right, sir. My car died, just off the warranty, of course."

"Stay put." The officer backed away a couple steps, setting a course to his car that allowed him to watch Stickman from the corner of his eye. The young deputy seemed uncertain of his next move. He may have checked the photos of Willford and Applebaum before leaving his car and is now taking another look, Stickman thought. He may be thinking: Is this one of those guys? Or he may have called in and wants to know if backup is on the way. And since the car's permanent license plates hadn't arrived, had Maple's theft of plates the day before been reported? Did the deputy already know the plates were not for this car? He didn't know how quickly information on license plates – new or stolen–worked its way through the system. But he could feel the sweat in his armpits as he opened the console and reached in.

Deputy Dumfries approached again, but this time stopped short, the Glock in his right hand. "Okay, put your hands on the top of the steering wheel where I can see them ... Now I'm going to open the door and I want you to step out slowly."

"Yes, sir, though I don't know what the problem is."

Following Dumfries' orders, Stickman assumed the position against the car. "I'm going to cuff you. Move both hands slowly behind your back."

Stickman slowly lowered his arms, leading with his left. When his left hand was nearly down, he sensed the deputy glancing at it and turning slightly, reaching with a ready handcuff. Stickman shifted his right wrist and a wooden handle dropped softly into his cupped hand. He spun suddenly, stepping back and into the deputy, left hand gripping the deputy's right wrist as the ice pick shot upward across his body. The pick found its mark, just below the sternum, piercing Dumfries' heart. The deputy's eyes went wide. Stickman's left hand firmly held his wrist as the Glock slipped away, clattering on the pavement. Deputy Dumfries stood quietly, unsteadily for a long moment before crumbling, the side of his face bouncing on the pavement. He rolled onto his back and then was still.

Stickman had released the pick with the strange thought that it would plug the hole in Dumfries' chest. Only the black handle protruded, sticking nearly upright in a small circle of blood. Though shaking slightly, Stickman took immediate pride in knowing all the practice he had invested in that quick move had created a muscle memory capable of saving his freedom. He had killed with his hands before, but this was the first against someone presumably able to defend himself, someone also trained to kill. Using the ice pick was personal, so different from directing a rain of destruction on unsuspecting victims. Stickman put his hands on his knees. As he steadied himself, he could envision wandering into the old-time pawn shop some years ago, seeing the elegant ice pick in a locked case. The polished black grip of ebony suggested India, the initialed shaft the work of an expert craftsman. He suddenly had wanted a backup weapon and didn't haggle price. Not until months later did he juxtapose ice pick with his name.

Less than a minute after his lethal attack, Stickman's methodical mind was taking control, charting next steps. The initial pride he took in the kill was also fading as he realized that his young victim barely qualified as a worthy foe, if that. Already, Stickman saw, the rose in Dumfries' cheeks was barely visible. "Officer Dumbshit," he muttered.

Given his late start, the day's shadows already were growing long. He needed to get the deputy and his patrol car out of sight soon, improving chances of nothing being found until tomorrow at the earliest. He worried that his luck wouldn't hold and a motorist – or other officers – would show up first.

In his car trunk, Stickman quickly located a plastic ground cloth and a pair of latex gloves. He started the patrol car and pulled it alongside the body. Thankfully, no one was trying to radio. Again, he wished he knew whether Officer Dumbshit had called in his location or description of the Toyota. He should have of course, but maybe he was playing the cowboy, seeking fame and fortune with a solo arrest. Or maybe he was plain careless.

Blood had continued spreading slowly in a circular pattern. There was a slight spurt when Stickman withdrew the pick. He tucked the ground cloth under one side of the deputy and rolled him over. Three lengths of rope tightly tied created the appearance of a plastic mummy. As strong as Stickman was, he struggled to wrestle the big man into the trunk. Though the day was turning cool, Stickman was sweating profusely when he again slipped behind the wheel. Seeing his license and registration on the dashboard was startling, but he didn't dwell on his oversight. A short steep hill was only a football field away. He wanted it to be rough downhill terrain, but found himself looking at rolling pasture, clearly visible from the road. He drove to the next, slightly higher hill. With relief, he saw the hill fell off steeply, enough for the car to go well off the road. If he could aim it between two mature red oaks, it should gather enough speed to hurtle through wild rose bushes and other brambles standing higher than a man. And if the bushes sprang back the car would not be visible from the road. Too many ifs but Stickman did not have time to find a better place.

He backed the patrol car to the opposite side of the road before easing it forward to the pavement's edge. He wondered if the car would high-center going over, but had to take that chance. Turning off the virtually silent radio and three other systems, he hoped he wasn't shutting down something he shouldn't. He put the car in neutral, killed the engine and eased his foot from the brake. The car didn't move. Stepping out, he leaned his shoulder into the door post. The patrol car moved an inch, another, then suddenly sprung away, leaving the road in a rush. Before Stickman could take a deep breath the car slashed between the red oaks, through the bushes and out of sight. A couple loud thumps reverberated, followed by silence. Stickman quickly scuffed away the faint tire marks in the shoulder. As long as there's not some sort of GPS signal, Officer Dumbshit may go missing longer than I hoped, he thought.

In the time he ran to his car an idea had hatched. He drove back to where he had pushed the patrol car from the pavement. Grabbing his road atlas, he tore a page from the Ts. Walking to the ditch on the opposite side of the road, he placed the page at the bottom of a woven wire fence, as if the wind had picked that spot to deposit the map of Texas. Hopefully, a bright investigator would conclude the page was connected to the deputy's murder and the search for the killer should be focused on the Lone Star state.

Stickman could think of just one more precaution in case Dumfries had called in his car's description. Two days earlier Maple had liberated another set of tags from a junkyard. They were on a Toyota of the same color and nearly the same vintage, close enough to pass muster in a casual traffic check – maybe. Stickman quickly switched tags and had just closed the trunk lid when a car approached from behind. No siren or lights, it appeared harmless enough. Stickman pulled on his ball cap as the car stopped.

"Everything okay?" asked a bulky white-haired man with what immediately smacked of a perpetual smile.

"Can you believe I just fixed a damn flat tire? Nobody has flat tires these days."

"Not unless you get real unlucky. No one should get unlucky on a fine day like this, even if it is April Fool's Day. Bye now."

Chapter 20

April Spring drove up to her mobile home, returning from another day of sketching and photographing scenes and subjects she might turn into miniature art. This must stop, time to start painting, she told herself. She needed to start with miniatures of the terrorists to get a sense of whether that would work. Admittedly, she was anxious about moving the fine-tipped brushes from oil to rock or tin, which carried the threat of failure. Especially for her, a rank amateur, even if showing promise. But the last several months had been rough, she rationalized. She deserved a few days in the sun. Tomorrow she'd start painting for sure, she promised herself as Maple drove in next door.

April waved hello and walked his way. "Have you heard from your friend?"

"Everything's under control, thanks, but I don't know his plans."

"Glad everything is okay. I just made a decision: I'm going to start painting tomorrow."

"Good for you. Have you decided what you're going to start with?"

She paused, reluctant to share her true plans. "I'd like to do that soaring red-tailed hawk, hunting, I think I told you about. But getting everything in such a confined space will be hard. I found an old iron bridge in a beautiful valley that I'm more comfortable with for starters. Say, it's cocktail time. Will you join me?"

Maple felt uncomfortable and pulled up a lame excuse. "Thanks, but I actually have quite a bit to do, several calls."

"Tomorrow then, if you can," April persisted as she turned away.

The next day went well. Working on stones, April painted the scenic bridge from a photo on her iPad and got a good start on an early 1950s Ford pickup rusting in a weedy field. Even so, there was a nip of guilt as her mind kept coming back to trying the terrorist portraits.

She had called Roy when she took a break for lunch, but got no answer. The afternoon was fading when she finished cleaning her brushes. Getting two beers from the refrigerator, she was sitting quietly in a lawn chair when Maple returned as dusk set in.

"Hi," she called. "I drank your beer. But come on over. I have more."

Maple walked slowly toward her, knowing he would be more at ease by himself. But being standoffish would draw unwanted attention at some point. What bothered him most, though, was he didn't really know how to talk about himself and was fearful of dropping a personal detail that didn't fit his simple cover story. His lack of experience with women, casual as well as sexual, made him uncomfortable in any one-on-one situation. He had a few girlfriends in and after high school, but his physical advances were clumsy and ill-timed. Other priorities crowded his immature love life, primarily his exploration of Islam and travel to Afghanistan, with the hardened radicalization that followed. Since then there had been only Mother Fist and her five daughters. It was much easier that way, never being challenged by the demands of a relationship. Never having a real conversation, let alone opening himself to someone else. Such interchange, he told himself, would endanger or make more difficult what was important in his life. Avoidance meant getting no more involved than water cooler chats about gas prices or how the Redskins were doing.

He wished Stickman had not left. Maybe April would see them as gay and wanting to be left alone. Or maybe Stickman would take an interest in her. He was closer to her age and, though never discussed, Maple knew he had occasional relationships. Now and then, Stickman would fail to come home and that would repeat itself every few days before abruptly ending. For whatever reason, Maple wondered whether those episodes involved men or women, though Stickman was not effeminate in any way.

"Unfold that lawn chair, Alex. Wanna Bud or an IPA?"

"I really don't drink much, April. Just water or tea would be fine."

Her hip brushed his shirt sleeve as he leaned to open the chair. She was quickly back with ice tea and another beer for herself. After exchanging summaries of their days – Maple's mostly a composite of things he sometimes did – the next hour went surprisingly fast as April took over the conversation, interrupting herself only for another beer.

Declining her dinner offer of stew, Maple pulled himself up from the low-slung chair and she followed suit. She moved to within easy reach. "You really shouldn't go."

"Yes," he began but was interrupted by the warm press of her body. Her hands took his face and she kissed him and after hesitating, he kissed her back, her tongue immediately searching his mouth. "That's better," she said, hands moving down his chest and to his sudden erection. He kissed her again and his hands cupped her ample breasts. She rubbed him, her other hand slipping under his crotch to squeeze gently.

"Oh God," he hissed as his cock began throbbing, then lost control. "Oh God, I am so sorry. I'm not very ...God, it feels good, so good ..." She hadn't turned loose of anything and he rocked back and forth, grunting softly. "Sorry. I'm embarrassed. I need to go now."

"No. You're coming inside. I'm going to tease you back to life."

Chapter 21

The call Stickman had made in search of a diversion was well-timed. His Northern California friends were restless. Led by Raymon Swale, there were seven men, down from nine. Two had become casualties of war. They hadn't planned on martyrdom, but both decided that was their best option. Diagnosed with cancer within weeks of each other, their prognoses were short. About the same time, Swale and his wife had returned from a wedding anniversary trip to Hawaii that presented an unexpected opportunity for jihad. Arrangements were made quickly, including getting false IDs for the cancer-stricken men. Little time passed before the Swales woke up to news reports of two Kapakahi Air commuter planes exploding in mid-air off the coast of Maui. No bodies were found, but Swale had no doubt who was among the missing. "The Swale people," as they were called by neighbors and the residents of a nearby town, had planned well. Officials could not pinpoint why the commuter planes went down. Most analysts blamed terrorists, finding no other plausible explanation for almost instantaneous explosions. In the public's mind, the tragedy accentuated the continuing threat of terrorism underlined by the attack on the Russian Embassy. Not since 9/11 had people been so fearful.

Swale took quiet enjoyment from that fear, even as it began to subside. After all, he and his people lived every day with something akin to fear. Bias against Muslims in Los Angeles was sometimes palpable even before 9/11. Post- 9/11, religious prejudice in their neighborhood grew much worse. Authorities, particularly the feds, kept mosques under close scrutiny. At times, undercover agents were believed to be operating in their midst. Suspected agents were shunned, and suspicions were confirmed when the agents, effectively neutered, quietly melted away.

Swale slowly created a militant jihadist cell in his Los Angeles neighborhood. It was not easy. The huge majority of Muslims who attended his mosque were not militant. Most applauded non-Muslims who refused to say "radical Islamic terrorism," seeing those words as falsely labeling all Muslims as terrorists and wrongly giving credibility to the Islamic State and other terrorist organizations.

Quietly, Swale counseled his small band of followers to believe they had every right to their fundamentalist interpretation of Islamic religious law, or sharia, and that what moderate Muslims labeled terrorism was a justified response to oppression. He rejected charges that practices of the Islamic State and al-Qaeda were barbaric, particularly when inflicted on fellow Muslims, but his militancy was more in line with al-Qaeda.

With maturity, Swale had learned the virtue of patience and deception and to keep his radical views from sight. Those in his cell appreciated his discretion, but they were younger and impatient to inflict pain on America. Occasional missions that took them far from California increasingly failed to hold Swale's cell in check or together.

Swale decided the answer was moving to a remote area where threats posed by law enforcement or by Muslims not sharing his radicalism were far diminished. He needed a rural community where it was not unusual to find small groups of people who had fled what they saw as societal oppression. He needed a place where people didn't ask too many questions, where being a little different was acceptable, where the barter system and living off the land, at least in part, helped mask the isolation they desired. He and his people needed to stay pretty much to themselves, where they could be in the community but not of the community. He found land for sale near a small town in Northern California that had a reputation for tolerance, and boasted enough "characters" that the Swale people did not stand out.

While not a commune, Swale and those who decided to follow him were definitely close-knit. They lived on properties adjoining each other, not separated by outsiders. Of the remaining seven men, three had wives and now there was a widow. Of the eleven children, those old enough were homeschooled. Swale sold most of the land to two of his men, who shared the farming equipment needed to grow small cash crops and support a few head of livestock. Everyone planted large gardens and fruit trees and some of the land already had vines producing small quantities of wine. Some of the Swale people worked full- or part-time, bringing them into casual contact with the broader community. The martyred Asian man and the skinny man had held jobs. When local residents asked about them, the response was a version of the truth: They had aggressive cancers and had left to exercise their preference for suicide.

The isolated and insular area had no mosque. The Swale people tried to practice their faith quietly, though it was difficult to advise their offspring about what to tell friends when religion came up. The unsatisfactory outcome was that everyone avoided the subject as best they could. The oldest of the children, a girl and a boy, were twelve and eleven. As they became more inquisitive, planning and carrying out missions became more difficult. At the same time, the children's growing acceptance of things American posed a huge challenge to radicalizing them. Before long, Swale thought, it would be necessary to return to a place with a large Muslim community where parental guidance had less influence on lifestyle choices. There, young people would gravitate more naturally in the direction of radical jihad, or not.

Meanwhile, his men, and sometimes Swale, continued to discretely carry out missions, though not as often as they wanted. Like Stickman and Maple's, missions typically took them far afield to avoid drawing local attention.

Though awakened by Stickman's call, Swale answered on the fourth ring and was glad to hear his old friend's voice. He slipped quietly from his wife's side and into the living room.

"Just a few days ago I had a notion I'd be hearing from you," Swale said, removing any doubt he had been following television news. There was no reason to believe the phone was tapped, but he and Stickman had long practiced extreme caution. They also had a simple three-part code for joining forces if need be. Swale figured they were finally going to use the code.

"Hope I'm not calling too late. Tired of reading and TV and can't sleep. I thought I'd take a chance."

"Nice to hear your voice, my friend."

"Did you and Fawn enjoy your wedding anniversary?"

"More than I ever expected. We were ready for a break, mon. Good food, good times, even came across a business opportunity. The timing couldn't have been better."

More chitchat and then part one of their code: "Your Giants are not exactly off to an explosive start. What odds do you need to pick them to make the playoffs?"

"That would depend on whether you want a friendly bet or are trying to pull me into serious money, mon. Oh ...assuming it's friendly and they improve, I might go for twelve-to-one."

"It would be friendly. But let's wait a bit. If the Giants perk up, maybe you'll be easier to get along with."

A little later, parts two and three: "I'm taking some time off. If you're not too busy maybe you'd like to meet at a mid-point."

"Sorry, mon, I've got to finish a couple projects for a guy. How about in a couple weeks? I could invite some neighbors, guys you've met. If I got four plus you and me, we'd have a good poker table."

"Not sure I'll still be loafing in two weeks, but we'll see."

They hung up a few minutes later. Swale, in giving odds on the Giants' less than explosive start, signaled he could deliver up to twelve pounds of C-4. Saying he was busy meant Swale was, in fact, not, and that he and four others could meet Stickman within a few days.

Swale sat back, remembering Stickman in his formative years, when he was a friend of several young Muslims that Swale also knew. They became acquaintances. After 9/11, those young men sought to understand the religious prejudice being heaped upon them. They found that reaction extremely unpleasant, particularly when it came from people long valued as friends and equals. It drove their conversations for months. Stickman joined them, mostly listening. So did Swale and other older men from the mosque, guiding the conversation as their own beliefs dictated. As Stickman's interest in Islam grew, so did his bonds in the Muslim community and with Swale.

Swale's subtly-expressed militancy was not lost on Stickman. Similarly, Swale saw how anti-Muslim prejudice was fueling the young man's growing anger. When Stickman showed an interest in travel, Swale was there to assist, contacting relatives in Brussels who welcomed Stickman and, in turn, fostered the next step of his journey, to Afghanistan.

The first conversation upon his return to Los Angeles was stilted, with Stickman and Swale trying cautiously to gauge the militancy of the other. As they probed, they slowly learned they shared an animosity toward the United States that, in their minds, justified radical jihad. It was one of the happiest days of Swale's life. Another was when Stickman headed east to rejoin Maple and embark on a very patient journey of homegrown terrorism.

The day after the late-night phone call, Stickman handed Maple an envelope and asked him to drive nearly to Pittsburgh to mail it. The envelope contained a single sheet of paper with a coded line of fifty-three numbers. The numbers included eight zip codes of five numbers each, written in reverse order. By previous agreement, the fourth zip code to emerge identified the key location. Also buried in the line of numbers – right after the key zip code – was a ten-digit telephone number, also in reverse order.

When the envelope arrived, Swale consulted a weary scrap of paper that nearly had worn out two billfolds. The scrap bore faded notes, meaningless to anyone else, but they jogged Swale's memory enough to identify the key zip code. He went to his computer and identified a medium-size Midwestern city. He deciphered the phone number and saw that the area and zip codes overlapped.

Swale knew the travel code worked out with Stickman would barely slow a cryptographer. But as long as their mail wasn't monitored, the string of numbers would mean nothing to anyone else. When confronting the vast resources of the federal government, it at least made them feel good.

Having a match, Swale called the telephone number and was relieved when a motel desk clerk answered. He was to meet Stickman at the motel. The fifty-first and fifty-second numbers gave him the date. The last number told him to come with a crew of four.

Just in case the mission dragged on, Swale made a week-long reservation for three rooms. His friends could double up.

Chapter 22

Swale took I-5 north into Oregon. Riding shotgun was Dog, whose baggy eyes and jowls and oversized earlobes gave visual confirmation to his name. The former Army Ranger had served in Iraq and Afghanistan and got out as quickly as possible after his third tour. He had grown weary of trying to help people who all too often didn't want help, who siphoned off money and, worse, materials that ended up on the black market.

Even worse were the indiscriminate attacks on civilians by U.S. troops and contract employees. Abuses were almost always brushed off as "collateral damage" – deaths covered up with no thought of disciplinary action. Maybe he just drew rotten units, but he knew too many soldiers who had raped, beaten and even killed those they were there to protect. Once, on patrol, he had scrambled in the direction of a shot, figuring a buddy was in trouble. Instead, he found his corporal standing over a dead Afghan. "He deserved it," the corporal said. "He mouthed off to me once too often." Dog did not file a report. To what end? The corporal would have his story.

Dog didn't know if his experience was typical. He did know that some locals were guilty of terrible atrocities against their own countrymen. But in pursuing combat deployment he had set a high standard for himself and those he served with. Perhaps that was unrealistic, even unfair, but it was his expectation. Mid-way through his last tour he uncomfortably became aware of harboring a seed of hatred against his own country. It was mixed with a fledgling belief that America was far too strong, far too indiscriminate about mixing in the affairs of others, far too arrogant in believing it had solutions to centuries-old blood feuds. He had no interest in deserting to join al-Qaeda let alone the ISIS butchers. Dog had been born poor and, slight of build, bullied from earliest memory. Now, with his training, he was seldom a victim. But his experiences as a Ranger had made the world a confusing and twisted place, more so because of America's overbearing policies.

Seeking respite after his discharge, Dog settled in Los Angeles near the beach. He found part-time jobs to stretch his savings but was largely content with simply having time to decompress. His apartment was cheap and his landlord, wanting to boost the rent, had hired a handyman/contractor named Raymon Swale to remodel the kitchen and bathroom. The job stretched over several weeks and an acquaintanceship became a friendship. As their talks grew more intimate, Dog revealed his festering opposition to U.S. foreign policy, and that he saw a growing need for someone to humble the United States. Swale expertly massaged Dog's discontent. A seed blossomed into a declared hatred.

When the time came for Swale to move north, he risked confiding in Dog. Not only did he, too, harbor such a hatred, Swale revealed, he was acting on it. Soon, Dog was in. Swale also tried to interest Dog in Islam, but failed. "Faith is for people who don't believe that dead is dead," he explained. When asked to join a mission, though, he accepted immediately. One reason was that he missed the tension of the battlefield. Over time, whenever Swale felt at risk, he put Dog at his side. Despite the man's forlorn appearance, he was by far the most dangerous in Swale's crew. Dog stepped up as a tutor, and the cell, including Swale, soaked up his lessons. Swale was not bothered that their skills fell short of Ranger quality. More important, they were loyal, radical jihadists who had his complete trust.

Intersecting I-94, Swale and Dog headed east for a critical stop in Fargo, North Dakota, before their final destination. Three other Swale men would meet them there, also covering more than two thousand miles but on a more southerly route.

That trio rode in a van driven by Ali Foster. His Catholic parents owned convenience stores in Hollywood, California. Working in the stores had given him an aversion to the risks and demands of a small business. He found other jobs, but often had to move back in with his parents. Studious, he accomplished little during those years except for exploring religions. He eventually chose Islam and regularly attended one of the LA mosques, where he met Swale. As a sign of his commitment, Foster abandoned his birth name of Robert and took the name Ali not long before 9/11. In its aftermath he felt the sting of suspicion and bigotry from friends and former colleagues. His views hardened. Swale recognized the young man's transition and gradually drew him into his confidence. When asked if he was ready for radical jihad, Foster said yes without hesitation. Swale trained him as a carpenter, as he later would Dog. After the long string of meaningless jobs, Ali took satisfaction in being able to see the fruits of his work. Most of all, he savored the periodic missions that gave release to his growing hatred for the United States.

Foster's front seat passenger was Issa Assiri. Having moved well into middle age, his girth had thickened and his full head of hair was turning gray. More important, confidence in his considerable physical prowess had slipped and with it, his zeal for trips he now saw as dangerous. Perhaps he should be home helping his wife with their small deli and grocery, Assiri thought as he watched the greening prairie slip by. Still, he was the one closest to Swale, not only in age but in temperament and was best suited to take over, if necessary.

Assiri came by his livelihood honestly. Most of his large extended family were shopkeepers in medium-size cities in northwest Iraq. His Sunni parents had immigrated to the United States when he was a young man and though visits to his homeland were infrequent, he saw his relatives become more and more radical as U.S. involvement in the Mideast dragged on. Over the years, those militant views rubbed off. Assiri had been an easy recruit. At the same time, he worried about his relatives in Iraq. Already, some were dead, their militant zeal found lacking by ISIS.

George Kobeisi's roots were much like Assiri's, his Sunni parents also coming to America from northwest Iraq. They, too, came from a large family of shopkeepers. They dropped the "al" before their name when they became citizens and when their son was born they christened him in honor of their new country's first president. The family never visited Iraq, but became friends with Assiri and Swale through the mosque. George's parents were killed in a car accident shortly after he graduated from high school and Assiri stepped up as the male role model in his life, something akin to a beloved uncle. His political views came to mirror Assiri's. When Swale announced the move north, Kobeisi assumed correctly that he was included. Financially comfortable from his parents' estate, he bought one of the two small farms that helped provide for the Swale people.

Kobeisi stirred from a light sleep. "Where are we?"

"Sioux Falls in South Dakota. We'll stay here tonight and have a short day tomorrow. Swale should be getting into Fargo about now. He has to get supplies, so we'll arrive before he does."

Chapter 23

Monsour Zarif was a careful man. He had to be. He was a terrorist.

Born in Fargo, North Dakota of Iranian immigrants, his parents moved the family back to Iran to protect financial holdings there after the U.S.-backed Shah came to power. Zarif received a mediocre education but learned a good trade. People always need watches repaired and, over time, Zarif graduated to watch making and then to designing and making jewelry. A Shiite, he was a fringe player in the religious rebellion against the puppet who allowed the United States to control his ancestral country and its oil. After his parents died, and with the Shah tottering, Zarif spirited his family's modest wealth out of the country. As U.S. citizens it was easy for him and his siblings to return to America.

By then, Zarif was radicalized. He vowed to take a slice of the Iranian Revolution with him to the United States. Before leaving he made arrangements to stay in contact with his friends in the Iranian Revolutionary Guard Corps and various other extremist factions. Perhaps it would take years, but Zarif could see himself as a middleman between radical Islam in the Mideast and homegrown terrorists in the United States. For jihad to one day flourish in America would require money as well as ordnance not legally available to U.S. private citizens. Weapons and explosives would have to be smuggled in.

When Zarif settled in Dearborn, Michigan's large Muslim community, he found little stomach for radicalism. He looked for opportunities to identify and shape young Muslims, but with limited success. Instead of fostering jihad as he envisioned, his life turned slowly around fixing watches and making jewelry and being active in mosque and broader Muslim activities.

Then he met Raymon Swale, the son of Saudi immigrants. The 1993 bombing of the World Trade Center generated heated discussions among Muslims about whether it was justified. Swale's portrayal of the West as morally bankrupt and his outspoken defense of the bombing heartened Zarif. Here might be a committed recruit.

Though Swale was Sunni, the profound separation between Sunni and Shia in much of the Muslim world had been lost on him. He worshipped in mosques in the U.S. that were accepting of both branches, and he had Shia friends. Zarif devoted himself to the deeply personal challenge of creating bonds of trust with the impetuous young man. After many long talks, Swale came to accept the value of patience and discretion and silence. He learned the carpenter's trade and moved to California in search of like-minded jihadists in order to form his own radical cell. Zarif stayed in touch.

Health problems encroached as Zarif neared retirement. He returned to Fargo where he still had remnants of a family support system. His timing was good. In the first decade of the new century, Fargo saw a large influx of Muslims. Among those thousands, Zarif found more opportunity to develop radical jihadists. He revealed himself to only a handful of potential recruits, the ones he perceived to be most committed. While many talked of jihad, their caution, and paranoia about being infiltrated, stifled action.

After the Arab Spring, as significant rebel factions deserted the call of democracy to join the ISIS tide, Zarif came to believe that radical Islam could be awakened in the U.S. His commitment to jihad in the United States was stronger than his commitment to traditional Islam.

He came to admire the efforts of al-Qaeda and ISIS, though he was appalled by ISIS bragging on social media of beheadings and other atrocities. That chest-thumping brutality stirred widespread condemnation from the Muslim community, making domestic jihad much more difficult. Even so, Zarif saw a new readiness by some radical Muslims to convincingly demonstrate an extremist presence in America. Successful terrorist assaults like those in Paris and Brussels would erase any doubt that extremists flying the banner of Islam were a potent force against the world's most prestigious target.

Enthused, Zarif reached out to old contacts in Iran that he had neglected to cultivate for many years. Some of those contacts didn't respond or couldn't be found. Others were dead. Zariff also failed to appreciate how much Shia-Sunni differences had worsened since his time in Iran. Some old contacts pulled him into contentious religious debates that made impossible any chance of buying weapons. The bottom line was that the extremist community in the Mideast, as he had known it, was topsy-turvy. He was completely out of the loop.

Asking for help from one of his former recruits, he was told of an arms dealer in Hoboken, New Jersey. Patiently, contact was made – and Zarif finally arranged a shipment of C-4 plastic explosives. Unfortunately for him, it was on a cargo ship that was thoroughly searched upon arrival in the Port of New York. Another shipment was negotiated and, eventually, the Department of Homeland Security's long-time failure to consistently secure cargo ships was exploited. Helpful hands in Asia were found to make slight additions to a few of the thousands of imported cars. Other helpful hands were found in West Coast ports to relieve those imports of their excessive cargo. Finally, Zarif was able to take a road trip to secure his first precious shipment. He alerted Swale and a couple other brothers that he had supplies. Zarif had learned that the money trail could be an easier path than one strewn with the landmines of religious dogma.

Detouring through Northern California, Zarif made a joyous delivery to Swale. He made other detours as he returned to Fargo. But except for Swale's success in Hawaii, Zarif had yet to see results. A plot in Florida had been discovered. Other favored recruits struggled to find the required nerve.

Recently, Swale had approached him needing another supply. During their cryptic negotiations, Zarif was startled by the apparent revelation that he shared his supplier with none other than America's Most Wanted. Zarif wondered why the infamous duo hadn't gone directly to Hoboken.

"When I have a choice, I will turn to a friend," was Swale's answer.

Now, an anxious Zarif watched as a nondescript car drove up his long driveway. Swale and another man climbed out, moving stiffly. Good, they're in time for lunch, Zarif murmured. He went outside to exchange an American-style hug with Swale and to meet Dog.

Over a simple lunch of falafel and lentil soup, Zarif said, "I was glad to see you and your lady weren't still flying around Hawaii when those commuter planes went down. Do I get some credit for that?"

"For us being back?"

"But of course, for you being back," Zarif laughed between bites. "What a shame about the planes. And wasn't the timing awful, coming just after the attack on the Russian Embassy."

"Yes the timing was tragic. But if you had given us a more generous anniversary gift we might have stayed longer. Then, who knows where we mightbe."

Swale was surprised and concerned about Zarif's apparent reluctance to speak openly in his own home. Could he be under surveillance? Worried that the house was bugged? Best to talk of benign things – or perhaps get out in the open.

"You told me once about a good hiking trail cutting through your property. After that drive Dog and I could use a little hike, if you can manage it, old man."

"You may have a hard time keeping up."

Zarif excused himself and came back wearing a loose-fitting hunting coat. "You're apt to be carrying that on a nice day like this," Dog ventured.

"You'll understand when your blood slows," Zarif replied.

With the dishes in the sink, they left the small house, walking toward the back of the acreage. Zarif asked Dog a couple of innocuous questions about his background and Swale gave a perfunctory update on his family. The trail wound through lightly timbered grassland with changes in elevation that took them higher.

Zarif slowed and spoke quietly to set the tone. "I think we're okay, even against long distance eavesdropping. When you made your request, I hope you did not make your first call from your home."

"No, I was in Sacramento, half a day's drive away," Swale answered.

"Good. The following day I noticed a little static on my cell. Not a lot and not on every call and I didn't dwell on it. It happened again after you called to let me know you were on the way. I was thinking I should get another disposable and then I get this other call. The Caller ID said U.S. Government, but there was no number. I tried to call back, but it wouldn't ring."

"It could have been a mistake," said Swale.

"Yes, but I'm treating it like it wasn't. Have you used your phone again?"

"Not that one. I shut it off and removed the battery. I almost called when we were an hour out, but didn't. I have a second phone that the boys and another colleague can call if they need to."

"That's good. But if your phone is being monitored, they see the call from Sacramento and then the second one and know you are moving this way ... What about your car? If I am under surveillance, they're already checking it out."

"It's clean, to the extent of not being stolen and being properly registered and the driver's license being for a real person. Even if they start looking hard I think the car will be all right for a few days. Time enough ...," Swale's voice trailed off.

"Certainly hope so," said Zarif, stepping into the shade of a large cottonwood tree. He removed his coat and pulled up his shirt, revealing four money belts. He unsnapped a pocket on one belt and pulled the flap back. Swale and Dog stared at the small, inch-thick blocks of C-4, wrapped in thin black plastic. With a knife, Zarif sliced the plastic, peeling it back to reveal the white explosive. So benign now, so deadly with the right encouragement.

"The bad news is that you may have to combine some of these to get them to the size you want." But, Zarif added proudly, "The good news is that you're getting a couple pounds more than you asked for and that could add to your success.

"To be honest," he continued, "this is the end of the shipment. Unfortunately, others I have tried to help haven't accomplished anything, at least not yet. But I still have hope, Allah willing. And I like turning what's left over to you, just in case this phone crap turns out to be real. I figure if I am being watched you guys are less likely to be stopped than I am to be raided."

In the attic of a deserted farmhouse several hundred yards away, a lone federal agent sat in shadows, watching as Swale and Dog left the house. He traded his binoculars for a camera with a lens long enough to need a tripod. He snapped several photos, just as he had when the two men arrived. They looked the same. Light jackets, slacks, ball caps. They carried nothing. He had listened to their lunch conversation and thought it a bit dull. Only momentarily did his ears perk up when the commuter planes were mentioned, but that seemed a coincidence of travel. There was a spot, as the three men neared the hiking trail, when he could see them for several seconds, as he did when they returned. He had called his supervisor with information on the car, wondering if this was a good use of his time. "We'll decide that," he was told.

Chapter 24

Maple's limited sexual experience had not prepared him for the pleasure and excitement April brought to the bedroom. Before their play grew too intense she enjoyed verbal banter that made him blush. Peals of laughter accompanied her orgasms.

He watched as she took enjoyment between his legs, her active tongue and large mouth slowly building his sensitivity. It was getting to be too much, and when his hips began to press toward her she stopped.

"Meow, 'Lil Pussy wants some of that cock," she said matter of factly as she straddled him, not yet touching him with her sex as she leaned in to kiss his nipples and drag her tongue around his chest. When his breathing slowed she took him in her hand, teasing her open petals with his tip and then slowly massaging her clitoris. She stopped. "I love your eyes in this light," she said. "They sparkle."

She resumed the motion and by tiny increments started to settle upon him. Her softness thrilled him and when he had reached her ...what was it called? ...that tight spot that squeezed in on him before he entered her deeply. A random thought whisked by, that his high school anatomy class was failing him when he most needed to appear worldly ...Okay, call it that nice spot. "Keep pushing past the nice spot, nice and slow," he told her awkwardly. "You mean into my vagina?" "Yes, into that," he whispered lamely.

When his hips started moving, she again stopped, and eased herself off and onto her back, legs splayed. "I don't want you to come yet. 'Lil Pussy wants kisses."

Across the yard Wilbur peered at the mobile home through the venetian blinds in their darkened bedroom. "I see a shadow movin' real regular in there, Violet," he said. "Must be some candles lit. Do you 'spose that June is getting' it on with one of those other renters?"

"It's not June, it's not even May, it's April, and I wouldn't know. It's not our business. Come to bed."

"Shadows still movin'. Do you 'spose it's the one we've barely met or that Alex, the one I thought looked kind of like the terrorist they show on TV?"

"Well, if somethin's going on, maybe it's both," she answered, sounding a bit wistful.

"Really, Mother, we never even heard anything like that about Kennedy, for all his philandering ...I just saw him once."

"You did?" interrupted Violet. "You never told me that."

"Didn't have to tell you, Mother. You were there."

"Where?"

"Why, at the twenty-fifth anniversary ceremony, of course, of Hoover Dam. It was real nice of the White House to fly us out so Kennedy could recognize me ..."

"Wilbur ..."

" ...just like Roosevelt did when the dam was closed twenty-five years earlier. Kennedy had done his homework, too. He knew all about how I had figured out makin' the blastin' as efficient as possible. And I have to tell you, he sure didn't look like a philanderer."

"But Wilbur, you ..."

"I know what you're going to say, Mother, and you're right of course, you can't tell what a person will or won't do by their looks. But

I got to tell you that when he looked me right in the eye and shook my hand, he just didn't look like what they'd been sayin' about him since he got shot. No. When I think about it, I've got to say based on my experience, I don't think any of it is true ...April, you say ...Shadow's still movin'."

Chapter 25

Stickman sat in his seedy room in a seedy hotel on the seedy side of downtown Milwaukee. Killing Officer Dumbshit had forced him to upend the leisurely schedule he had planned, he thought again with irritation. He needed to get well away before the stupid officer was found, then had to go to ground until it was time for the final push.

Stickman located a hotel that was across an alley from a parking garage. He requested a room on the garage side of the hotel, muttering something about that side having less light and he really needing sleep. The desk clerk had looked puzzled but complied. Stickman was pleased that he could see the front of his car from his room window, giving him at least a chance to spot police should the car draw attention.

After checking in he immediately left the hotel and found a convenience store, stocking up on enough snacks, soft drinks and magazines to avoid leaving his room. Turning on the television, he learned that Dumfries' body had been found. Video of the car being pulled through brambles and up to the road had a shot of a bulky white-haired man talking to a woman in uniform. The white-haired man was smiling, even as death visited his neighborhood. If Dumfries hadn't called in car and driver information as he should have, thought Stickman, the law now has at least a general description of him and the Toyota. He did find a silver lining: The story did not tie the officer's slaying to the search for the terrorists who attacked the Russian Embassy.

The hotel was home for two boring days, the most entertaining interruption being sounds of energetic afternoon coupling in the room next to his. Stickman did venture out once, for a hot breakfast at a greasy spoon down the street. He purposely set an alarm to wake him every two hours, then sat by the window to assure himself that his car had not attracted the police. Early tomorrow he would go, pushing against rush hour traffic toward Minnesota.

Chapter 26

Dog opened the door to Swale's room on the first knock. Hellos and handshakes greeted Stickman, who needed no introduction to the Northern California crew. The men stood in slight awe, giving him what seemed like full credit for the embassy attack. Swale never said it was Stickman's work, but what he refused to deny spoke much louder.

Everyone's timely arrival at the Bloomington motel on Friday allowed them to prepare the attack for the next day, targeting heavy weekend shopping traffic.

At Stickman's nod, Swale opened a handbag and removed the blocks of deadly C-4, lining them up on the bed like artillery pieces. Assiri, Foster and Kobeisi had no experience with the explosive. Only Dog was expert in its use. But expertise would eventually be of limited value. Once wired and secure in the worn backpacks Stickman had brought, the six men would primarily be carriers – unless detected.

"Thank you all for making the drive," Stickman began. He almost added an Allah akbar for dramatic effect, but decided the mission itself lent enough suspense. "As you entered Bloomington and approached our motel I'm sure you noticed the Mall of America. It is, of course, huge and an American icon of sorts. Most important, it is our target.

"Since the attack on the Russian Embassy and the mid-air explosions of the two commuter planes in Hawaii, a few of our brothers have been arrested and charged with planning violent acts. But unfortunately, there have been no major successful attacks against the United States. We are going to radically change that."

Stickman spoke calmly, with conviction but as a colleague, an equal. "Mall of America is a symbol of capitalist America. When the dust settles, the government and the media will – by speculation, not evidence – frantically conclude that the attacks in Washington and Hawaii and here are all connected. Because of you, my friends, most Americans will be gripped by fear. Anxiety will be their daily companion and this wretchedly excessive country will begin to slide into chaos."

He was a little amazed with himself. He had never been a leader, let alone a motivator. But he believed he was holding the crew's attention and mentally preparing them to accomplish more than they would have thought possible. Watching their faces, he found satisfaction in seeing their resolve harden. And he felt pride in his leadership.

"Americans are not like Israelis. Israelis have been fighting for what they see as their country for seventy years. They accept violence as a daily challenge. They are tough. Americans are weak. Americans freak out if their bus is late or the electricity goes off or there's three inches of snow in the forecast." He paused to smile. "Toilet paper becomes a scarce commodity, as if they can't wipe their sensitive asses with a page of newspaper."

There was amused laughter, and Stickman went on. "Those weaknesses are to be exploited but, my brothers, always remember to be cautious and patient. You can panic the general public, but law enforcement across the land – from local to federal – is very strong. Our network defeated them this time in order to deliver what we need to carry out tomorrow's mission. But we are always living on the edge, working against long odds.

"After we attack the mall your first task must be to get to your homes and resume your lives with no one being the wiser. But be ready to respond to opportunities spawned by the fear and chaos that we will ignite tomorrow. All of you are Internet-savvy," he continued, with a slight smile and forgiving glance at Swale, "so watch for opportunities to make guerrilla attacks that put you in little danger. Other shopping malls, sporting events. High school football games in Texas draw ten thousand people, can you believe it? Traditional old movie theaters seat a lot of people, too.

"If we can carry off new attacks, regularly, they will soon be a drumbeat. Brothers we don't even know, in every corner of this bankrupt country, will follow our lead. Some of us may fall, but that is all right. Our efforts will make Americans afraid. Some will be afraid to go shopping and won't spend their money. Some will be afraid to go to their jobs. Some will be afraid to leave their homes. And the response of law enforcement will have a huge price tag. Before long, that fear and that cost will combine to crush this evil country's economy."

There it was, a simple but possible outline for bringing America to its knees. The men were silent. Stickman relished the silence. They are weighing my words, and they are with me. It struck him that he had been thinking for a long time, mostly in his subconscious, about the potential for waging radical jihad. This is what my life has become, he suddenly realized. This is my vision. It is the product of the cold discipline he and Maple had imposed on themselves, quietly carrying out their disruptive, sometimes deadly missions, getting no credit over the years but relentlessly learning their craft until they were confident enough to launch that audacious attack on the Russian Embassy.

Swale had listened intently, hearing much of his own rationale for ji- had, realizing those motives were deeply felt but never had been fully expressed. He had thought often about whether his efforts, and those of his crew, amounted to throwing dust at a camel or whether some- thing more was possible. Now he believed they could help trigger a revolution. He knew, far better than Stickman, the resentment many Muslims harbored. His roots in his faith community were deep. He knew the anger that seethed, the resentment that kept building, as 9/11 was shamelessly used as an excuse for discrimination while demagogic politicians played the hate card for votes.

The men he led had never sought a broad perspective. They found excitement in their secret lives and the deadly intent they espoused. They were bolstered by the disruption they occasionally caused. If Americans died or were maimed in their sleuth attacks, their sense of religious righteousness and purpose was stroked.

Like Stickman and Maple, Swale did not make anonymous calls to claim credit for violence. He had avoided too much success, not wanting to become an oversized target for law enforcement. Also like Stickman and Maple, he and his people until now had committed acts as much for training value as to succeed at radical jihad. And while many Muslims were angry, Swale also knew his pursuit of violent jihad as a tenet of faith was distinctly a minority view among those with whom he worshipped. They held his definition of jihad in contempt, saw it as a black stain on the words of Allah. Hearing Stickman, such condemnation mattered less.

Swale accepted that trying to live deep in the shadows had blinded him to seeing how jihad by a few could be a catalyst for many. Stickman's words had changed him. Now he could see himself and his men not only zealously embracing radical jihad but also linked to a much bigger cause, a worldwide revolution.

Stickman broke the silence. "People going to the Mall of America do not routinely have their purses and backpacks searched. There is no special security for what is called Theatres of Mall of America. There are fifteen theatres. Tomorrow morning I will review the movie schedules. Six of those theatres will be our targets. The movies I select will start as close to the same time as possible. I already know which ones are most popular and will consider that in picking the theaters. In mid-afternoon we will go to the mall, with explosives in our backpacks. We will go to the movies and leave our backpacks near as many people as possible, where they can do the most damage. Try to get aisle seats so you can exit easily. We will be on the road well before the dust settles. It should be getting dark by the time the law can set up roadblocks and start searching cars. That's to our advantage. We'll go over all of this in more detail tomorrow. Dog will prepare the backpacks tonight."

He asked for questions but there were none. Swale was struck by Stickman's lack of emotion in explaining how they would go about dispensing death and mayhem. Cold. Effective. He's a harder man than I, Swale told himself.

Chapter 27

As Dog readied the death packs, April Spring shivered against the night air. "Alex," she called after her second sharp knock on his door. Lights were on but she heard no sound from within. She shivered slightly in her sparse clothing–cut-off jeans and a halter top. I want company, she thought as she tried the locked door. She knocked again. As she turned to leave she saw for the first time an opening in what she had assumed was a solid growth of multiflora rose.

Stepping closer, the lovely full moon easily illuminated a gap. April saw that a section of the brambles had been cut vertically and backed with light woven wire. Curious, she pulled gently on the wire, creating an opening she could slip through without getting snagged on the prickly bush. Inside, the brambles had been severely cut back to make an open air tunnel through the room-size bush. Regular use had worn a path. I should come when it's light, she told herself, but instead walked into the tunnel. I know Alex goes for a run nearly every day. This must lead to one of his trails.

She stepped into a clearing and a large hand gripped her shoulder. Screaming in horror, she flailed behind her with her right hand, hitting a hard body as she turned. "Alex!" she wailed. "You scared me to death."

"Sorry. I was just ready to go back to the trailer when I heard knocking. I didn't know it was you."

"God, I have never been so frightened. Why didn't you come out? I called your name."

"I didn't hear you. I must have still been up the trail when you called. This is sort of my place to run at night when the moon is out. There are cattle back there and they've made a good trail through the pasture."

As April caught her breath she inhaled a sticky scent and realized he was drenched with sweat. The fear that had sent blood racing to her throat suddenly changed direction. She stepped in front of him, then against him. "I came over because I want you."

She kissed him and he responded, slipping a hand inside the waistband of her cut-offs to find her bare. "I see you're nearly ready."

"All the way ready," she said, reaching for the front of his running shorts, pulling downward. "You, too."

"We'll be eaten by chiggers. Let's go inside."

"No, you just need to be on the bottom."

Eager jerks removed their skimpy clothes as they sank to the ground, April shoving him down. She straddled him, knees spread wide as she began rocking slowly, her hard nipples punctuating the gray light. The cool moist grass felt sensual beneath him and he moaned softly as he admired her undulating body. They quickened, bringing each other to orgasm, Maple showing far more finesse than only days earlier. He lolled back, unruly dark hair falling from his face, eyes half-closed, content, still slightly moving with her.

April studied him, his sensual lips, the drowsy eyes, hair falling back. There was a mole beneath his right hairline. She shuddered, seeing his face with a new familiarity. She heard the TV announcers, heard a terrifying chorus of them as she stared slack-mouth, *"dime-size mole beneath his right hairline."* She stifled a gasp and shuddered. "Nice aftershock?" His soft voice stirred a fear beyond her control. My God yes! The scores, perhaps hundreds of times, she had seen his mugshot on television washed uncontrollably before her. How had she not recognized him? How? The way his hair fell ... somehow she had never seen the mole. She fought within to tell him yes, nice aftershock, and calmly save herself. But she was screaming "You! You! No! No!" and of course he knew. She lurched away and rolled but he rolled with her, like circus acrobats. They rolled again and when on top she struggled to her feet. He was too quick, too strong, grabbing an ankle and jerking violently. She went down on her back and he scrambled between her legs, then straddled her.

"Stop. Stop," he demanded, grabbing her wrists, holding them down above her shoulders. She kept fighting to raise her arms, bucking to throw him, yelling for help and that he was a murderer, for someone to save her. "Stop. Stop," he pleaded. She wouldn't, and with her strength ebbing he flipped her over and pressed her face into the damp grass that no longer felt sensual, quieting but not ending her pleas. "Please stop ..." She kept arching her back against him, futilely, but Maple lost hope. She wouldn't stop fighting him. Within reach was a stone that barely fit in his hand, and he used it.

"Did ya hear that, Wilbur?"

"Hear what, Mother?"

"I thought I heard a yell," said Violet, undressing for bed. "There, did ya hear it that time? More like a scream."

"Probably an owl catchin' a rabbit. They set up the most pitiful squealin' when they die."

Maple lay on his back, eyes wide in alarm. He reached for his running shorts and was disgusted by the smell of their orgasms that hung in the air. She was totally still now, so soon after so much passion, so much fight. His eyes ran over her and he felt chilled. Scudding clouds passed before the moon and he could barely make out the indentations where he struck her. He assumed the slight glisten was blood. "God," he said aloud, "what have I done? What do I do?" He began shaking, gripped by waves of confusion and anxiety. Never had he killed with his bare hands. Never had he killed someone he actually knew. I didn't want to but there was no choice, he insisted to himself. Stickman will understand. He'll tell me the years of training had stuck. Affection and need had turned to desperation and survival as quickly as flipping a switch. I had no choice, he told himself again. This time he knew it to be true. Had she escaped, the police would have been swarming within minutes. He started shaking again, decided he would think more clearly in the trailer, over the beers April had left on her last visit.

Inside, he wrapped himself in a blanket and drank deeply. His shivering stopped but not the shaking. They could feel nearly the same but Maple knew better. He needed to call Stickman, knew he could not. He didn't know what Stickman planned, only that it would happen tomorrow, Sunday at the latest. No way could he disturb the mission now. Once it happened, he and the entire world would know about it soon enough. Knowing where it happened would give him an idea of when Stickman should be back. Okay, he continued, talking quietly to himself, there's still the matter of April. I can't just leave her out there. He went through options and then knew what he needed to do. But first he headed for the shower to scrub away the chiggers and whatever else he could.

At Point of Rocks, the river had been their friend, his and Stickman's, for disposing of threatening evidence. The river would be his friend now. He gathered what he needed and went back through the makeshift multiflora rose gate. He felt strangely disoriented to find April was just like he had left her. If she had moved, none of this would have happened, he reasoned, starting to shake again. The back of her head sparkled more but didn't appear to have bled to the ground. He found that surprising but had no idea why. He pulled a penknife from his back pocket and scraped beneath her fingernails to remove any skin claimed by her scratches as they wrestled. This is crap, he thought: I may be leaving blood traces or her DNA on the soil. If they find her in the river will my cum be gone? What the hell do I know about any of this? Stick with what you do, Maple told himself as he began carefully slipping an extra-large heavy duty black garbage bag over April, from her feet up. With nylon rope, he lashed the bag tight beneath her breasts. He slipped another bag on from the head down, tying that below her breasts, too. The second bag overlapped the first, and a third, up from April's cold feet, overlapped the second. This is what I know, he said aloud as he carried her to her car. He cut what was left of his nylon rope into three long lengths. Those he braided before tying one end of the braid around the plastic garbage bag at her waist. He circled her trailer looking at the cement blocks it sat on. As the trailer had settled, some blocks had loosened. Maple gathered those, laying them neatly in the trunk around April. He leaned against the closed trunk, anxiously wondering what else to dump. Shit, driver's license, purse, plastic, whatever. Maple rushed inside and soon returned with a small, zippered bag. He was surprised when he found twenty-seven thousand dollars in cash, no doubt from her winnings at the casino named Downstream. The wad of bills bulged from a back pocket of his jeans. Fuck, this is taking too long, he thought, realizing he had to untie the knots securing the braided rope and at least one of the large black bags to put the small bag in the bundle that was April.

Okay, think a minute. Done this way, what's next? If someone comes looking for her, what's my story? I saw April drive away with someone. At least I thought it was April. It looked like two people in the car and her place was dark. End of story. That way I won't have to dispose of her car. Not the most stable creature, it's doubtful she'll be missed soon.

He felt depleted, this time not from April's pleasures. The strain of events starting before the embassy attack were taking their toll. Sweat broke out during the short drive to a state park. Though closed, Maple knew a service road that took him to a trail along the Youghiogheny River. The area was deserted. On a steep embankment, he stacked the concrete blocks at the water's edge. The river was fast and deep, a dark stretch where a weighted object would sink and rest. Ready, finally, he tossed April over his shoulder and walked to the waiting stack of blocks. After making sure the braided rope was tight around her waist, squeezing her middle between rib cage and hips, Maple began weaving the rope's loose end through openings in the blocks, one, a second and more and more. The concrete far outweighs her, Maple thought smugly, starting to regain confidence. Almost home now. He balanced the black plastic bundle on top of the stack and got on his back, knees bent nearly to his chest, feet solid against the concrete blocks. He kicked violently, tumbling the blocks over the embankment and into the inky water with surprisingly little splash, April streaming in behind and immediately disappearing from sight.

Getting up, Maple released a huge sigh. As he trudged back to her car a thought struck him: The total weight of the blocks may not be as important as having looped the braid through the first block only once. Would the endless motion of the current, pulling at April's one hundred thirty pounds, fray the rope until it snapped? He tried to put the thought aside.

Chapter 28

Darrell Stickman opened his mini-computer and searched for Mall of America. His room was quiet, good for taking yet another look at tomorrow's target and putting together a final to-do list.

The mall is the perfect target, he thought, capitalism with a capital C. Opening more than a quarter century ago at a cost of six hundred twenty million dollars, its long-term building plan still called for it to double to nearly five million square feet. As if it already isn't huge enough, he thought as he read the site's "Facts" section, envisioning a story of self-indulgent extremes run amok: More than five hundred twenty stores where Americans gorge themselves on overconsumption and more than fifty restaurants where they pile on calories. Just spending ten minutes in each store would take eighty-six hours to get through the mall. There was space – captured in a photo gallery that struck him as gauche and garish – big enough for thirty-two Boeing 747s or seven Yankee Stadiums or where two hundred fifty-eight Statues of Liberty might lie.

The mind-bending statistics rolled on: The "nation's largest indoor theme park" with twenty-seven rides and attractions. A one million two hundred thousand-gallon aquarium. More than forty million visitors annually. Mall of America "has revolutionized the shopping experience," the site bragged. I like that word, revolutionized, Stickman said to himself. I like hitting this place even more than I would like hitting

Wall Street. Wall Street symbolizes wealth and power and pompous CEOs making up America's 1 percent. Mall of America is the remaining 99 percent. Friends and neighbors and everything they see as good about their country. Good times and clean fun and well-deserved relaxation. Job opportunities. A civilized pace. It is the heart of the Heartland, where people trust one another and value having a safe place to raise their children and are not so driven by ambition and greed. After tomorrow, he thought with satisfaction, that sense of security will be shattered long-term, more than it was by 9/11 or by our successful attack on the Russian Embassy. New York and the nation's capital know they are targets. Tomorrow, all of the United States will feel like a target. Will? Could. Tomorrow could bring a new day, one to inspire others to radical jihad. But much, Stickman reflected somberly, depends on how well Dog is doing his work.

Swale was with the other men, giving up his room so Dog could be alone to prepare the C-4. Dog had lined the blocks up neatly on the bed, along with fuses, detonators, timers and the tools he needed to assemble six deadly packages. Stacked on the corner chair were six used backpacks, all different, one nearly new, one well-worn and the others somewhere in between. When Dog was done, each backpack would carry more than two pounds of C-4.

One challenge he faced was constructing bombs with redundancy. To achieve that, there would be three scenarios for ignition. Each timer was set for five seconds, with a safety lock to prevent accidental detonation. As the men went to their assigned theatres, there was the danger of being stopped by security officers or police. If being searched became a near-certainty, one option was to flip off the lock and detonate enough C-4 to demolish a dump truck. Put another way, each man could choose martyrdom or hurl the backpack at passing shoppers and scramble for cover. To bolster chances of escape, each man would be armed with a handgun and knife. An explosion would signal other carriers to detonate their C-4 and retreat to their cars. That scenario promised so much confusion that, in reality, it would be every man for himself.

Dog molded the small blocks into a total of six, each armed with an electronic fuse. All were set to the same frequency. Under the second scenario, the men would plant their backpacks in the theaters, return to their cars and leave the mall. Stickman would call both cars to confirm they were on the road – and hit a toggle switch. He had declared that he, and only he, had the honor of remotely igniting the six death chambers.

But before leaving the theaters, the carriers would reset the timers, for five forty-five. If remote detonation failed, the timers would determine the mission's success. Option three.

Dog whistled as he molded the six blocks of C-4 to form-fit a bottom corner of each backpack. He smiled as he used much-disparaged duct tape to hold the explosive in place, further anchoring the tape to the backpacks with large safety pins. "Baby, it doesn't get any better than this," he chuckled at his little joke.

The C-4, by itself, could cause extensive damage. To the backpacks Dog added ugly projectiles that Stickman had brought from Pennsylvania. There were roofing nails stolen from construction sites. Screws similarly liberated. Ball bearings and buckets of nuts and bolts and washers picked up for a little of nothing at garage sales. For years, Stickman and Maple inconspicuously collected common pieces of metal that already-destructive C-4 would turn into ugly projectiles of mayhem. They were packaged in thick canvas bags to prevent punctures by nails and screws. "A backpack looking like a porcupine could turn a cop's head," Dog said aloud. For best results, the C-4 needed to be against a solid surface, like a wall, with the metal aimed to carry the force of the explosion outward, sending hundreds of small missiles on haphazard flights to kill and maim.

His companions, after checking in, had each picked up several books from the motel's small library. Adding the Gideon bibles in their rooms, Dog used the books to fill out the backpacks. He set them in rows of two on the desk and declared, "Job well done."

In the morning, Dog would brief the men. "Your job is not complicated," he would tell them, "but how well you do it will mean the difference between setting off some fireworks and petrifying the nation."

Chapter 29

Monsour Zarif tossed on his single bed, bothered by the noises on his phone, the clicking, the static. Bothered most by having seen Caller ID flashing U.S. Government. He searched for a response, if not a solution.

Finally grasping an idea, he was up forty-five minutes before dawn. As quietly as possible, he made tea in the dark and settled in his favored rocker at a window on the front side of his west-facing house. It was a bright night, stars backlighting the ridge several hundred yards away. If someone were watching, the sun's first rays could catch a camera lens or binoculars, a reflection not detectable when the sun got higher. He sat still, not rocking, occasionally sipping his tea as the early morning slowly turned gray and the mature elms in his front yard gradually loomed into focus. Another ridgeline was behind the house. He could imagine it turning pink. Minutes passed and then it was there, light flashing off something halfway up the west ridge. Having explored the area when he moved in, Zarif knew the reflection was coming from near an old homestead. The flash became a constant reflection, then suddenly disappeared as if someone had turned a lens away from the rising sun.

Zarif's palms were clammy. Far, far too many coincidences. The sun was just coming up, not high enough for the reflection to disappear so abruptly. And he remembered the young man at the mosque who for several weeks hinted at supporting radical jihad. Zarif had engaged him in a cautious conversation, not hinting at recruitment, nothing like he had done with Swale and others, but neither did he disapprove of the young man's incendiary comments. If an undercover agent, had I said enough to cause suspicion? Probably not, usually not, but if they didn't have someone better to watch, an agent could be sitting up there to justify their existence. Or maybe his recent conversations with Swale hadn't been circumspect enough. Now, there's no way to tell.

He shuddered, suddenly wanting to charge up to the deserted farm to assure himself no one was there. Maybe a piece of broken glass did catch the sun's first rays for a few minutes every morning, when he typically slept. He forced himself to be calm, to think. If he found someone at the farm, he could be arrested. They would no doubt know of Swale's visit and have a full description of his car, probably identifiable photos of him and the one called Dog. Given their brief stay, Zarif had to think they needed to keep moving, that whatever was planned would happen soon. Tipping his hand could threaten that mission. No, I must stay here as if all is right. Stay right here and prepare.

Nine a.m. – Joining the others in Swale's room, Stickman examined Dog's handiwork. It looked good and he offered his praise. Dog grinned with pleasure. "That plastique is going to bring down some major shit."

Ali Foster and George Kobeisi had been out early, liberating three sets of license plates. In the motel parking lot shortly before the mission, they would find the space offering the most concealment and switch plates. They would join the rest of the crew and go to the mall early to familiarize themselves with parking, walking routes to their targets, and whatever they could learn about security. Stickman expected to encounter private security guards, possibly backed up by police. Should a serious, unexpected problem arise, the mission could be delayed or aborted. But he was confident that security would be light. Heavy security would discourage spending, God forbid.

Eleven-twenty a.m. – Stickman, Swale and Dog stood in line at Theatres of Mall of America, patiently waiting to purchase their tickets.

As directed by the mall website, they parked in East Ramp, Level 5 and walked the hallway between Dick's Last Resort and Hooter's Restaurant to the theaters on Level 4. That was more than an hour ago, after making the short drive from their motel on I-494. Assiri, Foster and Kobeisi followed not far behind.

They had had time to get comfortable with the mall, particularly alternative routes for returning to their cars. Now they were purchasing tickets for six movies with starting times between four-ten and four-thirty-five. Movies that by five-forty-five would be chambers of death. Five-forty-five at the latest, and then only if the remote igniter failed. Five-forty-five assuming the timers in each backpack became, by default, the conduit to destruction.

The men returned to the motel, to finish packing and loading their cars. But mostly to pick up the immoral backpacks. The wait was tedious but necessary. All things being equal, Stickman reasoned, the pre-dinner movies draw the biggest crowds. They did not check out, keeping their rooms another night. Best to have them available if things go wrong, if hunkering down becomes the best option. If things go as planned, the West Coast contingent will be miles away when chaos strikes. Only Stickman will still be close to the mall – his price for the privilege of igniting the C-4, the privilege of radical jihad.

Eleven-thirty a.m. – Surveillance photos from Fargo were waiting for Special Agent in Charge Franklin Terrell when he arrived at his FBI office in Brooklyn Center, northwest of Minneapolis. Scrutinizing them had been delayed by more pressing matters. Besides, his agents in Fargo had yet to come up with a concrete lead tying Monsour Zarif to any illegal activity, let alone terrorism.

Terrell had approved the stakeout because he liked and respected the young agent who had been approached by Zarif after going undercover at the Fargo mosque. The agent had little to go on, really nothing beyond his instinct, in urging the surveillance. Terrell agreed, in part because the agent he assigned the task needed more on his plate. Then the young agent was gone, on extended leave for a family emergency.

The folder cover gave no hint that the photos could be of value, just the basic logistics of the investigation, who took them, when and where. Nevertheless, Terrell followed his thorough nature, looking at each long lens photo carefully. Two men getting out of their car, being greeted by Zarif, going in his house. Even longer shots as they left for the woods behind the house and then their return. Exiting the house, brief farewells, the men getting back in their car. But wait. Terrell squinted hard. The two men wore the same jackets they did when they arrived. As they departed, were there short strings of bulges pressing through their jackets as they bent to get in the car? Two short strings on each man? Terrell picked up a magnifying glass and peered even more intently before flipping back to the first shots. No strings of bulges. On either of them. Why weren't they openly carrying whatever they had picked up? A chill ran through him. He called for his secretary, orders quickly piling up in his mind.

Two-fifteen p.m. – Six vans roared into Zarif 's front yard and SWAT teams poured out. A car followed closely behind, carrying the agent in charge and three others. The SWAT teams had been quickly cobbled together from law enforcement agencies in the Fargo area, scrambling to get to a staging area near Zarif's property. Their ninety-minute response time was doubly impressive because the teams included two specialists trained to disarm explosives.

Terrell was on his way in a small plane, hoping to arrive before anything dramatic happened. He had been handed a transcript of the lunch conversation in Zarif's house and was alarmed by the mention, though casual, of the commuter planes in Hawaii. But also, he was pleased with himself, for he had never assembled a response so quickly or decisively. He had sensed there was no choice and, as he was still barking orders, photographic specialists confirmed his gut, that Zarif's visitors left with something concealed beneath their jackets. Who knew what, but one possibility was that they were wearing belts with pockets, filled with deadly explosives.

The SWAT teams quickly surrounded Zarif's house and the agent in charge, Michael Bellow, pulled out a bullhorn to identify himself and demand that Zarif surrender with hands raised and empty.

"Why, why are you here?"

"To question you about any ties you may have to terrorism."

"I am not a terrorist. You are welcome to enter my house."

"Then come out with your hands raised."

"I can't. I can't walk. My right leg is broken."

"I could care less about your leg. Hobble or crawl if you need to. Just get out here or I'll fire tear gas."

"It is bad. I can see the bone. I couldn't crawl if I wanted to."

Bellow was not trained to talk. He was trained for combat. He weighed putting everything on hold, bringing in a negotiator, maybe someone who deals with hostage situations. But his orders warned that he could be dealing with a terrorist who was suspected of making a delivery, possibly of explosives. There was no way to know if time was short, but Terrell's sense of urgency had come through loud and clear. Zarif must be brought in for questioning as quickly as possible.

"Last chance. Get your sorry butt out here or tear gas comes in."

"Please ...the pain. I can't. I want to but I can't."

Bellow looked at a SWAT team sergeant. "Fire the tear gas."

Canisters crashed through the front windows of Zarif 's house, overwhelming the three floor fans Zarif had running on high. One was on either side of him and he held the third in his lap, aiming it to blow tear gas from his face as best he could. He had tied a wet towel around his face. Still, he coughed violently, eyes watering as vomit ran down his shirt front.

"Please, stop," he called. "I can't walk I tell you. No way. I don't have a gun. Please believe me. Please. Your tear gas is killing me. Please."

All right, thought Bellow. We've got the bastard. He turned to the SWAT team commander, ordered the demolition experts, now in body armor, to take Zarif. They would be backed up by a SWAT team, with the others moving into position at windows and the back door.

"Sir," asked the commander, "how about bringing in a negotiator? If this guy is a terrorist it seems he's giving up too easy. Let's bring in more support and a trained negotiator."

"You questioning my order?"

"No, but ..."

"Just do it!"

In their protective gear, the demolition team climbed stiffly up the steps and to the front door as the SWAT teams took position.

Bellow jumped to the porch, handgun drawn, standing to the side of the door behind the demolition team leader. "Pound on the door," he hissed. Then yelled, "Zarif! Open the door. You are surrounded. Give up."

"I can't walk. I don't have a gun."

"Okay," Bellow shouted. "We're coming in. Scratch your nose wrong and you're a dead man."

He motioned to the demolition leader who tried the doorknob and the unlocked door swung open. From a slight crouch he took a quick glance inside, seeing a small man in his sixties sitting in a straight back chair, his right leg propped on a pillow on another chair. He was wrapped in a blanket.

"He's just sitting there."

"Okay," said Bellow, still shouting. "We're coming in. I want your hands in the air."

He wheeled into the doorway. The last thing he saw was Zarif raising his right hand as he pressed an igniter. Violent explosions tore off the front of the house and erupted from window wells at the back and on either side. Most of the officers flattened against the frame house on either side of windows were killed instantly or horribly injured.

Terrell's plane was just landing in Fargo when the emergency call was patched through from Zarif's acreage. On the line was one of the agents who had arrived with Bellow. "We've got every damn ambulance in the county on the way," the agent said, voice cracking, "but what we really need are fucking hearses."

As he wired his house, Zarif carefully picked times when the window wells at the front were in shadows. Those in back and on the sides didn't matter; the long lens couldn't reach them. He had been careful to conceal the explosives under black plastic, like that used to keep rain out. He had wished for some of the C-4 he had given to Swale and Dog, but knew old-fashioned dynamite, purchased to blast tree stumps out, would work fine.

Three-twenty p.m. – Nearly time to go. In the bathroom of his room, Swale was reaching to shut off the radio when the urgency in the announcer's voice stopped him.

This just in from Fargo, North Dakota. Several police officers, most of them on SWAT teams, reportedly were killed when a house they were raiding exploded. First reports are that the SWAT teams were called in on short notice to assist the FBI. The bureau reportedly was making an arrest in connection with a terrorism investigation. We'll bring you more details as we get them.

"Damn. Poor Zarif."

Five p.m. – Stickman walked casually toward the car where Swale and Dog waited. Assiri was at his car several spaces away. All right, thought Stickman, four back, only two to go. It's too bad there won't be time to hear their war stories about how things went.

An hour earlier, he had briefly faced martyrdom when a private security guard stopped him and asked to see the backpack slung over his shoulders. A trickle of sweat immediately formed between his shoulder blades and traced his spine. The guard had stepped suddenly from a boutique doorway, just feet away. He had a backup and Stickman doubted he was fast enough to get to the five-second timer inside the backpack. "Of course, officer," he said, forcing a friendly smile. He pulled open the main zipper and held the backpack out so the officer could see inside, ready to reach under his light jacket to the holster at the small of his back. The guard opened the backpack wider and peered in at the books.

"I read In Cold Blood a long time ago," he said, straightening.

"Me, too," said Stickman. "The way things have been going for you guys, I thought a reminder was in order that there are some real bad guys out there."

"Right on, man. Have a good day."

He caught a glimpse of Dog, ticketed for the earliest movie, going in Theater 7. Stickman said, "Theater 3" as he approached the ticket taker and, small popcorn and cola in hand, entered. The lights were still up. He looked around at the half-full theater. People were scattered randomly, but it should fill in pretty well, he guessed, looking for an aisle seat. Spotting one in the back row, right side, he started up, but lost out to a man changing seats. Damn. At the opposite end of the back row the aisle seat was still empty. Stickman walked down and across and started up again. A young man, hot date in tow, also liked the idea of a back row aisle seat. All right for you, Stickman thought as he slipped past them and sat down, I'm going to sit right next to your chick and send the both of you to hell.

He put the backpack on the empty seat next to him. He wanted an opportunity to slide it under his seat and firmly against the back wall, where it would be out of sight when he left. The couple got into themselves, rubbing against the bounds of intimacy in public.

Stickman unzipped the backpack and, aided by a small flashlight, set the timer offering redundancy. A silly caution popped to mind: Never yell fire in a crowded theater. He zipped up the backpack and slid it between his legs and against the back wall, the C-4 well-positioned. The young couple – she whispering in his ear, he teasing the inside of her knee – took no notice. Anyway, stowing a backpack was no big deal.

More important will be whether they take interest after he leaves and doesn't return for a time. Whether they notice his backpack and start to worry about it. Security officials in airports and metros had driven home all too well the danger of deserted luggage. It is what it is, Stickman mentally shrugged. I just hope everyone else is doing as well.

The theater steadily filled in. An old man sat next to Stickman and promptly nodded off. Munching his popcorn, Stickman tried to picture the scene when this theater and five others exploded. Scores, maybe hundreds, of people killed instantly. Body parts flying, decapitation. Walls disintegrating and ceilings crumbling. Floors collapsing. Water pipes bursting and electrical circuits shorting, throwing terrified survivors into total darkness. Splintered seats and twisted metal and fire, flying debris and dust. Temporary silence, maybe. Fire spreading and debris settling and more dust. Moans and whimpers and cries and screams and pleading. Fires getting worse, reaching victims as they blindly wandered in the darkness. People horribly seared, in shock with shattered bones, groping down aisles, feeling their way over bodies and body parts and theater rubble creating horrible obstacles. Survivors desperately seeking a tortuous path that in a few short yards offered life-giving oxygen and safety, but yards beyond the reach of many.

A brave or foolish few struggling against the tide, fighting through the wreckage and carnage to get in – to do what? They had to know the futility of it but the call of loved ones inside proving too strong. Determined souls quickly starting the agonizingly slow process of rescue, saving some, holding others, comforting the dying and those piteously maimed. Still, hands grabbing some who could be saved, dragging out their broken bodies at sometimes fatal cost. A few arming themselves with fire extinguishers to spew weak streams of hope against the well-fueled inferno. Untrained rescuers soon hearing the sirens, a gazil- lion-alarm fire bringing in every emergency vehicle from miles around. Every cop joining the rescue or scrambling to locate attackers gone without description, without a trace.

And what happens in here will be just the start, he said to himself, looking around a theater nearly full. Hopefully, some of the C-4 explosions will breach walls, spreading death in hallways or maybe even the lobby where people will be checking their tickets or going to the restrooms or using a water fountain. Besides those killed or injured at the blast's fatal edges, there will be panic, people running, or freezing in shock. Injuries from falls, tumbles on escalators, people crushed in tight spaces. Responders will add to the mayhem, bulling in as movie goers fight to get out. Fear will bring heart attacks, strokes, seizures. The confusion of parking lots looking like bumper cars, with more accidents, more injuries, more deaths.

Stickman's imagination cataloged all that mayhem and more, with satisfaction, even as another reality crowded in. The courage of some in the face of the theater massacre would also inspire millions of people. He put the thought aside. Can't be helped. That's short-term. Long-term is the awful wrath, the long-term fear unleashed by C-4. Wrath and fear beyond my imagination. Long-term with a capital L. He munched his popcorn and sipped his cola and waited.

The previews started, then the movie, full of action with gunfights and car chases and plenty of explosions, which seemed fitting to Stickman. After a while he pressed a stem on his watch and, shielding the face with his hand, saw it was nearly four-fifty. Time to go. He reached under his seat to reassure himself, unnecessarily he knew, that the backpack was still there. He pardoned himself and slid by the doomed lovers.

Reaching the lobby, Stickman wondered nervously if by some weird coincidence he would bump into one or all of his colleagues as he walked from the theater. He saw how empty the lobby was and worried about six men drawing attention if they left within a few minutes of each other. He was pleased to see none of the crew.

As the outlines of Swale and Dog, waiting in the garage, came into view he heard popping sounds, like a car backfiring in the distance. He didn't change his casual pace, but stiffened at the sound of rapid steps, someone catching up with him. He turned to face Foster, panic in his eyes, his face flushed. Stickman motioned him to slow down.

"Kobeisi, the dumb fuck, got himself shot."

Stickman took a deep breath. "Did he get his backpack planted? Is he dead?"

"I have to believe he did, at least he didn't have it when I bailed. He was shot bad, I think, but alive."

"Walk slow and tell me what happened."

Foster reached out with his hands and spread his fingers wide as if ordering himself to be calm.

"I left the theater and about halfway back saw Kobeisi ahead of me, thirty, forty yards. After a bit he started walking a little fast I thought, and then I saw a cop and two private guards a little ahead of him on the right side of the hall. Dammit, he should have just kept strolling, cool, but I think they saw him speed up. Then I see his jacket is hitched up over his holster at the back of his belt. Fuck! They're going to see his gun if they ain't fucking blind. I slowed to look at a sign to get my shit together. As he walked by them they saw his holster and gun. Whew, sorry ...They pulled in behind him no more than five yards away. 'Sir,' I heard one say, and Kobeisi turned. They had their hands on their guns and he knew he was in deep shit. He reached for his gun but snagged his hand in his jacket. When he finally got his gun out he had no chance. The cop who said sir shot twice. It looked like he took them in the stomach, at least one of them. Then there was a crowd. I stood on the edge for just a minute or so. I couldn't hear or see Kobeisi and just eased on by." As they reached Swale's car Foster was a sweating wreck.

Stickman looked around. Few people were in sight, none close. "See Assiri at his car? Get him and come back here. Don't run."

"Give me a minute," he told Swale and Dog as he leaned against the car.

With Assiri and Foster back, Stickman said simply, "The cops got Kobeisi. He's gut shot and could give us up. The four of you can't caravan. Assiri, Foster, head home. Swale, as we leave I'm going to ignite. Then drop me at my car and you and Dog head home, too. You know the routes, but it won't be long until roads are a mess. Checkpoints. All you can do is follow your noses. We don't know whose phones may be compromised, so no phone contact unless you've got something that will save someone else's ass. I'll be in touch as soon as I can. You have done great, my friends. Thank you. Good luck."

No one felt a need for goodbyes. They were all ready to leave. Who knew whether Kobeisi was coherent, what he was saying. Whether the cops were coming their way. Shutting down or evacuating the mall were both possibilities. Getting caught inside was a bad option. As Swale trailed Assiri's car down through the parking garage a siren could be heard, growing louder. "That could be an ambulance for Kobeisi," Dog said from the back seat. Stickman would rather it be a hearse, but said nothing.

"When we reach the street, drive as slow as you can," he told Swale.

As Stickman had hatched the mission, he had wished for details on how the mall was constructed, to know if there was a liklihood or even a chance that his igniter would not work. An opportunity to test the igniter in the mall would have been even better. But he had put the plan together, assembled the crew and secured the C-4 all too quickly for a trial run. Or so it seemed. After Swale relayed the news flash about the raid near Fargo, news that neither had shared with the crew, Stickman was convinced he made the right call.

They were turning out of the garage, the igniter ready in Stickman's hands. He was trying to judge when they were parallel to the Theatres of Mall of America. If he waited too long, went too far, missed on this pass, going back carried more risk than he wanted to think about. "Now," he hissed through clenched teeth, and pressed the igniter. The three men strained as one to hear ...then spat out "Yes!" virtually in unison, believing a muffled clapping sound had penetrated the drone of traffic. For Dog, it was not a matter of believing. It was a certainty. The explosion was faint, but it still was the ugly roar he had heard many times in war-torn lands. A holocaust had been delivered in the name of domestic terrorism.

"For Zarif," Swale said grimly, easing into the traffic of I-494 for the brief ride to Stickman's car. With a nod, he was out and both cars were soon westbound. Sirens were in full throat, seemingly from all directions, and Stickman knew with certainty his ears had not deceived him. As he reached the I-35 exit to go south he could still see Swale, westbound.

Chapter 30

Traffic was moving well as Stickman tuned in an all-news station to monitor still-sketchy reporting on the attack at the Mall of America.

Early reports are that more than two hundred people may be dead and scores more injured, many critically, in today's bombings of at least six theaters at the iconic mall. The death count is expected to rise significantly. Officials immediately blamed terrorists for the attacks, but did not name a particular group. So far, no terrorist organization has claimed responsibility. Investigators are searching for possible links to an explosion at a house outside Fargo, North Dakota. There, more than a dozen officers were killed as they moved in on a suspected terrorist. Several more officers were critically injured in what was described by the FBI as a raid on the house. At the mall, a man suspected in that attack was shot twice by police or security guards. He is in critical but stable condition at a nearby hospital, and is expected to live.

We caution you that some of the information coming in from the mall and from law enforcement sources is preliminary. We have not, repeat, have not independently confirmed all details. That said, a plastic explosive such as C-4 is believed to have been used. It appears the bombs had been loaded with nails, ball bearings and other metal objects. That metal extended the carnage far beyond the actual blast areas, causing wounds similar to those inflicted by a grenade. Some of the explosions also brought down walls and ceilings, apparently causing electrical fires and immedi-

ately turning the theaters into infernos. One official said at least some of the bombs appear to have been under back row seats. They said that when the blasts took out walls, patrons in hallways outside the targeted theaters also were killed or wounded. Because the blasts appeared to be simultaneous or nearly so, officials believe a remote igniting device was used. However, the use of sophisticated timers on individual bombs has not been ruled out. Given the massive impact of the blasts, the perpetrators are believed to have used several pounds of explosive. The possibility remains that several suicide bombers carried out the attack. But, the wounding of a suspect before the explosions, in a retail area well away from the theaters, does not support that scenario, one official said.

First responders and witnesses are describing scenes of unimaginable horror as survivors attempt to crawl through bodies and wreckage. Many victims suffered terrible wounds from the metal objects loaded into the bombs as well as from flying debris or fire. A couple using wheelchairs, celebrating their sixty-fifth wedding anniversary, was among those killed. Also dead is a four-year-old going to see her first movie, a Disney film.

It's now been more than an hour since the terrorist attack. Sources tell us every officer who can be summoned, has been. Some are helping deal with the absolute chaos at the mall, one of the nation's most popular shopping and recreation venues. Federal agents, including those of the FBI and Department of Homeland Security, have been called in. Officers from around Minnesota are responding, as are some from surrounding states including Iowa and Wisconsin.

Our reporting thus far indicates law officers have few leads – no indication of how many terrorists or what kind of vehicles were involved, let alone descriptions – assuming of course that suicide bombers were not to blame. Officials are not saying whether they believe the attacks were carried out by homegrown terrorists. The other likely possibility, of course, is that an international group was responsible for or inspired the massacre. We know that a huge dragnet is being thrown up around the Minneapolis-St. Paul area. That includes road blocks on interstates, county roads, state and federal highways and even some city streets. SWAT teams have been dispatched to bus and train depots and airports have been shut down. Major facilities and institutions – from universities and their dormitories to hospitals and sports venues – also have been shut down or are under a high security alert. Check our website for details on closings.

You gotta love the American media, Stickman thought. Freedom of the press and transparent government help me every time. But perhaps not enough. Seemingly without warning the interstate ahead lit up in a river of red. Traffic check coming up, no doubt. Think, think. Car papers in order. If I toss my guns someone will no doubt see. Can I slip through with them? I'll want them if bad goes to worse. But I always have my ice pick, he thought with a nervous chuckle. Again he thought about the guns, not wanting to give them up and the difficulty of tossing them. He wondered how long traffic checks could last. Americans are impatient. Count on this through tomorrow, then easing up the next day. It he could find a safe place for a day or so ...But that's not the problem. Not right now.

He hadn't thought to get in the right hand lane, but as he crept ahead he belatedly realized an exit was approaching. Take it, an internal voice shouted. The car on his right had dropped back slightly, far enough to nose in, and he laid on his horn. The startled driver braked, giving Stickman room to cut in and then whip into exit lane traffic.

Between listening to the radio report and getting out of traffic he had lost track of exactly where he was. A Northfield exit? He felt a bit disjointed, told himself that's probably to be expected, that this hasn't been an average day. The exit emptied onto a street and a nearby motel boasted a restaurant and lounge. He found a space in the corner of the parking lot beside a car hooked to a rental trailer. He didn't know if the sense of concealment really meant anything, but it felt good.

No rooms were available. A Masonic group from southwest Missouri had booked all available space to avoid paying downtown Minneapolis prices. "I think there will be vacancies tomorrow, sir." Stickman politely thanked the desk clerk. Getting back into traffic made no sense. He headed for the bar.

Chapter 31

At the bar, Stickman felt lucky to cage the only empty stool. He ordered a light draft. On his right was a young man trying to read a paperback in the dim light. On his left sat a woman of perhaps 50, well endowed, not fat but sturdy, with virtually no waistline. She ordered another Scotch as the bartender brought Stickman his beer. A large man at the end of the bar, perhaps perched there too long, had seen more than enough non-stop coverage of the terrorist attack. He loudly declared it was time to change the channel, which was fine with Stickman. It was only a question of time before his and Maple's mugshots would pop up. Seeing himself wherever he went was getting old.

The woman wasn't exactly chatty Kathy, but it took little prompting to learn she was from Des Moines, in pharmaceutical sales. She was driving north as she did every quarter for a week of rounds at doctor's offices, clinics and hospitals in the Twin Cities. "The business is getting more and more impersonal with the computer and all, but we still see value in going face-to-face." Stickman nodded appreciatively. He learned her name was Wendy and told her he was a computer programmer, between jobs and seeing a part of the country that was new to him. He had planned to spend a few days exploring the area but now that may be too much hassle, what with the awful attack. They had another drink and Wendy allowed it was time for her to find dinner. "I was thinking the same thing. Perhaps you'd like to join me."

Swale and Dog drove west, picking up radio reports about checkpoints, sometimes learning their general locations. They took U.S. 169 southwest toward Mankato, thinking roadblocks might be less likely off the interstate. "Best we find a place to stop and get our legit plates back on," Swale said as he turned off the highway onto a gravel road. Not long after rejoining highway traffic a helicopter passed overhead. The sun was getting low. "Even with our own plates I'll feel better when it's too dark for the bastards to read them," Dog said.

Swale was suddenly panicked. Zarif had worried about being under surveillance. The focus was on strange noises on his phone or a possible wiretap. But what if someone also had been watching and photographed Swale's car. Now, the legal plates could be putting them at serious risk. He ran his concern by Dog, wondering if they should put the stolen plates back on. "Shit," Dog said quietly.

They didn't have time to stew, or find a spot to again switch plates. Without warning the helicopter suddenly reappeared, its chopping blades making it hard to hear the orders blaring from a loudspeaker. It was easy to figure out, though, that the voice wanted someone to pull over. That someone has to be us, Swale said to himself. "So Dog, what now? Should we give up?" He sounded like an old John Wayne movie, and knew it, but glancing at Dog he saw a resolve to overcome the fear even as sweat rolled down his face. "I got caught by the Taliban once. I never was hurt so much. Only fool's luck got me out. Let's run like hell."

They topped a rise to see flashing lights a mile or more ahead. It was getting dark. If they could buy a little time, disappear for a minute to bust out their brake lights, maybe they could slip away. Swale saw a paved county road coming up and at the last second swerved sharply to take it, the helicopter in close pursuit. They raced down a tree-lined lane at sixty, seventy, eighty. When they suddenly came to a series of curves, Swale had no choice but to apply the brakes. The pilot spotted them and within seconds was hovering overhead, weaving back and forth, up and down to keep pace. So far, no patrol cars had joined the chase.

"Think you could bring them down with your Glock?" "Hell no," Dog answered, wiggling between the bucket seats and jerking out the back seat for the AK-47. Slamming a clip in, he rolled down the window on Swale's side, waiting for open space between trees to squeeze off several rounds. Sparks popped off the copter's landing gear. "Keep at it." Dog emptied the clip and slapped in another, emptied it. "Seems like I should be hitting something." But the helicopter had climbed to an elevation of several hundred feet, making an accurate shot more a matter of luck than skill.

Rounding a curve, two patrol cars blocked the road not a half-mile ahead. Swale braked the car for a rapid three-point turn, reversing direction. He saw a road to the left and took what quickly deteriorated into a double dirt track leading into a pasture. He made a wild U-turn, bouncing over uneven terrain. The copter again hovered overhead, and the patrol cars were going to beat him back to the intersection with the paved county road.

Dog fired desperately at the copter. On board were two SWAT snipers, now convinced of the futility of taking the terrorists alive for their intelligence value. They set their rifles on full-automatic and each of them emptied a clip into the back half of the car. Dog was ripped with pain by the first shots, then felt nothing as his corpse was riddled. Again the loudspeaker, "Surrender! Give yourself up!" Swale veered left into a copse of trees, having the presence of mind to grab a bottle of water as he threw open the door and scrambled from the car. He ran a zig-zag course into the woods.

The copter hovered overhead, spotlight sweeping, circling. Swale could hear officers from the patrol cars clambering after him. He angled left, uphill, the direction least expected, he thought. When the copter neared, he sought cover in a narrow gully, hugging the cool earth, Glock at the ready. The officers worked away from him, downhill. He trudged stoically on for a few hundred yards, the dark countryside growing quiet around him. Twice the helicopter flew back in his direction, then changed course yet again, at a loss for his location. He could hear trucks in the distance, maybe on Highway 169. Somewhere in the distance he saw the staccato lights of an emergency vehicle and picked up the warp of a siren. He knew dogs would be after him soon. Knew he needed to find a stream to break his scent, or get back to a road, maybe commandeer a passing truck or car. The thought of dogs made him sad.

They were in her room, on her invitation for a nightcap. Dinner had been pleasant. Wendy had not shown much curiosity about Stickman as she sipped her way through two glasses of wine. He had another beer, content to mainly listen. Now they continued chatting, each with a Scotch. She finished hers and got up from the bed, rounded his chair, leaned over and kissed him without invitation. He kissed back. Satisfied with his response she said, "Let's shower." "I'll join you in a minute. I need to make a call."

Waiting until he heard the shower, he picked up the house phone. "This is Mike, Wendy's husband. We're in 210. Can we get the room for an extra night? ...Good. Please leave a message that we won't need maid service tomorrow ...Thanks. Good night."

They soaped one another and stood under the hot water, pressed against each other, before stepping out to towel off. She giggled as the towel lingered in sensitive spots, accentuated by his mischievous grin. She made clear, though, that foreplay was pleasure delayed and their sex was hot but perfunctory. After he rolled off she quickly fell asleep, flat on her back and breathing heavily. Stickman kissed a nipple. "Darlin', I'm going to my car for an overnight bag." She didn't stir.

Outside, he crossed the street to a convenience store. Food selections were predictably bad, the last ham and cheese on multi-grain and two slices of pepperoni pizza. He added chips and mixed nuts, granola bars and three bottles of water. It all fit easily in his overnight bag. Wendy was still breathing heavily when he returned to bed.

In the middle of the night she slid her hand between his legs. She teased and he responded. "Give it to me," she murmured with a hint of urgency. "Come get it." She rolled on top. Stickman remained motionless, prolonging his sensitivity, and slowly she satisfied them both.

"Do you suppose I could bring you around again in the morning?"

"Yes, but I want you to start with some kisses."

He slept soundly, too soundly he guiltily thought later, awakening to the pleasure of Wendy burrowing between his legs, her circling tongue already making him hard. "Nice, that's so nice."

"No baby, that's all you get of that. Mama wants some more action."

The early sun was turning the room grey. It was a nice light for watching her hover over him, rubbing herself with his hardness, then settling herself and encouraging him to vigorous coupling that left both of them gasping with satisfaction. Ah, she had a talent.

As Stickman's pulse returned to normal he asked, "Can we stay here another day, mix in a movie or two with lots of love?"

"No way, sorry. My twin grandsons in St. Paul are five today. I'm going to surprise them and their single-parent mom. And I have appointments starting early Monday. I would have driven on in yesterday but knew traffic would be a mess because of the terrorist attack. It's probably still a mess."

"I'm glad you decided to share your room."

"Me, too. I'll leave my contact information. You can call me during the week if you decide to stay in the area."

She reached over for a quick kiss before settling on her back, arms limp at her sides. Her breathing quickly turned heavy. Stickman eased out of bed and went to the bathroom to wash. Coming back he slowly unzipped his overnight before returning to bed. It was getting lighter, Wendy's contours more distinct. He gently lifted the sheet, slowly pulling it down to reveal her thick pubic hair. She was snoring softly.

Propping himself on his left arm, he positioned the tip of the pick toward her heart, just below her sternum, just above her soft flesh. He looked at her face, oh so satisfied from three rounds of sex. Oh so relaxed. What a way to go Stickman thought as he swiftly pressed the ice pick in nearly to the hilt. Wendy's eyes snapped open and froze. She made no sound. No motion. He gazed at her silent face and down the length of her body. He felt himself getting hard again, and thought about it, and told himself no.

He let a few minutes pass, then showered before removing the inner plastic curtain and taking it to the bed. He maneuvered the damp curtain under Wendy's dead weight, no small task, and wrapped it around her. He was grateful there was little blood. "Gotta love the pick." Cutting lengths of chord from the window blinds, he secured the shower curtain around her. "Darlin', you're starting to look like a mummy." He used a sheet to drag her to the bathroom and wrestled her into the bathtub, on her back. "Your favorite sleeping position."

Stickman made sure the Do Not Disturb sign was on the door, then microwaved pizza for breakfast. It would be a long and hopefully uneventful day. He settled on the king bed to watch the news.

A breaking development on the terrorist attacks on Theatres of Mall of America. Here's our reporter Hank Anderson outside FBI headquarters in Brooklyn Center.

Sources here have confirmed that the chase and shootout west of the Twin Cities near Highway 169 are believed to be connected to the attacks at the mall. One man in the fleeing car opened fire on a police helicopter. Sharpshooters in the copter killed him. He has not been identified. The driver fled on foot and a manhunt with dogs, aircraft and more than one hundred law officers is underway.

The car involved in that chase has been linked to the explosion near Fargo that killed more than a dozen SWAT team officers who were attempting to arrest the occupant of a farmhouse. The car reportedly had been at the farmhouse recently and investigators are working on the as-

sumption that there is a link between the house explosion and the attack on the mall. The occupant of the farmhouse, who apparently had wired his house with dynamite, also was killed. Utility and other public records show a Monsour Zarif lived in the house. He reportedly was born in Fargo and was believed to be in his sixties. Zarif was said to be active in a local mosque. His parents were Iranian immigrants.

The man shot by officers at the mall yesterday died early this morning. He has been identified, but his name has not been released. According to a source, the man is believed to be from Northern California. Investigators believe the attacks were carried out by at least six people, based on surveillance video taken in the mall parking lot closest to the theater. If the six includes the man killed at the mall and the one killed during the chase near Highway 169, at least four terrorists remain at large.

Federal officials on the ground increasingly believe they are searching for homegrown terrorists. International connections can be made, however. The Fargo man whose house was raided apparently lived in Iran for several years. Some of the attackers are believed to be Muslims who have stayed in touch with their ancestral countries. But neither the Islamic State, al-Qaeda or any other international terrorist group has claimed credit for the attacks on the mall. No group has claimed credit for last winter's attack on the Russian Embassy in Washington, D.C., either. Federal officials find that so out of character that they increasingly believe homegrown terrorists are to blame.

As reported earlier, four more people have died of injuries suffered in the mall attacks. That bringing the death count to more than 220 – by far the largest act of domestic terrorism since 9/11. That gruesome count is expected to go up because rescue workers are still digging through wreckage and because many of the injured remain in critical condition. An estimated 350 to 400 people were injured. From Brooklyn Center, Hank Anderson reporting.

The noose is tightening, Stickman told himself grimly. If Assiri and Foster hear such reports, and they must, they surely will have the good sense to change direction. If Swale's little community hasn't been located already, that's just a matter of time. A short time. By comparison, Stickman felt fortunate, although he didn't like the apparently heightened interest in homegrown terrorists. That could mean more resources being poured into following domestic leads. Still, there's not much about me to attract attention, unless someone watching too much television hones in on the Most Wanted photo. Fingerprints from Swale's car will match those from the embassy investigation. Even a good wipe-down of this room will miss at least a few prints. A connection will be made between the embassy, the mall attacks and Wendy. Once the cops know all that, the wanted photo will really be out there, a veritable electronic and paper blizzard. And here I was going to create a national diversion to take the heat off. So much for that. But connecting all those dots doesn't help them make an arrest of someone with an altered appearance that seems to be holding up. The phone, he thought with mild alarm. If–when–they get Swale, and his phone, they will call numbers he has called to pinpoint current phone locations. Stickman impulsively grabbed his phone from the nightstand and totally disabled it, as if police were already punching in those traitorous numbers.

Swale's phone was in the car with Dog's body, left behind in haste. Shortly after seeing the lights of an emergency vehicle in the distance, Swale lost his footing going down a hill in the darkness. His left ankle was broken or badly sprained, a painful swollen mess in any case. The night had turned unusually cold and he alternately shivered and broke into a sweat from his tortured efforts to walk, pushing toward the traffic noise. Each step sent pain shooting from foot to knee, forcing him to stop every few limping steps in a frustrating search for relief. Just let me come to a road or a farmhouse, he pleaded through rasping breaths. He came across nothing, finally realizing he must be in a park or nature preserve or something like that. How could it be so big? he wondered, at the same time knowing he had not gone far since his fall.

Stumbling, he fell again, then pulled himself to the nearest tree. It was on a slope and he could not get comfortable. He saw the sky turn rosy and must have passed out because he opened his eyes to a bright morning. He looked with longing at the water bottle. Better save what little was left. He felt nauseous and pity for himself and worry for his family. Tracing the car to his home will be a snap. The women and children don't know about any of this, not the specifics, but the FBI will be hard to convince. The neighbors will be brutal of course. What has it all accomplished, these missions, particularly this one? What did killing all those people change? A friend was dead, maybe two. He was being hunted, no doubt, as were the others. He stopped, reminding himself he was a soldier, at war with an America that on the other side of the world was an imperial invader, taking unfair advantage to control its precious supplies of oil, running roughshod over the people of Islam. I will be remembered as a martyr, he told himself with satisfaction. Americans will now live in fear, wondering when the next attack will come. Other attacks will come, inspired by his actions. He remembered the words of Stickman in the motel room ...Damn, I wish I had my phone. I would call Stickman or Assiri and they would pick me up – except where would I tell them to go? I can't even find a damn road.

He thought he heard dogs, then the chopping of a helicopter for sure. The branches of the oak he sat against started high on its trunk. They'll see me easily. He crawled to the other side of the tree. As the helicopter approached above a nearby tree line, the pilot spotted a man's leg on one side of the oak. A voice on a bullhorn demanded, "Come out, hands in sight." Swale edged around the side of the tree and emp- tied his Glock. The helicopter spun away, none the worse off. "We've got SWAT teams on the way. Give yourself up." Swale inserted anoth- er clip and took a look around the tree. The helicopter was staying too high to bother shooting. Somewhere back in the woods he could hear a vehicle approaching slowly, probably on a service road he missed. Not that it would have mattered. He opened the water bottle and drained it in two large swallows. It tasted good, still chilled from the night. Swale gently placed the Glock in his mouth and pulled the trigger.

As Assiri and Foster drove west, radio news reports made it clear they were going the wrong direction. Even if they made it to California the FBI would certainly be waiting. Home was out of the question. As they had left the motel for the mall, Swale had slipped Assiri an envelope. "Should there be problems and you need help, try this number if you're okay with Chicago. Ask for Mr. E and hope he hasn't had to toss his phone. I've given him your name and Foster's, too. He will hook you up with brothers you can stay with. Allah be with you."

Los Angeles was another option, many old friends still there, but it was a long way. The feds will certainly be looking for them there, too. Chicago was looking better all the time and they wanted to get out of sight somewhere, fast. Law enforcement had already sifted through surveillance tapes at the mall and released a description of their car and identified the likely attackers as being from Northern California. Assiri and Foster were living right, encountering only one road block before a description of their car went public, and getting through without a problem. But the nation was in a state of alarm and rage. Shorter was much better. Somewhere they weren't known was, too. They reversed direction, toward Chicago.

Stickman spent the day with Wendy's body, picking up the news that Swale and Dog were dead. By early afternoon, television reports had surveillance footage from East Ramp, Level 5 of mall parking. The video was grainy, taken by a camera with a dirty lens or in need of being replaced. Whatever, Stickman was thankful. He could tell who was in the footage by body shape and size, but facial features appeared too blurred for identification. The video showed five men, no doubt taken after Kobeisi was shot. Stickman learned that Kobeisi died of internal damage that the doctors could not bring under control. A young woman reporter speculated that his death was unfortunate if only because investigators had been denied potential information. Stickman took the opposite view. The reporter said the FBI was still saying no connection had been made between the embassy and mall attacks, but Stickman scowled as his and Maple's photos flashed on the screen, anyway.

... And this side note just in. Officials now say bombs exploded in five theaters, not six as has been reported since the attack.

Stickman sat upright on the bed, his attention solely on the television.

...and it has been difficult to know with certainty where the destruction from each of the multiple bombs started or stopped. But now, in one of the damaged theaters, responders have found a backpack, tucked under a back row seat, containing a homemade explosive that did not detonate. That bomb – tentatively identified as C-4 – was found in Theater 3

"Damn! Damn it to hell! My bomb didn't go off, my fucking bomb didn't go off!" Stickman leaped from the bed in a fury, his usual calm shattered. He was beside himself, overwhelmed by a woeful sense of failure.

"Damn you, Dog! You fucked up my bomb. Damn you to hell." He barked his shin on the frame of the bed. He gritted his teeth against the pain and took deep breaths as he continued swearing. The reporter's voice slowly recaptured his attention.

...and so it isn't known why that bomb failed to explode. It could have been wired improperly or had a faulty detonator. It's believed a remote igniter was used and it's possible that signal didn't reach the bomb in Theater 3 simply because of how the mall was constructed. Investigators are trying to sort all of that out.

Stickman had largely regained his composure, but could still feel the flush of anger tingling in his cheeks. He turned the TV screen toward the desk chair and sat down.

...Officials are hopeful the contents of the backpack will be helpful in tracking the killers still at large. Officials refused to say what the backpack contained, but we have an unconfirmed report that there was a Gideon Bible. Without doubt, investigators will be visiting motels in the area. You can also be sure they'll be looking for fingerprints, DNA and sources where the terrorists could have obtained bomb components, the backpacks and their other contents.

"Good luck with that," Stickman said to the TV, switching it off as the announcer went to other news.

He felt empty. A failure. He sat quietly, wondering what he might have done differently. Perhaps he should have gone over each bomb and backpack with Dog. Maybe they would have noticed a defect. Maybe not. Could the lovers beside him have noticed the backpack and called for help? No. That would have been on the news long ago. He thought about how he would have reacted if one of the other men's backpacks had failed. He knew he wouldn't have cast blame. At that point, all of them were little more than carriers. He still would have praised Dog for five out of six, probably. Gradually the guilt and anger subsided. He felt better, but still inadequate, and, in a way, fortunate to be alone.

Toward evening, broadcasts were suggesting that the intensity of the dragnet had eased. Stickman had eaten the stale ham and cheese sandwich. He put the last slice of pizza in the microwave as he called up another movie. He nodded off, wondering if Wendy might soon become a bit odiferous. He started awake near midnight. The hotel had honored his request for no maid service and now wouldn't be by until morning.

He gathered his belongings and checked to see that the Do Not Disturb sign was still in place. He attached the door chain, thus ensuring someone from maintenance or security would have to be called and would be present if the maid found the body. See, I am a nice guy, he told himself. In the early hours he slid open the balcony door as he silently thanked Wendy for scoring a second floor room. Stickman eased over the railing, tossed his overnight bag to the ground and briefly hung from the balcony to position himself for the short drop. He glimpsed a humping derriere through the window of a dimly lit first floor room before dropping to the ground and walking to his car.

Chapter 32

After leaving the motel, Stickman had stopped at first opportunity and bought two disposable phones. He was fine with using a phone once or twice and tossing it, minimizing the danger of a call being traced, his location being jeopardized. He reached Assiri and Foster in Chicago and kept the call short. They were hunkered down with sympathetic jihadists in a rental house on the city's gritty south side. Stickman urged Assiri and Foster to destroy their phones, and to call him back from another part of the city on a new phone. They moved fast, calling back later in the day as Stickman continued driving east. He asked if they would join him on another mission, time and place to be determined. They agreed. Okay, he said, start putting together another crew.

When Stickman pulled alongside the trailer house it felt like home. Weird, he thought; he had done nothing to make this place a home. But given the stress he had been under since leaving, the quiet tin shell at the edge of the woods was a welcome haven.

Maple came out and they fist-bumped. "Guess I know where you've been. All over the damn tube, flashing your damn mug shot – and mine – though the FBI isn't making a connection with the embassy, at least not publicly."

"Things didn't come down like I wanted, our dead I mean. And my damn bomb not going off. Otherwise, not bad."

"Not at all bad, indeed. That was a hell of a hit. I want to hear about it, and I also have something to tell you."

After Stickman kicked back with a cup of tea, Maple told him about April, concealing nothing.

"Do you think she'll stay under?"

"No guarantees, but yes. I do think we should get her stuff and her car out of here. So far no one has been snooping around."

They watched the evening news. The mall attack had claimed two more of the injured. Swale, Dog and Kobeisi had been publicly identified as among the attackers. The FBI was interrogating all of Swale's people. At least three terrorists remained at large, with news reports giving no hint that law enforcement knew where to look. Mall of America had tightened security.

"No shit," said Maple.

"When I said that was a hell of a hit, I meant it, and I'm hoping it has legs. But the government is so huge, I worry that they can take these body blows for a long time. Hate to say it, Mr. Stick, because I don't want to be a martyr, but we'll probably come to a bad end."

"You're probably right."

"But what if I'm wrong? What would you replace the government with if you had the chance?"

"I've thought about that, but I really don't know. I'm more a tactical guy. But the thing is, anything would be an improvement. Big time."

They cleaned out April's trailer the next day, loading all of her clothing, art supplies and other personal effects into her car. Stickman followed Maple on the drive to Pittsburgh International Airport. In a remote corner of long-term economy parking, Maple found an empty space, betting weeks would pass before April's car would be checked out.

Stopping on a quiet street as they left Pittsburgh, Stickman used his new phone to call Assiri. Though he and Foster had been in Chicago only a few days, they could see the mall attack was having a profound effect. "We have hooked up with a few brothers and, man, they are kissing your feet!" declared Assiri. "You can't believe how hyped they are. They have totally bought into you being the dude who did the embassy, too. I don't know if you like that, but man, this is a big deal. You are becoming a big deal."

Stickman was taken aback, not sure he wanted that much notoriety among radical jihadists. He assumed he had Assiri or Foster or both to blame. But no sense yelling at them. He was going to need their help. Also, he had to admit liking the flattery, although he didn't know how to respond. Except for his computer prowess, he had done little in life worthy of notice, let alone compliments. He wondered if the brothers knew it was his bomb that didn't explode. Probably not. Assiri and Foster may well have forgotten who was assigned to Theater 3. In any case, he wasn't going to bring it up.

The personal attention made him uncomfortable and he decided to ignore it, try to at least. The important thing was whether the scale had been tipped, or at least tilted, whether others would pursue violent jihad. He had used the argument of inspiring others to pump up the Swale people at Mall of America. He thought about what Maple had said the previous night and had to admit the likelihood of an emerging movement remained well in the future.

"That's, that's very encouraging," he finally said. "You and Foster need to be proud of what you accomplished. But success means increased risk, so be careful not to attract attention. Let me ask you, is anyone actually doing anything?"

"Well, a few of the brothers here are talking kind of crazy, like wanting to shoot up a ball game or a parade."

"Listen to me, you must tell them in no uncertain terms that this is not easy, it is not glamourous. It is dangerous. Look at our operation. I thought it was pretty well planned. We had success but three of our six are dead. The FBI and the others are not easy to fool. Their resources are much greater than ours. We cannot afford loose talk."

"I hear you, but I'm not sure I can control a couple of these guys, and no doubt there are others. There may be a lot of them, all around the country, guys we don't know anything about."

"What happens around the country is the whole point and it's beyond our control. I just don't want your local hotheads putting you and Foster in jeopardy. Please, Assiri, do nothing until I have another plan. I don't know when that will be, but I will need your help, no doubt. Please keep your head down until then. If things start looking too shaky there, you and Foster may need to find another place."

Having developed a phone phobia – justified or not – Stickman tossed the one he was using and bought another. When making purchases now, he and Maple used a simple disguise of sunglasses, false mustache and ball cap. Photos taken at a check-out counter might not fool investigators, but at least they wouldn't have one better than what was being splashed on the news.

Stickman and Maple took their own advice to go low profile, and monitored with satisfaction reports of militant incidents. Some were committed by Muslims, others not. Some reports suggested without attribution that radicals had been inspired by the mall and embassy attacks. There was no way to know.

In Boise three days after the attack on the mall, a lone gunman walked into a supermarket and opened fire with a 12-guage shotgun. Seven people died before an off-duty police officer, interrupted in his search for garlic-stuffed martini olives, fatally brought down the shooter. Investigators learned the man, born in Iraq, belonged to a mosque in the upper Midwest and had visited Pakistan the previous year.

The next day an out-of-work plumber walked into the headquarters building of the Transportation Security Administration in suburban D.C., pulled two handguns from his jacket as he approached the magnetometer and shot and killed three officers. Running deeper into the building, he came to a cafeteria and emptied both guns, killing four customers and wounding two. Building security officers who were eating breakfast gunned him down. Investigators found no connection between the plumber and Islam, let alone any terrorist organization. That didn't keep conspiracy theorists from loudly pointing out he had twice visited the Mideast several years earlier.

At the University of Missouri, Columbia, a student from Syria calmly walked into a men's locker room, pulled a handgun from his gym bag and shot two fellow students dead before he was overpowered by members of the wrestling team.

Nearly two weeks after the mall attacks the tone of the violence shifted when the son of Iranian immigrants attempted a suicide mission in a sold-out playhouse in northwest Des Moines. The would-be bomber suffered second degree burns when he detonated an improvised explosive device that was defective. No one else was injured. The young man had visited Turkey the previous year and the CIA found indications that he taken a side trip to Afghanistan for several weeks.

A well-organized operation surfaced a few days later, the kind authorities feared would be inspired by the attack on Mall of America. In Houston, four assailants clad in black and wearing pullover masks stormed front and back doors of a large restaurant hosting a wedding party. Firing AK-47s, they killed employees and guests at point-blank range. Then, two attackers kept firing while the other two threw homemade bombs among the trapped guests. The bridesmaid managed to grab one of the bombs and threw it back, killing an assailant who turned out to be female. When another of the terrorists stopped firing to reload, members of the wedding party charged him and beat him unconscious. The other attackers retreated by the back door and escaped. The two who did not get away, authorities concluded, were in a cell of homegrown militant jihadists. Raids on cell members resulted in arrests and the seizure of a large cache of weapons and explosives that, the investigation showed, had been stockpiled for more than two years.

In Los Angeles, several young men wearing masks took a page from the Boko Haram playbook, grabbing two Hispanic girls as they walked through a slum neighborhood after dark. The girls, in their early teens, were blindfolded and gagged and taken to a house where they were repeatedly raped over the next two days. Each was made to watch as the other was violated. The men made clear their allegiance to radical jihad, declaring "God is good," "Death to all infidels" and other slogans. Again blindfolded, though now so submissive that gags were not needed, the girls were driven to a dangerous neighborhood and dumped in an alley. They began wandering and luckily were spotted by a Good Samaritan. Except for several DNA samples, authorities said they had no leads for identifying the rapists.

Wilbur and Violet Banks were watching the ten o'clock news from their bed when the story of the Hispanic girls aired. "That is just awful," said Violet.

"Yes it is, Mama," Wilbur agreed. "If I were a young man again I'd be glad to go after those animals, just like I went after that Jap machine gun nest at Guadalcanal. I had no choice. The Japs had my platoon pinned down."

"I wish you wouldn't call them that, Wilbur. They've been our allies for a long time now."

"Today they're Japanese. Back then they were Japs. Remember all the newspaper headlines after they bombed Pearl Harbor? Even General Douglas MacArthur called them Japs when he pinned on my Silver Star."

"You got your purple heart when you were still in the hospital, Wilbur. Well deserved, too. Mickey Ailes got the Silver Star."

"That was really somethin', signing up for the Army with Mickey after we graduated from high school and then goin' through the whole damn Pacific together. Two Silver Star winners from one little high school."

"Wilbur ..."

"Course I didn't get mine right away like Mickey did. Got stuck in that damn hospital with malaria. It was worse than takin' a little shrapnel."

Other news followed, as did weather and sports, but Wilbur's mind kept wandering to the virility of the young men, while stepping around their despicable abuses. It put him in a time when he and Violet sometimes enjoyed each other more than once a night rather than seasonally. Getting up, he went to the bathroom and then to their office before returning to bed.

"Well, Violet, seems like somethin's going on," he said, eyeing the sheet over his lap that had taken on tent-like contours.

Violet peered in his direction. "Oh my, yes," she said. "Wilbur, have you been looking at that porn on the computer again. I jus' hate it when I turn on the computer and all those porn sites come up. We've got to get that machine cleaned up and keep it cleaned up. You hear me Wilbur?"

"Why are you looking a gift horse in the teeth? I declare we best not tarry 'cause it's not going to last forever, don't ya think?"

Violet's eyebrows went up. "My, yes," she agreed, reaching for the light switch.

Chapter 33

The repetitive violence put much of the nation on a discriminatory footing against Muslims. Across the country, they were shunned and treated with suspicion, at best. Others were attacked, some viciously. Mosques and Muslim centers were torched. Muslim-owned businesses were vandalized and the targets of arsonists. Many Muslims lived in fear, and those that didn't harbored uncertainty and anxiety they had never experienced before.

Never mind that the huge majority of Muslims strongly condemned the brutality practiced by al-Qaeda, let alone the barbaric practices of ISIS. Or that the huge majority were loyal American citizens or aspired to be citizens. Too often, the ideals of usually tolerant non-Muslim Americans collapsed under the weight of suspicion or fear or panic or a thirst for revenge. Picking up momentum was the view that Islam was not a religion but a political movement using religious teachings as a front. Embracing that canard made it easy to then ignore constitutional and legal safeguards against religious discrimination.

Fueling intolerance were demagogic rants of unscrupulous politicians and others of influence who crassly manipulated public insecurity to advance their twisted agendas. President Tower issued calls for restraint and calm, while promising to relentlessly track down perpetrators of mass violence. He poured voluminous resources into bringing to justice anyone known to foster violence or to have ties to foreign terrorist groups. To those ends he cast the widest possible net, particularly in cities targeted by an attack. In theory, those efforts should have targeted homegrown terrorism equally, from those of the alt-right to militant survivalists to radical jihadists. But that was not the case.

Dormant campaign promises to crack down on Muslims and those from predominantly Muslim countries came to life. The Immigration and Naturalization Service was issued orders that effectively banned Muslim immigrants, including students, visitors and those with work visas. Federal agencies created joint task forces to round up and expel Muslims for the flimsiest of reasons, relying on sympathetic judges who found their dockets overflowing. Executive action was supplemented by harsh legislative remedies handed down by a Congress where nativist conservatives ruled.

Other immigrants, particularly Hispanics, also came under increased scrutiny. Only because illegal Hispanics numbered in the millions, and were so important to the economy, did they have a limited buffer against the harshest enforcement efforts of the vast federal bureaucracy.

The country was rapidly moving toward isolationism and, at the same time, federal policing that clearly skirted–or violated–the Constitution. Those priorities, though bearing pregnant seeds of repression, had disturbingly wide support. Polls showed a majority of people ready to take restrictive measures against Muslims, be they American citizens or in the immigration pipeline. There were calls for a constitutional amendment to permanently ban Muslims from immigrating. Calls, too, for wholesale deportation of illegal immigrants, whole families, men, women and children, Muslims as well as others. Monitoring or scrutinizing activities of mosques in clear violation of Constitutional religious rights had alarming support. With public anxiety at a fever pitch, the potential for political gain was too appetizing for demagogues to resist. Not since Senator Joe McCarthy, with his witch hunt for communists in the 1950s, and Alabama Governor George Wallace, playing the race card in the 1960s, had the country seen such shameless efforts to inflame the public's ugliest passions.

Outnumbered voices waved red flags against policies condemning an entire religion. They warned that fear-mongering and incendiary political rhetoric would spark formation of hate groups targeting Muslims and other minorities. Indeed, during the just-past presidential campaign, the number of fascist and similar groups had nearly tripled. Outnumbered voices warned against the U.S. failing its constitutional and legal responsibilities to minorities. They pointed out that minorities were on an unstoppable demographic path to the majority, and that trying to recapture a monolithic culture was a futile dream. They warned against casually throwing away a proud heritage – regardless of its admittedly ignoble stains – that had long survived as a beacon to oppressed people in all corners of the world.

Those voices argued that the world was complex, not easily or skillfully or humanely negotiated with sloganeering and simplistic solutions. Most specifically, they predicted that a global backlash would be unleased if Muslim extremists could point to the U.S. blatantly practicing discrimination and prejudice. Recruiting for radical jihad would be the clear beneficiary, both at home and abroad. All those warnings, and more, were made, loud and clear, and too many Americans chose to ignore them.

Both sides all too often took to the streets with competing demonstrations that further incited and divided a frightened public. Happy to participate, on both sides, were anarchists and other activists who found benefit in violence. In that climate, police too often lost control. Abuses were inevitable, often against blacks, and rioting broke out in several cities.

Even when terrorist attacks – and demonstrations and demagogic rhetoric – lessened, anxiety remained high, the potential for fresh outbreaks of violence just beneath a simmering surface.

Most Muslims held to their faith and their love of country. There were those, however, whose views hardened against the United States.

They took many paths, from harboring or supplying extremists to actively joining their ranks. Those who chose violence found it becoming easier and easier to coordinate with the international movement.

Chapter 34

Stickman and Maple kept their heads down, seldom venturing out except for groceries or an early- or late-day run. Had it not been for terrorist attacks dominating the news, their lives would have been totally boring. There was time to think, to devise a new mission. As assaults by unknown compatriots around the country slowed, they decided radical jihadism needed another inspiring jolt. They saw their time approaching again.

Their plan was the most ambitious yet. They would strike another soft target. And again, it would be in the Heartland, seeking the biggest impact by hitting a part – perhaps the part – of the country where people feel the most secure. More isolated than the coasts, more prosperous than the South, enjoying individual control often lacking in the federally-owned West, families of the Heartland had basked in a sense of security for generations.

Like the attack on Mall of America, the aim would be to destroy that sense, to replace security with fear and anxiety that are the handmaidens of vulnerability. But Stickman and Maple decided to not target another symbol of capitalistic largess or excessive consumption. This time there would be no symbolism. They would simply and methodically kill and maim to inflict maximum pain. Perhaps that would send a rumble of fear across the country, inspiring other jihadists as never before.

The plan would put the attackers at great risk and, to succeed, Stickman and Maple knew they must secure far more firepower. For starters they needed fully automatic AK-47s and a second rocket-propelled grenade launcher. They also needed a somewhat bigger team than Stickman had used at Mall of America, which meant more Glocks and ammunition.

Because they had been so cautious, their contacts among the jihadist community were extremely limited. When talking to Swale before the mall attack, Stickman said he had a munitions supplier in Hoboken, New Jersey, but was uneasy about having only one source. Hoboken caught Swale's attention. "Small world," Swale had said. "Mohammad Rouhani is Zarif's supplier for the C-4 we're using." Swale went on to say he believed Rouhani not only trafficked in arms, but was committed to jihad. He couldn't recommend an alternative supplier, but now Stickman had a name and not just initials.

After driving nearly an hour to a pay phone, Stickman called the number for Mohammad Rouhani. A man picked up and Stickman, after identifying himself as he had in the past, dispensed with MR and asked for Mr. Rouhani by name. The line went silent. Stickman, worried that he had overplayed his hand for no good reason, finally hung up with little hope of a return call. He and Maple loitered near the pay phone, with growing concern about attracting unwanted attention. Finally, mercifully, the phone rang.

"I did not call back sooner because I was driving myself to a pay phone of some distance," said the man, speech heavy with a Mideast accent. "If you think your phone is safe we can talk but do not say that name of my employer again. He is not happy with what you did. Also we must quickly to do business. Why do you call?"

Stickman told him what was needed. "That can be done," the man said, naming a price. "It could be less. My employer's anger is less because he is honored to have business with men of such demand. The day you want to come, call that morning to see that all is right. You will be given directions." He provided a cell number Stickman had not used before and hung up.

Obviously, Rouhani has pieced together enough information, probably starting with what he got from Zarif, to conclude that Maple and I share the distinction of being Public Enemy No. 1, Stickman said to himself. Perhaps that's why the price was more generous than expected.

Unfortunately, Rouhani still wanted more money than they had. They could scale back their plan or find another target. Or they could raise more money. Stickman thought back to the day they returned from ditching April's car at Pittsburgh International. They met an armored bank truck on a county road south of the city. Maple had noted the time on that Wednesday, musing that sometime they may need to make a bank withdrawal. They found it curious that the truck was using a fairly remote road. Perhaps it was a shortcut between stops, a route taken regularly.

Early the following Wednesday, Maple and Stickman were on the same county road, patrolling a stretch of half a dozen miles connecting two state highways. It was hard not to be conspicuous. Maple hoped if the armored truck showed, it would be sooner rather than later. No such luck, but they found an abandoned corncrib on a hill that allowed them to watch the road for more than a mile in each direction. Parking their car out of sight in the drive-through crib, they waited through the morning, then well into the afternoon.

"Sometimes it strikes me strange that Muslims, the ones we work with, seem to really like us, mainly you, Mr. Stick," Maple said abruptly.

"Where did that come from?"

"I don't know. Too much time to think, I guess ... Anyway, to like us they must think we're true believers, when we're not."

"I'm not sure that's what they think. I think they like us because we're hurting the United States. As long as that doesn't change, they're okay with us."

"I think we use them. You don't think they're feeling used?"

"Nope. I think Muslims come in all different stripes, just like Lutherans or Catholics or whatever. Some are more religious than others. Or they interpret their religion in different ways. Like the huge majority of Muslims are against violent jihad. But Swale and his guys? They weren't praying five times a day. If anything, mon, when they look at the damage, they may think they're using us."

"Maybe that's right ...Don't know about you, but I never got much out of praying by my lonesome, like the real devout ones do. Wherever they are. When I was a kid, sometimes going to church, or later, to prayers at the mosque was nice. It made me feel calm, like things were okay, at least for a while. Do you know what I mean, Mr. Stick?"

"Maybe. Growing up a Catholic seemed all right for a while. Same with trying Islam. Then trying yoga, kind of nice for a while. Then herbal tea. I still like tea ...Anyway, I've been thinking that we need to move on, from the Banks' place I mean."

"I have the same feeling, Mr. Stick. Wilbur and Violet seem fine with our story about April. But I keep waiting for her to pop up downstream and deputies trying to ID her, talking to people all over the county."

"I'm about ready to call it quits today, too."

"Maybe," Maple said with little hope, "the bank guys have been picking up a ton of money."

Then there it was, red and black and beautiful to their eyes. Maple quickly went to the trunk and removed the rocket launcher armed with a high explosive anti-tank round. He stepped back into the car, door open, and Stickman drove the short distance to the road, parking at a slight angle. Maple waited until the armored truck was within a quarter mile before he stepped out. He poked the launcher through the open window, resting it on the door.

Suddenly suspicious, the driver slowed to a stop. Fine, Maple muttered, nothing like a stationary target. He fired. The front of the armored truck erupted, bullet-proof glass shattering and a large jagged hole coming into view as the smoke cleared and flames licked out of the interior. Stickman accelerated down the road and past the burning hulk, braking to a sliding stop at a safe distance. Maple quickly went to the trunk, reloaded and fired again, creating a cavernous hole in the back door of the armored vehicle. Paper currency blew into the air like confetti and Stickman backed to within a car length. Tossing the launcher in the trunk, Maple pulled out a fire extinguisher and laid several bursts of foam on the growing flames, knocking them down at least temporarily. He stepped past the dangling back door, Glock in hand. He didn't need it. The driver, or what was left of him, remained strapped in his seat. The other guard, also dead, had been blown behind the seats.

Several cash boxes were open, others intact. Maple started tossing those out the back door and Stickman hurried them to the trunk. After chucking more than a dozen, Maple hopped out to help finish loading.

As they drove away in the direction the armored truck had been going, Stickman saw in the rearview mirror a decades-old station wagon approaching. The car slowed to a stop. Half a dozen children poured out, running down bills of all denominations that were skittering in the light breeze.

"How long do you think it will take the parents to call the sheriff's office?" Stickman asked with amusement, watching the prancing children.

Chapter 35

They were in the next county before picking up a radio report on the heist of the armored bank truck. "You're right. Mom and Dad let the kids collect their allowance before calling police," Maple said drolly.

Back at the trailer they waited until well after dark, when the lights in Wilbur and Violet's house were off, to unload the cash boxes. Using a diamond tipped bit, Maple drilled the lock on the first box. With trepidation that exploding dye might greet him, he slowly lifted the lid. No problem. He exhaled and turned the box to show Stickman the neatly wrapped packets of one hundred dollar bills. "Sweet, huh?" Maple grinned, reaching for another box.

Within an hour, over a million dollars in mostly hundreds, fifties and twenties were stacked in rows on the kitchen table. The cash boxes were back in the car trunk, filled with bricks and strapped tightly shut. Soon the boxes would disappear in a deep and remote inlet of Youghiogheny Lake.

Money raised, other preparations went swiftly. Not trusting either of their cars to carry the weight they would pick up in Hoboken, Maple went on Craigslist in search of a heavy duty pickup. He had a Ford F-150 with a hard, one-piece bed cover by the next day. With modifications to the tailgate the F-150 was ready.

Stickman called Assiri and, after brief chitchat, asked, "Can you put together two tables for bridge?"

"I still don't play very well, but yes."

"Oops, I have to take another call. I'll get back to you within a couple weeks, maybe sooner and we'll find a time to play."

Yielding to a restless night, Stickman roused Maple before dawn to pack for the quick trip east. Two-lane highways took them to I-70 and they pulled in at the first rest area, where Stickman got on a pay phone. Lounging against a wall, Maple heard just one end of the conversation.

"I called about some supplies several days ago."

"I recognize your voice, too. Is what I need still in stock?"

"I'm on the road."

"Alone."

"Yes, all of it."

Stickman pressed the phone to his ear with his shoulder and scribbled in a note pad. "I think I've got it," he said, quietly reading back the directions before describing the pickup and estimating a time of arrival.

Back on the road, Stickman explained that, again, he hadn't spoken directly to Rouhani. "His man gave me directions to a city park. We're to call from there. Then we'll follow him to Rouhani's place."

Maple glanced from the driver's seat to ask, "What's the story on Rouhani?"

"I wish I knew more about him. I had a chance to talk to Swale a little before we hit the mall. It turns out his old friend Zarif and Rouhani go back a long way, to Iran. Zarif was on the fringes of Hezbollah, but Rouhani had strong ties, maybe was active. Swale did have one interesting tidbit: Zarif knew of just one time when Rouhani got at odds with a customer. He said Rouhani can be as mean as he is huge. Swale seemed to say that as a warning."

"Has he been busted?"

"Swale didn't mention it. Besides a warehouse, Rouhani owns a couple small businesses that he has others manage. They give him a good front, low-key. And he buys from an importer, so he doesn't touch anything until he takes delivery. That helps keep his profile low, too."

Nearing Hoboken they exited I-95 to gas up, wanting to be able to get clear of the metro area once they were loaded. Following directions from Rouhani's man, Stickman got to the city park a few minutes later, alone in the cab. He waited five minutes, ten, thirty, and was wondering if the deal was off. An SUV parked half a block away flashed its lights twice. Stickman hadn't noticed anyone in the car. Not sure what to do, he flashed his lights twice in return. A minute later the car pulled slowly into a space beside him. The driver's window opened and a swarthy, middle-aged man peered out.

"Let's play twenty question. How many times previous have you had contact with my boss?"

"Three."

"You and my boss have a mutual acquaintance in the Midwest. In what state does, or I should have said, did he live?"

"North Dakota."

"From what country comes my boss?"

"Iran."

"Game over. Follow me at a distance to not attract attention. We're going to drive around a while."

They did, rather mindlessly it seemed, presumably to ensure not being followed. Stickman was at a loss to see how the exercise prevented use of an electronic tracking device or a surveillance drone. Oh well ...He followed the SUV into a warehouse district. The street was empty, not surprising on a Saturday. As they entered the second block, the overhead door of a warehouse on the right began to rise. The SUV entered and Stickman followed slowly. In his rearview mirror, he saw motion behind him as the door came down, casting the interior in an ominous dim light.

A huge man with a full gray beard – Mohammad Rouhani, no doubt – moved along the passenger side of the pickup. His gait was uneven, his six and a half foot frame struggling to support well over four hundred pounds. He carried a five-foot wooden staff, probably for balance, and a scowl dominated his face. Saying nothing, he motioned for Stickman to reverse his direction by turning left into an empty bay and then backing up to one covered by a large tarp stretching perhaps twenty feet high. Stickman began the simple maneuver, keeping Rouhani in the corner of his eye as the large man shuffled to one side of the olive tarp. Stickman stopped well short of the bay and at a slight angle that gave him a bit of protection. Finally, Rouhani boomed, "Welcome, sir!"

As Stickman swung his left leg out of the cab, Rouhani reached to a supporting column and jerked a rope tied in a slipknot. The tarp fell to the concrete floor with a rush of air, revealing three evenly spaced men, assault rifles waist high, pointed directly at him. Stickman jerked his leg back, grabbing the Glock he had tucked in his belt. He slid down in the seat a few inches, fearing a hail of gunfire. When nothing happened he risked a peek, saw the men had not moved. Rouhani, too, now had an assault rifle. That glance left another impression, that the men looked too bulky, as if wearing body armor. Rouhani may have been, too, though on him it would be hard to tell.

"Now, Mr. Stickman, you need to relax as I explain a couple of things. I do not know if you have heard but the reward for you and your colleague, Mr. Maple, has been raised to twenty-five million dollars for each of you. The names Stickman and Maple are not used, of course, but I prefer the familiar ones by which we have come to know you, the ones by which you were known to Monsour Zarif and his friend Mr. Swale, may God rest their souls. The higher rewards were just announced a short time ago. If you were not aware of your new worth, I can understand. But for your own sake, I feel duty bound as a companion in jihad to say if the two of you are going to be such public figures, you really must stay more abreast of current affairs. I felt very fortunate when I heard, knowing that you were already on the road."

Stickman felt sweat running down his spine, but could not push aside an untimely thought: Rouhani's ponderous, reassuring style reminded him of someone from another age. Alfred Hitchcock? Orson Wells?

"Now, Mr. Stickman, you have nothing to fear," the fat man went on pleasantly, Stickman's mind's eye seeing the scowl obscured by a pasted-on smile. "I had planned a simple sale, and at a generous price, I am confident you agree. But twenty-five million dollars can buy a lot of destruction. It can substantially help fund the needs of brothers other than you who are also responsible for the disarray beginning to sweep this country of infidels. You notice I said twenty-five million. You will not be harmed if you assist us in capturing Mr. Maple. And I promise, his end will be swift and humane."

Maple is no doubt relieved to hear that, Stickman told himself. His nerves starting to settle, he automatically began looking at the difficult situation from a distance and was first struck by how Rouhani had overplayed his hand. If he had waited until I cleared the pickup to drop the tarp, I'd have been in the open and out of the picture one way or another. Maple would be on his own. Buy a little time. Rouhani may make other mistakes ...

"I have a contact, Mr. Stickman, a cleric with a radical past who appeared to reform and, after many years, was able to enter this country. The authorities trust him because of his efforts, on the surface, to discourage militant jihadism among our young men. This cleric can deliver Mr. Maple's body to federal officials and collect the reward. So, my friend, please step out. There is no need to raise your hands or any such nonsense."

"Wouldn't fifty million suit you better than twenty-five?"

"No, Mr. Stickman, and I will explain why. I am sure Mr. Maple has many abilities, but I believe you are the planner, the strategic thinker, the man with the tougher core. Why do I say this? First, I had no problems in my early dealings with you. I appreciate a man who does what he says he will do. Second, our departed brother, Mr. Swale, spoke highly of you to Mr. Zarif, who carried those words back to me. Third, when you needed a rocket launcher, I believed it would be for something important, and it was. Fourth, according to my last conversation with Mr. Zarif, when you called on our brothers in California for help, they responded without question. That speaks very highly of you. And finally, without doubt, your well-planned attack on the Mall of America was the most successful on American soil since 9/11, by far."

Rouhani really does like the sound of his own voice, Stickman muttered, starting to wonder if he would see an opening.

"I must admit I felt slighted that you did not come to me to supply the C-4 for that mission. I rationalized that Mr. Zarif was much closer to the mall. But, you do know that I deliver. Anyway, that success brings us to why you are here today. The shipment you are picking up portends another audacious attack, perhaps even bigger than the one on the mall. It will elevate our cause even higher, spawning other attacks and prove to be a boon for recruitment. No, Mr. Stickman, you are far too valuable to kill. You are worth far more than twenty-five million dollars."

"And Maple isn't? We've been together every step of the way for a long time. He had the harder task by far at the Russian Embassy."

"I have no doubt that he is valuable, but the question is whether he is of more value alive or of more value dead ...I just had an idea, Mr. Stickman. Perhaps we could give Mr. Maple the opportunity to demonstrate his commitment to jihad. An attack on a school, perhaps, with the understanding that someone sympathetic to our cause would step in just ahead of the police and, ah, qualify for the reward. The timing would be tricky. It's just a thought at this point, but what do you think, Mr. Stickman?"

I think, Stickman thought, that you are way out there on Maple's wrong fucking side. "He wouldn't think much of your opportunity, is my best guess. And pardon my suspicious nature, but if I gave you Maple, you could then kill me, too. Perhaps make me tell you what we have planned."

"There, my friend, is yet another reason why you are so valuable. You see possibilities, even when you are in a stressful situation. But let us change the subject for a minute. Take a peek, Mr. Stickman. Look to the right side of the tarp. You will see three boxes. They contain your merchandise and I believe they will fit nicely in your pickup's large toolbox. Take a peek. It is okay."

Wiping sweat from his eyes, Stickman looked, and agreed the three gray boxes would fit. He also noticed that Rouhani had moved for protection behind a support column. Unless I go along with him, things are quickly going to change, he thought. But there is no way I am going to give up Maple and I sure as hell can't trust Rouhani, anyway.

Glancing in the rear view mirror, he had to smile at Rouhani, amply protruding on either side of his supposedly protective column.

"Mr. Stickman! Time for a decision, my friend. Come now, be reasonable. You are badly outnumbered and outgunned. I don't want to have to force you to take me to Maple."

Stickman put no stock in Rouhani's promise to keep him alive. At best, that would only buy time. The only reason he was here, that he had met Rouhani instead of a flunky, was the reward money.

Taking another peek around the door frame, he saw one of Rouhani's men kneeling, holding a weapon as he attached what appeared to be a canister. Teargas.

Stickman had driven so slowly into the warehouse, in part, to not disturb the bed cover. It was not latched at the tailgate, giving Maple a wide but thin view of Rouhani and his men. The one who had readied the teargas awaited only a signal from Rouhani.

"All right, Mr. Stickman, time to decide."

When several seconds of silence followed Rouhani's ultimatum, he motioned to the teargas man, who slowly moved to his left toward the driver's side of the pickup, crouching low. He stopped, and it was Maple who sniffed opportunity.

Teargas man laid his weapon on the concrete floor to pull on a gas mask. As he finished, Maple saw Rouhani signal his man at the far end, on the passenger side, who cautiously put his weapon down to don a mask. No reason to let these fuckers get masked up. The thought jolted through Maple's mind as he slammed up the hard bed cover and snapped off three shots from his AK-47 at the armed man waiting his turn. The man fell silently, except for the clatter of his weapon, blood streaming from his face.

Maple fired three more rounds at Rouhani, who screamed as one ripped through belly fat that sagged beneath his body armor. As Maple swung back to his left, the second man masking up was already firing. Maple felt a jolt in his left shoulder and went to the bed of the pickup, behind a protective steel plate welded inside the tailgate.

Stickman rolled from the cab, trading shots with teargas man. Stickman's Glock won. Teargas man screamed in pain as he grabbed his groin and thrashed on the floor. The man who shot Maple turned on Stickman, who scampered behind the rear tire of the pickup as bullets ricocheted off the floor next to him. Hearing the exchanges of shots, Maple unsnapped a latch securing the tailgate and pushed it open, firing a lucky – and painful – shot to the knee of the last gunman. Stickman ran to him, kicking his weapon out of reach and jerking loose a holstered handgun. Rouhani was clutching his stomach, the fight easily gone out of him. Teargas man was bleeding out from a severed upper leg artery, nearly unconscious in a spreading pool of blood.

Maple scooted painfully from the pickup, rested on one knee, AK-47 in hand, as blood streamed primarily from the exit wound. He watched Stickman walk to the huge man whose eyes were filled with fear. Rouhani barely muttered "My friend" before Stickman shot him in one knee and then, ignoring an anguished howl, in the other. Making sure no weapons were within Rouhani's reach, Stickman got plastic cuffs from the pickup and secured the man with the knee wound to a support column.

Surely someone heard the shots, Stickman thought, listening briefly for the whine of an approaching siren. Nothing yet. He decided to not flee the warehouse with Maple, recognizing several things that could work to their advantage. He started with Maple, who was sweating profusely but not in debilitating pain. Using the medical kit they always carried, Stickman treated the wound as best he could, then helped Maple into fresh clothes. Turning to the cargo they came for, he was surprised to find the three gray boxes were filled with their order, making him think Rouhani did want the next attack carried out. If only he hadn't foolishly thought Maple was legal tender. Stickman carried the gray boxes to the pickup. With room left in the metal toolbox, he quickly poked around Rouhani's stores, adding more guns and ammunition. Checking the tailgate, Stickman found two bullet holes and that a brake light and cover had been shot out – problems with no immediate solution.

The handcuffed man was wearing a cell phone, which Stickman put at the base of the column. "When we are gone you can call for help. I hope you don't call the police. Better call your friends and make good use of Rouhani's supplies for jihad. Whatever, just know I can see you and the phone. Touch it before that door comes down, I'll kill you." The man nodded gratefully.

Maple continued watching, propped against a back tire, as Stickman walked to Rouhani. "I heard what you told my young colleague and I thank you," he managed to say hoarsely through the pain of his shattered knees. "You misunderstand," Stickman answered, staring hard into Rouhani's eyes. The fear that eased just seconds ago returned in triplicate. Rouhani's lips began to quiver uncontrollably and his multi-layered chin jiggled. Stickman raised his Glock, centering it on Rouhani's forehead. "Please, please ...," the fat man begged, tears suddenly sprouting from his squinting eyes. He forced his eyes open and saw Stickman lower the Glock. Rouhani let out a deep sigh just as Stickman fired at the base of his pants zipper. A huge roar burst from the fat man, echoing off the warehouse walls and ceiling, repeating itself again and yet again.

Stickman turned and walked over to help Maple get buckled into his seat. He looked around the warehouse, saw three bottles of water on a crate and put them in the pickup. Finally, he walked slowly back to the weeping Rouhani. "Kill me, please kill me." This time when Stickman centered on Rouhani's forehead he pulled the trigger. It was a matter of tying up a loose end, not an act of mercy.

Chapter 36

Leaving the warehouse, Stickman kept an eye on the handcuffed man in the rearview mirror. He stepped from the pickup and walked back to the overhead door, reaching in to press the control button. He returned to the pickup, feeling the man's eyes, knowing he would snatch the cell phone when the door closed.

As they headed toward the interstate, they passed an automotive store and, on impulse, Stickman circled the block to pull in. The clerk did, indeed, have in stock a brake light for the popular pickup. Stickman also found a compound to fill the bullet holes. They looked like splatters of mud when he finished the patch job in the store's parking lot a few minutes later. He was opening a small toolbox for a screwdriver when a patrol car cruised past. With his nerves fraying, Stickman opted to repair the brake light at the first rest area.

"How you doing?" he asked, getting back in the pickup.

"I'll make it," Maple said weakly. "You wouldn't know what to do with a twenty-five million dollar corpse."

"You've got a point. I'd better keep you alive."

Stickman wasn't confident Maple would make it without a doctor's care. The direct hit had done a lot of damage, cost him a lot of blood. Stickman wondered if an emergency room visit were possible, but seeking help for a gunshot wound was a huge risk. Even in the fading light, he could see a sheen of perspiration on Maple's face. Rosy seepage blemished the front of his shirt from the bandaged shoulder, the back no doubt worse. Stickman wished they had spent more time on medical training over the years.

The pickup blended into rush hour traffic, just another big honking pickup slowly making its way home. Or so they wished. A New Jersey State Police car parked on the right shoulder suddenly was moving, flipping rooftop lights on as he pulled behind their right rear bumper. "The pickup with Pennsylvania plates, pull to the side of the road. Now!"

Stickman immediately followed the order. A tall patrolman unwound himself from the marked car and approached. He was so tall that he squatted rather than bent over to draw even with Stickman's window. "I need to see your driver's license, sir. Do you know you have a brake light out?"

"Yes sir. I noticed it not long ago. I think it was vandals, the way the cover is smashed," Stickman answered, handing over the license. "Anyway," he continued, gesturing at the boxes on the dashboard, "I stopped a few miles back and got what I need. Planned to fix it at the first rest area."

"I see. That will be fine," the lanky officer said, handing Stickman back his license. Leaning in slightly, the officer peered intently at Maple. "Your friend doesn't look so good. Looks like his shoulder is bleeding." As he took a half-step back and raised himself to a crouch the officer's right hand moved to the butt of his handgun. "I want both of you to get your hands where I can see them, then step slowly from the vehicle. You, driver, first."

Stickman's hands came up slowly, a Glock in the right one. As it cleared the door the patrolman found himself looking down a gun barrel for a slice of a second before his world went black. The round struck the bridge of his nose and he sat straight down, jaw dropping as he flopped backwards into the roadway. A SUV veered sharply to avoid him, hitting the front fender of a car in the next lane. The SUV driver stopped and began screaming at Stickman, "I think you killed that man! You killed that cop!"

Stickman ignored him. The exit ramp just ahead offered escape and he gunned the pickup to the right, roaring down the shoulder past the slow-moving traffic. The exit had two lanes but all the traffic was on the right. A lagging driver gave Stickman room to cut left between cars, clipping the front car's rear bumper. Speeding up the open lane, he caught a yellow light and turned left, crossing over the interstate. Almost immediately they were in a residential area and, with exit ramp traffic still in sight, Stickman turned onto a quiet street. He took the first right and casually drove a few blocks before returning to the street he had exited. They were below the sight line of the ramp traffic.

Without doubt, a flood of 911 calls had frantically reported an officer being shot, and every squad car within miles was rushing to assist. Maple was only semi-conscious, mumbling that he wanted to help. Telling him to rest, Stickman drove with one hand and one eye on the road as he punched GPS buttons to call up a map showing their location. Not far ahead was a larger road. Stickman took it with no clear idea of where he was going, but satisfied to know it was west and away from a dead cop. Within a mile he met two police cars, sirens blaring and lights flashing. "Good," Stickman told the incoherent Maple. "They're still in rush-to-the-scene mode. Maybe we can get far enough out to avoid roadblocks."

He stopped at a municipal park and in the shadows of a bandstand changed the brake light. He hadn't wanted to stop so soon, but the repair was the best thing he could do to avoid being stopped again. Stickman worried, though, that the patrolman could have radioed in why he was stopping the F-150, with a full description.

He kept nosing west, roughly parallel to Interstate 78 until traffic grew light, then started fretting about any Ford F-150 being suspect. Near Spruce Run Reservoir in western New Jersey he stopped at a remote copse of trees. Changing Maple's bandages, he didn't see signs of infection, but couldn't be sure. All he could do was make him comfortable in a sleeping bag.

Awake much of the night, Stickman kept tapping the "seek" button for radio reports that barely changed. The 39-year-old patrolman was the married father of two small children. A dragnet had been thrown up but as best Stickman could tell, it was behind them. A couple reports speculated about the killer being involved in the embassy or Mall of America attacks, but had nothing supporting that from law enforcement. The unchanging reports encouraged Stickman, who reasoned that police were struggling to find a warm trail. There was no news about Hoboken police investigating a grisly murder scene in a warehouse. Apparently the handcuffed man called friends and was now an arms dealer, whether to jihadists or others.

Chapter 37

When Stickman and Maple pulled in shortly after sundown, an older model sedan was parked next to the trailer April had occupied. Lights were on, but it was not the time for introductions. Stickman parked out of sight of the new neighbor and quickly helped a sweaty and dysfunctional Maple into the trailer's relative safety.

The final leg of the trip, which seemed to last forever, was on two-lane roads. Once, they saw an array of flashing lights at what had to be a major traffic check. They worked around it but clearly, the dragnet had been expanded. Their path was zigzag, trial and error across Pennsylvania, along the way meeting three sheriff's deputies who luckily didn't slow.

The biggest development in news reports about the patrolman was that his union was offering a twenty thousand dollar reward for the killers. Small change, Stickman smiled. More personal details about the patrolman crept into the reports. Eagle Scout as a teen, he had been awarded a citation the previous year for saving an elderly couple from their burning car. His brother said he had always wanted to be a law officer, that he had died doing what he loved. He was active in his community, doted on his children and was always in church on Sundays. "I killed a freaking saint," Stickman said aloud after one broadcast. More important to him was the absence of coverage about Rouhani and his men. Stickman could only conclude that police were not called, the deaths were being covered up, and the checkpoints were solely for the patrolman's killers.

If true, that would suit him fine. For the first time ever, he was starting to feel overwhelmed. The steady drumbeat of tension the past few months had taken a toll. Decision making wasn't as crisp as it should be, or at least demanded more concentration. He wasn't sleeping as well as usual, even excluding the previous night. With Maple shot, he knew the next mission had to be delayed. That was all right with him if it meant a few weeks of relative calm.

Though the long day of driving had caused Maple pain, he had improved slowly from incoherent rambling to feverish sleep to finally being semi-aware. He was very weak, but Stickman was relieved that his admittedly unpracticed eye still saw no infection as he carefully changed the bandages.

With Maple sleeping again, Stickman shut off lights to discourage a visit by his new neighbor. He sat quietly with his thoughts for more than an hour until first the lights and then a TV's glow went dark next door. He did not think about the man he had killed, which was done, but about what he needed to do next. As quietly as possible, he eased through the trailer door and went to the pickup, lifting the hard cover from the bed. With the aid of a small flashlight he found three shell casings overlooked in getting out of the warehouse. Missed, too, had been smudges of Maple's blood and he scrubbed them out as best he could with lubricated wipes, then moved to the cab to do the same. Satisfied that the pickup would pass cursory inspection, he fell into bed.

A car starting for an early morning commute awakened Stickman. He sat up reluctantly to face the gray that telegraphs dawn. A groggy Maple refused breakfast. After suffering through another change of bandages, he took a few sips of herbal tea and returned to bed. "Sorry, mon, but I'm going to have to get you up soon," Stickman warned. Outside, he washed down the pickup bed with soapy water, then scrubbed the cab.

He gently shook Maple. "I need to hide our cargo and I need a lookout." Maple nodded and slowly followed Stickman to the corner of the trailer. From there, the driveway could be seen all the way to the county road. Stickman unfolded a lawn chair and put a block of wood in Maple's right hand. "Sit here. If anyone pulls in the driveway, clap the block twice on the arm of chair. Hard. Do it hard and then go back in the trailer."

Stickman unwired the makeshift gate and walked into the clearing where Maple had killed April. He followed the trail into the woods only a few yards – still within easy distance for hearing a signal from Maple – before stepping around a huge multiflora rose bush and into another clearing. Using a spade, he peeled back a large patch of sod, which he carefully rolled and laid aside. He dug a hole for four boxes – the three gray ones plus a black metal one for the additional guns and ammunition he had taken from Rouhani. He tossed a foot of soil over the boxes before replacing the sod. It fit a little above ground level, enough to allow for settling. Fertilized and watered, he hoped the sod would not turn telltale brown should there be an unwelcome visitor.

It was mid-morning before he could trundle Maple, badly in need of rest, off to the trailer and turn to other tasks. Locating a Ford dealer who had a new tailgate in stock was easy. He picked it up and drove back to the trailer to make the change. With an eye to the future he salvaged the sheet of extra armor from the tailgate before taking it to the river for burial. Stickman had just returned to the trailer when his new neighbor pulled in. "Might as well get this over with," he said, walking forward for introductions.

Wally Cornell wore the uniform of a heating, ventilation and air-conditioning technician. With protruding Adam's apple punctuating a skinny neck, stooped shoulders, over-long legs and arms, and middle-aged paunch on a lanky frame, his body poked in every which direction. But his eyes were bright and Stickman, having worked start-up jobs with many technicians, immediately took him to be smart, or at least not to be underestimated. Being an HVAC tech demanded not only keeping up with challenging changes in the field. To repair and install heating and cooling units and often fashion their frameworks, techs were plumbers and electricians and welders and metalworkers and God knows what all. Hands down, Stickman would take a flighty neighbor like April, and tell Maple to keep it in his pants.

Cornell was a talker, which wasn't all bad. Stickman felt little pressure to carry the conversation. But the man's slow drawl masked a curious streak and, combined with an assumed familiarity, put Stickman on guard.

"Violet and Wilbur said ya have a roommate."

"Yes, I do." Stickman went on to answer the obvious question. "He's got Montezuma's revenge, we think from the deep-fried shrimp we had last night."

"Ugh, bad seafood is the worst. I've had dynasty myself, a couple times. Thought I'd never get plugged up."

"Yes, well," Stickman began, not sure how to respond. "Well, as I'm sure you know then, dysentery can actually be dangerous, but hopefully he's not that bad."

"Where'd ya get them shrimp? I'll try to avoid that place."

"I can't remember the name. It was a little roadhouse about halfway back from Pittsburgh."

"Did ya get caught up in any roadblocks? I hit two today. One this morning that 'most made me late for work. So I took a different way tonight and danged if another one still didn't get me. Radio says that's going on all around the Northeast and even down to D.C. and Virginia. Such a big area, they're just random. John Law is really worked up about that patrolman getting shot. I figure ya heard about it."

"Of course. Turn on the radio and you can't hear anything else."

"Know what I think? I think ole Johnny Law has made a connection to something else. Bigger. Like shooting up that commie embassy maybe. Or they've got it tied in to something that's coming up. Domestic terrorism, ya know?"

"You could be right. They sure are worked up. We saw a lot of patrol cars, but were lucky that we weren't delayed, I guess."

Cornell spat a thin stream of chaw and went about explaining the world of heating and plumbing, slipping in enough questions to get the story Stickman and Maple lived under. When he thought Cornell had covered ample ground, Stickman turned to leave, saying he needed to check on his sick friend.

"See ya got a new tailgate. Unusual to have to get a new tailgate. Most folks get along if they'll just close. What happened to the old one?"

"You're right about tailgates, but I couldn't get it bent back in line enough to close. There was nothing to steal from an empty bed, so it must have been vandals. But why would someone want to bend a tailgate? Sometimes it's hard to figure people."

Finally getting away, Stickman found Maple in a deep sleep, as had become his wont. His slow progress created problems a couple of times when Cornell showed up at the door, inquiring after the neighbor he had yet to meet. Stickman felt like telling him to get a grip. Instead, he patiently speculated that Maple must have e-coli or something worse than they first thought. "He's coming along but very weak. I should have taken him to a doctor, but he refused. He did say he'd like to grab a beer with you as soon as he feels better," Stickman lied.

One afternoon as Maple slept, Stickman drove to an interstate rest stop, ignoring the reduced but still uncomfortable traffic checks by law enforcement. He used a pay phone to reach Assiri, who was still in Chicago, and told him their bridge game had been delayed. "My friend had an accident. He's slowly getting better, but we're weeks away from hooking up with your crew for a nice weekend, maybe more."

Stickman's worry about Maple grew as he continued to eat very little, mostly surviving on sips of water, tea and broth. More than once

Stickman came close to insisting on taking him to an emergency room. Maybe they could say he had been in a hunting accident in the West. Stickman was still toying with that idea when he was pleasantly shocked one afternoon when Maple appeared in the bedroom doorway and declared, "I'm hungry." Nearly a month had passed.

After a few days on soft food he began light exercises – endlessly walking the trailer end to end and doing cheater sit-ups, then what passed for a push-up. He wasn't whole by any means, but claimed to move without discomfort.

"You really have to shake hands with our not-so-new neighbor. He's the curious sort and you need to put his mind at ease," Stickman prodded. "Just don't forget, the bug from that roadhouse shrimp turned out to be really nasty."

The next day, when he returned from an errand, Maple was sitting in the sun, waiting to have the niggling meeting as soon as Cornell got in from work. Maple was purposely reserved and Cornell, his curiosity satisfied, took the hint that his neighbors weren't interested in adopting a new friend.

Ignoring Maple's progress, Stickman decided he should be the one to take the rent to Wilbur and Violet that month, eschewing their mailbox just as Maple had. When he explained that Maple was recovering from food poisoning, Violet allowed she would find her soup recipe featuring pig intestines, a sure-fire cure from a Greek friend. "They use tripe for hangovers, but it's even better for a bad stomach. Just leave the spices out."

"One good thing," said Wilbur, "is we finally get to spend a little time with you. You know, you look a lot like that movie star we see on the TV."

"Really? Which one is that?" Stickman tried to keep his tone nonchalant.

"His name escapes me but I see him every once in a while. By the way, how's your vacuuming going?"

A confused Stickman was rescued by Violet. "You don't have to answer that," she said firmly. "Wilbur, you really shouldn't ask people you barely know such personal questions."

Stickman caught on. "No problem, sir. I don't mind. Actually it's going quite well. How about yours?"

"I quit the vacuum. Violet's in charge of it now. I finally decided anyone who has a presidential award could quit the vacuum."

"Wilbur, you are confusin' our guest. Just try to ignore him, young man, while I get that recipe for tripe soup."

Several seconds passed. "I don't think you're confused, young man, and I would recommend quittin' the vacuum even if you don't happen to have a presidential award."

"I don't, sir. I have had a chance to see the outside of the White House, but I'm sure I've never done anything the president would give me an award for. What were you recognized for?"

"It was my work on Hoover Dam. Roosevelt himself gave me credit."

Seeing an unwanted story coming, Stickman quickly searched for something else to talk about. "With all respect, at your age you and your wife must have a large family," he said presumptuously.

"No, but not for lack of tryin'. Violet lost her babies. Now it's too late, of course." After a pause, a twinkle lit his eye. "Of course, we can still try. That girl gets hot enough to boil water. And I don't need any little blue pills, not by a long shot."

Stickman wished he had encouraged the Hoover Dam story.

"I just can't believe someone like Bob Dole comin' on the TV to sell little blue pills. Maybe you're too young to remember, sonny, but he was a United States senator and a presidential nominee. To think he would advertise that he can't ... Those TV people must have paid him a load of money ... Speakin' of TV, we were watchin' the late news not all that long ago and there were stories about this domestic terrorism stuff.

"One story was about a gang rape of two young girls in L.A. or some place. Now it was awful, mind you, but I got to thinkin' about what I could do when I was young and virile. Not rape, of course, but underline virile. Those were the memories flittin' through my mind ..."

Stickman was feeling an information overload when hit by the random thought that his nerves handle shooting a cop better than this inappropriate ramble from a man easily old enough to be his grandfather.

"...and spare me any of those 'how old people fuck' stories. They're not just crude. They're not real."

I've never even heard such a story. They must have been popular with an earlier generation, Stickman thought, desperately wishing for Violet's return. Even if she, too, had confused him since his own grandmother's tripe soup called for ox stomach and not pig intestines.

But Wilbur was not to be denied, recounting in detail a night not long ago when a shadow in one of his rental trailers kept moving. Stickman fidgeted uncomfortably, thinking he likely knew who was starring. "...Anyway, I told Violet we probably didn't have much time. You know what she did? She shut the light right off."

As if on cue, Violet returned, recipe box in hand. "Had a little trouble findin' it. Kept lookin' under the Ps and the Ts and shoulda been lookin' under Soup. Now you just give me two minutes, young man, and I'll copy it for you."

It was a slow-moving two minutes, prolonged by chances of Wilbur starting yet another unwanted story. Once armed with recipe and receipt, Stickman found himself backpedaling out the front door, more than ready to return rent duties to Maple.

Chapter 38

Maple exercised diligently at least three times a day, doing small sets that incrementally grew larger. When he was wounded, the buds of spring were still in high gear. Now that season was past and the heat of summer was setting in. The hot weather seemed medicinal, lifting his battered spirits and massaging his torn shoulder.

In the two months since being shot, Maple had also come to more fully appreciate Stickman's loyalty. Rejecting Rouhani's treacherous plot to collect the reward came as no surprise. Money, in and of itself, had never been a priority for either of them. But the risks Stickman unflinchingly took, his careful nursing, and his patient handling of life's nuts and bolts while Maple healed, all combined to strengthen their bond. Not to be forgotten was the exhilaration of their first firefight, when nothing less than survival hung in backing each other. There was even something to be said for Stickman's amusing discomfort while delivering the rent money. Only briefly did Maple's mood darken at the still-clear memory of the instant of fear in the patrolman's eyes before he died.

One morning without ceremony Maple unpacked a rocket launcher, cleaned it and spent much of the day carrying it about. He simulated movements needed for firing, broke it down and reassembled it, repacked it and unpacked it and repacked it again. Everything felt good as he relived raining RPGs on the Russian Embassy, torching the patrol cars at their rental house near Point of Rocks, blowing away the bank truck with its confetti of hundred dollar bills. He declared himself ready. Stickman was not convinced, but calculated that could be true by the time they finished preparations for their next strike and hooked up with Assiri.

Using the coded system that worked well in coordinating the attack on the Mall of America, a time and place to meet was set. With Maple suffering cabin fever, Stickman suggested driving west of Pittsburgh to call Assiri from an interstate pay phone. Assiri confirmed getting the meeting information and said the needed crew was ready. It went without saying that the mission would be risky.

With some trepidation they had packed the rocket launchers and some other weapons in the tool box. On the return trip they searched back roads, eventually locating a remote area where approaching traffic could be seen nearly a mile out. They quickly test-fired the weapons and sighted them in for accuracy. Maple happily fired the rocket launchers last.

A few days later, they were loading duffle bags and fishing gear in the F-150 when Cornell walked out of his trailer, bound for work.

"Looks like you'll be gone fishing a few days," he called.

"That's the plan," Maple answered.

"I'll keep an eye on things for you. Have a good trip."

Stickman and Maple again headed west. A long day's drive took them to Cahokia Mounds State Historic Site in Collinsville, Illinois, just east of St. Louis. More than one hundred mounds dot the twenty-two hundred acres that is believed to be what remains of the most sophisticated native civilization north of Mexico. After inhabiting the area for hundreds of years, the natives mysteriously left, or disappeared, about 1400 A.D. One theory is that they were victims of a massive flood. There won't be much mystery about the next catastrophic event in this area, Stickman thought as they pulled into the Interpretive Center parking lot. It was nearly closing time and Assiri and his men, having enjoyed their down-time as tourists, were just leaving the building.

During brief introductions, Stickman was impressed by the seven men Assiri had gathered. In age from mid-twenties to forty, they were to a man in at least decent condition. Clearly, Assiri, too, had been no stranger to working out. But there was much more. This bunch was mature and, perhaps to a fault, had a hard edge, most noticeable in their eyes. It was a quality born of experience and perhaps suffering, sustained or inflicted on others or perhaps both. It made Stickman wonder how Assiri had collected them without drawing attention. And maybe he hadn't, a bothersome prospect. Unlike the Swale team, there were no virgins here. Even in this unflinching crew one man stood out. He went by the single name of Abu. His size and heavily muscled frame, the curved scar that hooked from cheekbone to nostril, and the maniacally bright dark eyes made him a malicious presence. Stickman was glad the mission would come off the next day, hopefully before a redneck with a phobia for Muslims shared his hysteria with local police.

Five rooms were reserved at a nearby motel. "Let's gas up on the way. I'll check us in and Assiri will hand out your keys and give you the room number for Maple and me. We'll meet there at seven-thirty."

Chapter 39

Cornell lounged on his worn sofa, a perspiring beer in hand, an empty on the vinyl covered coffee table. He was watching the evening news, where the announcer was reading a tragic story about five members of an Ohio family being murdered, killed execution style in their beds. The local sheriff had few leads, no suspects. The announcer speculated that this could be yet another of the terrorist acts roiling the nation. Gratuitously, photographs of Stickman and Maple flashed on the screen. *And these two men remain at large, each carrying a twenty-five million dollar bounty.*

"Holy Mother of Christ!" Cornell yelled. Though the photos were shown for only a couple of seconds, he was sure. "My next-fucking-door neighbors!"

Suddenly, he was shaking, in part from fear but mostly from anticipation. All that money. And fame. "I'm gonna be America's next hero," he shouted, thumping his concave chest. He leaped to his feet and uncontrollably broke into a pitifully uncoordinated dance, beer foaming. "I'm gonna be bigger than Bryce Harper, Madonna and Donald Trump all rolled into fucking one. I'm fucking going to be something, baby!"

Finally willing himself to be calm, Cornell drained what was left of his beer and snapped open another. "Slow down, now. You've got to think, Cornell, about how best to do this. Okay, all you have to do is call the sheriff's office and tell them where to find these bad-ass dudes. No risk. No fuss, no muss. Easy-peasy, the money is yours."

But fifty mil is an awful lot, he muttered to himself, an awful lot. Who knows how some dipshit sheriff could arrange things to steal the credit and leave me pounding sand. Might even disappear me, for fifty mil. He walked in small circles, talking quietly, urgently. "I've got the upper hand. I just got to be smart. I'm a vet, man, a pretty mean mother. Did a tour in Afghanistan, or most of one, until that chicken-shit major got me drummed out. That bitch corporal had wanted it until she didn't. She'd have got it, too, except for her lucky knee. They knew her case sucked. That's why they let me fucking walk with a dishonorable. But I do know I carried my weight, bro, every time we were in the field. I shot the shit out of some of those al-Qaeda ragheads. And I learned some heavy shit about explosives, how to wire them up. Learned well, man. Messing with my bad-ass terrorist fifty mil neighbors don't bother me, not a fucking bit.

"Maybe that's the smart way. Really mess them up. They're wanted dead or alive. Get 'em dead and then get some unselfies with them. That would be proof. Proof no dipstick sheriff could mess with. I've already got dynamite and my tool box has everything else I need to hook it up. They're gone for a few days. Convenient. Fuck yes! I can do this, man. I can be ready when they come back. I get the unselfies and then I call the TV. Yeah, call the TV. No way can fucking John Law screw me once I'm on the boob tube. After what these dudes have done, that will go virile, man. Truly virile."

Cornell stopped circling, got another beer from the fridge. Stood silent. Rocking in place as he thought hard. What if something does go wrong? I mean, things do go wrong, even good plans. I need a little insurance that these fuckers would still get nailed. I'll take my chances because I know I can do it. But if something did happen and they still got caught I'd still be the all-fucking-American hero. That's worth something even if you're dead. Like, you know, being in the historical books. And I won't be dead 'cause I'll be so ready for them.

He studied his beer for several minutes before finally smiling. Out the door with a slam, swift strides took him across the rough lawn to the nearby house. Wilbur answered the loud knocks, Violet behind him.

Recognizing Cornell, Wilbur swung the door wide. "Come in, young man. I have been waitin' to show someone my pin collection and you are the lucky someone."

"Wilbur, Cornell doesn't want ..."

But Wilbur was already hobbling down the hall to the small office that doubled as a nonagenarian's man cave. Cornell followed, then the reluctant Violet. They went to the only side of the room with enough wall space for a four-by-four-foot cork board. "This is my pin collection," Wilbur said proudly. "I doubt there's another that equals it."

A red linen cloth was thumb-tacked symmetrically in place, almost covering the cork board. The cloth was nearly full of horizontal row upon horizontal row of silver straight pins. The little balls atop the pins were perfectly aligned, with the top left row starting one inch from the top and one inch from the side of the cloth. But while the silver balls were in perfect order, the pins pierced the cloth, in and back out, at different places on the shaft and at various angles – to the extent that some of the shaft points overlapped. The result was conflicting – shafts and points in disarray, silver heads perfectly aligned.

Cornell stared at the rows, blinking. Was Wilbur's pin collection perfectly imperfect or imperfectly perfect? He shook his head. This could be unorienting, he thought.

"Don't you love the colors?" Wilbur asked. Colors? Not just silver? Cornell peered harder, saw Violet lower her head, shaking it slightly.

"Which color do you think is best?" Wilbur asked. "Personally, I like the orange ones best. I do believe I have every color in the rainbow except for chartreuse. I'd have that one, too, if I knew what it looked like."

Cornell gave that a moment of thought, felt himself tottering on the edge of a profound discovery, but it slipped away. True, he decided. "Wilbur, that's a good point."

Wilbur moved to his desk and picked up a century-old wooden cigar box. He opened it to show Cornell more pins, hundreds of them, maybe thousands.

"This is the rest of my collection – so far. Far too many to get on that cloth," he said, indicating the only area still empty, at the lower right. "I'm goin' to have to clear this wall to get more space," he said, waving at what appeared to be family photos. Violet's mouth pursed at what obviously was news. Not welcome news.

"Well, sir, this certainly is impressive, not be underestimated for sure. Now, if you have a minute, let me tell you why I came by."

"You're here to pay the rent, four days early."

"Actually not, but I will be on time. Yes, actually, that's a good thought...No, I'm here to tell you I'm having a little difficulty with my neighbors. I don't want to bother you with details..."

"It would be no bother," Violet assured him.

"Really, I'd rather not. It's just that if I'm not up here to pay the rent in four days, you could tell the sheriff's office that my neighbors would be a good place to start investigating."

"Investigatin' what, Cornell? Oh my, you think you could be in ...Oh, my. Alexander and Demetri seem like such fine men. I barely know Demetri, mainly from when he got my tripe soup recipe, but Alexander is always so considerate of Wilbur's, of, well you know."

"Know what, Mother, you're confusin' me."

"Without goin' into details, if you really don't want to, can you let us know why they concern you?" Violet fished. "I mean, if you're concerned maybe we should be too, ya know?"

"I didn't mean to upset you, ma'am. No, I can't think of no good reason for you two to be concerned, none at all." Cornell cocked his head in a practiced way, to show he was being thoughtful, chewing on whether he should toss out just a little information.

"I'll just say this: When you're watching the TV you might stay extra alert, just in case any mirages catch your eye. If they do, don't do anything right then. Just sit tight until after rent day. Then do whatever you think is best."

"So if we see something unusual or suspicious we should wait for you showin' up on rent day and if you don't we might want to do somethin' the next day. Like call the sheriff, maybe. Got that, Wilbur?"

"I got it. Simple enough. Sounds like a good plan. Oh Cornell, how's your vacuuming going?"

Chapter 40

The meeting started well. Stickman and Maple slipped weapons – rocket launcher, anti-tank round and RPG, M-16 and an AK-47 – into their room to play show and tell. Assiri's men handled them with expertise and approval. As they should have. All were military issue and came at a high price, not in dollars as it turned out but in the blood of Mohammad Rouhani and his men.

Stickman and Maple had easily rejected getting the civilian version of the M-16, the AR-15. It was readily available over the counter in gun and discount stores. But those purchases meant transactions in the glare, as it were, of surveillance cameras, to say nothing of background checks. Some AR-15s could have been purchased legally as fully automatic or converted with an "auto sear" that modifies the trigger assembly. Both options would have meant going through an extensive approval process by the federal Bureau of Alcohol, Tobacco, Firearms and Explosives. No way was that going to happen. Rouhani had AR-15s for sale, too. But none of those options ensured getting military-quality weapons.

That left choosing between the Russian AK-47 and the U.S. M-16. Both military assault rifles were select-fire, allowing the shooter to select full automatic or semi-automatic, with each trigger pull firing one round. The slightly more reliable AK-47 – one malfunction every thousand rounds vs. two for the M-16 – offset the slightly more accurate

M-16. Another key factor was effective lethal range, 380 yards for the AK-47 and 500 for the M-16. Hundreds of millions of the Russian assault rifle had been manufactured over the previous half-century and it was less expensive and more readily available. Stickman and Maple took the coward's way out and split the difference, ordering an equal number of each – before everything became freebies because of Rouhani's treachery.

Reflecting lethal range, shooters assigned M-16s, which were outfitted with telescopic sights, would have primary responsibility for targets at the far end of the killing ground, those with AK-47s responsibility for closer targets.

As the weapons were passed around, the crew discussed thoroughly their pros and cons. Maple and Stickman were in no hurry. The enthusiasm for the weapons was good for morale, good for getting the men pumped for the next day's ugly work. In due time, Maple and Stickman huddled with Assiri. Maple and three others would fire the rocket launchers. Three other Assiri men were assigned M-16s. AK-47s went to Stickman, Abu and Assiri, a notoriously poor shot. If he sprays enough ammunition he might hit someone, Maple reasoned.

"Now, let me show you a real gun!" It was Abu, loudly commanding the attention of the crowded motel room. That done, he unzipped a small duffle bag and pulled out a monstrous revolver. "Anyone know what this is? Assiri, don't give it away."

"Abu, I told you not to bring that thing."

"This, my brothers, is an 1847 black powder .44 caliber six-shooter, the Walker Colt revolver. It is one of the guns that tamed the Old West."

Abu held the gun high in both hands, delicately, with something approaching reverence, so all could see his beautiful toy. The metal barrel gleamed from polishing, the grips had a rich sheen. Assiri fell silent, knowing it was better to let Abu put on his show.

"Only 1,100 of these bad boys were manufactured. If you were in the United States Cavalry and lucky enough to carry one, chances are it was in a saddle holster," Abu continued, warming to his subject. "It weighs four pounds, nine ounces, unloaded. That's an awful lot to lug on your hip. It was the most powerful, the most feared pistol out there until the .357 magnum came along just a few decades ago. If you've got a clear eye and a steady hand, this horse pistol will drop a man at a hundred yards. This baby can do some righteous damage. And that's ..."

"But not nearly as much as the AK-47 you'll be using tomorrow," Maple interrupted, not happy with the monologue that showed no sign of abating.

"I don't know about that, shot for shot."

"We're not talking about shot for shot. You've got a job to do tomorrow and it doesn't include a black powder throwback."

Abu's complexion turned a darker shade and his left eye began to twitch. Assiri had seen anger settle on Abu before. It was not pretty.

"I am here with Assiri," Abu declared. "We don't ask how high when you say jump, so don't fuck with me."

"You listen. We're all depending on each other tomorrow and there's no room for horse pistol nonsense," Maple said with more heat, taking a step toward the big man.

"I can make room easy enough little man. I can ..."

Stickman had heard enough, too much. "Abu, I'm here to tell Maple that I'm sure you can be relied on to do what's right tomorrow. Tell me I'm correct. Abu?"

"You've got that damn straight."

Chapter 41

The next day began with a final equipment check and briefing. But by mid-morning the men restlessly watched television or tried to read, mostly succeeding in getting on each other's nerves. Well before the late checkout arranged by Stickman, Abu and a swarthy, spidery man called Mohammad lobbied for a beer run. Stickman flatly refused, telling them to "just suck it up." They did, grumbling.

As they checked out, Maple suggested returning to Cahokia Mounds for a walk to burn off nervous energy. He and Stickman led the way, taking advantage of the spacious grounds to go over their plan of attack yet again, confident they were not being overheard. Away from prying eyes they spread maps of the multi-state region on the ground, marking routes they might use to scatter in three directions. They knew their flight would be determined, in part, by the response of law enforcement. In part, too, by the condition of their vehicles and, of course, by who was standing after the attack.

Finally, at four-forty-five, with rush hour traffic in full flow, Maple moved the F-150 alongside a large van in a far corner of the Cahokia Mounds parking lot. In the van's visual cover, the sedans that had delivered Assiri and his crew pulled in by the pickup. Within a minute the deadly contents of the tool box were distributed.

The F-150 led the caravan onto Collinsville Road. Maple took state highway 157 north to get on Interstate-55/70 at Exit 11. Even with heavy traffic it took only a few minutes to reach Exit 10 – their destination. They joined traffic moving slowly to a stoplight, where they turned left and immediately flipped a U back to the light. When the light changed to stop the main flow of traffic, they turned right and went up the entrance ramp as if heading back to I-55/70.

But at the top of the ramp Maple stopped and the crew piled out on the overpass, weapons in hand. No one had followed them from the cross street. When the light changed, the main flow of traffic started across the intersection. With no hesitation, Maple and an Assiri recruit named Omar took out the lead cars with high-explosive anti-tank rounds. Milliseconds before Maple fired he made out the face of the driver grimacing in fear as she saw weapons pointed at her. Her car and its shadowy occupants – children picked up after soccer practice? – disappeared in a flaming explosion the attackers could feel.

The other men armed with rocket launchers stepped up for long shots of more than a quarter-mile. One hit a car head-on but the second missed – a rocket wasted – and Maple quickly stepped in, firing on target. A large SUV exploded. Suddenly a killing ground had been created with burning vehicles at either end, virtually trapping all traffic in between. Stickman and the others opened fire – three fully automatic AK-47s punishing the closest cars, three more accurate M-16s deliberately seeking individual targets farther out. Men, women and children bailed fearfully from their vehicles, making the terrorists' jobs easier. Abu was in his glory, the machine gun jumping in his strong hands as he rained bullets at the innocent, a crazed laugh rolling from deep in his belly as he slapped in a fresh thirty-round clip.

Drivers desperately fled the roadway, seeking cross-country routes to escape the carnage. They high-centered in ditches and collided after zig-zag patterns that smacked of bumper cars. People leaped from disabled vehicles, exposing themselves to the gunmen's deadly intent. Some people frantically sought cover behind vehicles or hugged low-lying areas, anywhere offering hope of protection. The underbelly of a small overpass gave respite to a lucky few, who shoved out others threatening their sanctuary. Screams mixed with gunfire and the explosions of gas tanks. An eighteen-wheeler became a battering ram as it backed up in a clumsy three-point turn, crushing two teenagers in a tiny sports car before an anti-tank round turned the truck into an inferno. Another truck loaded with explosive material went up in a tower of sparks and flames, incinerating everything and everybody for yards around. Panic was in order. The dead were suddenly counted in scores.

But this stretch of gore was not the primary target. That distinction went to interstate traffic approaching from the northeast. Heavy gauge fencing topped most interstate overpasses, but not at Exit 10. Stickman had selected it for the clear view that would make the attack much more effective, deadlier, than one where fencing obstructed lines of fire.

On Stickman's signal, Maple and the three others with launchers took positions to punish oncoming interstate traffic with close-in and long-range shots. The interstate's multiple traffic lanes were a bigger challenge to sealing off a killing ground. The result was sloppier, with more vehicles finding escape routes. But a fertile killing field was soon accomplished, with vehicles exploding in flames, painful screams of the dying and wounded, undiluted panic. Again, deadly AK-47 and M-16 fire sought out fleeing victims, some falling to withering bursts, others to the sniper's cold efficiency. Hapless victims of a sluggish rush hour fell under the relentless onslaught of the terrorists.

With rockets dwindling, Maple and Omar picked their interstate targets carefully – a gasoline tanker, a tour bus, a U.S. Army van, a bright yellow school bus. Maple surprised himself when he momentarily teared up as he put the school bus in his sights. But after that passing nod to mercy, he calmly fired. Without reaction he watched the school bus explode.

Meanwhile, a lone rifleman, still working the first killing ground, methodically found fresh targets, bolstering the death count.

Above the din of slaughter, sirens could be heard and, quickly, their threatening whine drew close. If the sounds of gunfire and explosions hadn't alerted a passing law officer, there no doubt was a barrage of 911 calls from still-surviving victims. Suddenly a police car was coming up the ramp the wrong way. Stickman and Assiri fired long bursts, shattering the car's windshield. It veered out of control, rolling off the ramp.

Sirens grew louder. Stickman shouted an order to quit firing, to leave. Major damage had been inflicted. Remaining targets were in the margins, not worth the accelerating risk. Stickman shouted again to be sure he was heard. Maple took no convincing. He moved to the driver's door of the pickup with a spare M-16 liberated from Rouhani, firing every few seconds at fresh targets on the interstate. Assiri raced to one of the sedans, scrambling behind the wheel, most of his men hard behind him. But Abu and Mohammad wanted more blood. "Allahu akbar!" Abu screamed, firing the AK-47 with delight, raking the closest burning cars though they showed no signs of life. "Allahu akbar!" The spidery Mohammad stood at his shoulder, trying to wave others back to the slaughter, pointing as if to say there still were targets to bring down. Abu emptied his clip and instead of reloading, reached beneath his loose-fitting shirt, jerking the Walker Colt free from the back of his waistband. He gripped the horse pistol in both hands, squeezing off shots at someone, something in the killing field.

Maple saw him and boiled with anger. He raised the M-16, ready to execute this fool who was putting them all in jeopardy. Instead, he shouted, "Assiri, get your men out of here! Leave those assholes!"

Without warning a police helicopter swooped in from the opposite side, the empty side, of the interstate, its approach muted by the mayhem. Abu and Mohammad, oblivious in their blood-fueled zeal, were clear targets. A police sharpshooter expertly riddled their backs with gunfire. They crumbled, face-first, dead before they hit the pavement, Abu's beloved horse pistol still in his hand.

The sharpshooter turned his fire on the fleeing terrorists as Assiri punched the accelerator, deserting his man still firing on the first killing ground. The sniper's frantic sprint for the car ended in another hail of gunfire from the helicopter, one overlapped by a barrage from Stickman and Maple. The helicopter heaved away from them, wobbling over the second killing ground in a stream of smoke that angled into the school bus Maple had destroyed. Impact brought yet another explosion.

On the clear side of the overpass, the ramp gives interstate-bound drivers the option of turning left onto a state highway. That was the terrorists' preferred escape route, with success tied to blending into the flow of rush hour and not getting caught in gridlock. The swiftly executed attack that left hundreds dead had also generated a massive volume of phone calls, from passing drivers as well as victims. Descriptions of the terrorists' vehicles varied so much as to be worthless. But some approaching drivers frantically reversed direction to flee the carnage, adding to the confusion and helpful to the fleeing attackers.

But gridlock did threaten as Maple and Stickman came to the first stop light on the state highway, Assiri and the packed sedan right behind. Maple squeezed into the intersection on yellow and forced a left turn against a woman laying on her horn. She was not to be twice denied and Assiri was stuck at the light. When it finally changed, oncoming traffic immediately blocked him from turning, but he saw no advantage in trying a caravan escape, anyway. That was fortunate for Stickman and Maple. A camera in the downed helicopter had captured and transmitted the license number of Assiri's sedan, but not the pickup's.

Every responding lawman had that number and soon a patrolman spotted Assiri's car. Approaching each other slowly in the traffic, the patrolman rammed his car into Assiri's, then hopped out in the protection of his door. Handgun leveled, he ordered Assiri and his remaining crew to step out with hands raised. Assiri signaled Omar, sitting beside him, to attack. As Assiri ducked low in his seat, the patrolman saw Omar's Glock and opened fire. Omar and the man behind him jumped out, returning fire. The patrolman's rapid fire poked spider holes across the sedan's windshield before he fell, blood flowing from head and neck. Assiri hadn't ducked low enough. His forehead was neatly punctured. One man in the back seat was badly wounded. Omar slipped back in the car and seeing his leader dead, reached across to open the door and unceremoniously shoved Assiri onto the pavement. Finding the sedan not entangled with the patrol car, Omar backed up and swerved out of the traffic lane, fleeing along the shoulder.

Luck was running out. The sedan's radiator had been pierced in the collision. Omar thought about abandoning the sedan and commandeering another car. It would be easy enough. Facing three armed men, with no compunction about killing, a family would be more than happy to give up their mini-van. What then? Another barrage of 911 calls, with the van's description and license number. Omar did not hesitate. Shouting, "Akbar! Akbar!" he drove wildly, bouncing off creeping cars and skidding around a corner as steam rose from the radiator. The street fed an industrial park, with broad streets and open space that afforded little cover. He sped up briefly until the engine coughed, ignoring his violent entreaties on the accelerator. Making a shredding sound, the sedan rolled to a stop. Omar jumped out, AK-47 in hand and still in full throat, "Akbar! Akbar!" A police helicopter swooped in. Omar squeezed off an errant burst before a sharpshooter cut him down, his head exploding.

"You in the car. Step out with your hands raised."

The terrorists did.

Chapter 42

Stickman and Maple's erratic route was easterly then north, picking up U.S. 40 near Vandalia, Illinois, not returning to Interstate 70 until they were past Effingham. Fiddling with the radio, Stickman searched for snippets of information to help navigate around the wide, hastily tossed up dragnet.

Authorities now say upwards of 400 men, women and children are believed to have been slain in the vicious terrorist attack...

"Who says the attacks were vicious or the work of terrorists?" Maple countered. "The attacks were the work of warriors, putting it all on the line."

Authorities believe at least ten men carried out the massacre. Six are known to have been killed and two surrendered. A massive hunt is underway for those still at large...

"Damn," Stickman said. "That's up from three dead. I wonder if Assiri surrendered."

None of the attackers – dead or alive – has been identified...

"I'm betting he didn't," Maple allowed. "And I hope to hell he took some cops with him."

We have confirmed that at least four officers died in gunfights with the terrorists. Three were in a helicopter that went down near the interstate overpass where the attacks were launched. Another officer was killed in an exchange of gunfire after he spotted the car in which five of the attackers were fleeing. The officer heroically rammed them with his patrol car, then shot it out, killing two terrorists before he went down. The car fled to a nearby industrial park. There, the driver was shot from a helicopter by a sharpshooter and two of the terrorists surrendered. We'll bring you more details of the deadly exchanges between law enforcement and these killers as we learn them.

The terrorists at large are believed to be in a dark, late model pickup, but eyewitness descriptions vary. Some witnesses describe the pickup as dark blue, others as black. And it is variously said to be a Ford F-150, a Dodge Ram or a Chevy ...

"That helps a little," muttered Maple. "But how about some witnesses seeing a red pickup and the ubiquitous white van?"

Authorities now say an officer was killed when he drove his patrol car into harm's way against the terrorists slaying motorists at Exit 10. No details, but that brings to five the number of lawmen known to have died battling the interstate killers. None of the lawmen has been identified yet.

It's unfortunate that the massacre was unleashed as responders, including police, were dealing with two other serious incidents in downtown St. Louis. The apartment building fire in which, miraculously, only two people died, and the train derailment had pulled numerous officers off their regular beats, some of which were in the direction of Exit 10. Under normal circumstances those officers would have been able to get to the interstate faster and perhaps prevented some of that terrible carnage.

Investigators speculate privately that two of the attackers – now on the run – were involved in other recent terrorist acts, including the bloody assaults on the Russian Embassy and the Mall of America. So far, no international organization has claimed responsibility for the interstate attacks, leading officials to believe we have again been the victims of homegrown terrorists ...

"I like that, the assault bit I mean," Stickman said with a grin. "Much more military sounding than 'vicious' or 'massacre'."

"Well, fine for you, but I'm getting falsely accused in the mall attack."

Stickman glanced at his partner, not sure if he was joking. "You're getting much more credit than you deserve," he belatedly quipped, tuning in another station as a talk show host ended his commentary.

When the ringleaders of these terrorists are finally identified, it will be fascinating to learn what motivates them. Did they grow up in families full of hate for the United States? Are they sons of extremist survivalist parents? Did they have a series of life experiences that they think justify cold blooded murder? Or perhaps they were motivated by learning about Hitler or Lenin or bin Laden. Or maybe these guys just have some loose screws. I say guys, but we really don't know. The ringleaders of the slaughter on the interstate may be the same killers who attacked the Russian Embassy and Mall of America. Given the scale of today's slaughter, I can tell you that federal investigators are working on that assumption. Let's hope these terrorists are brought to justice before they can strike again.

"Have you been brushing up on your *Mein Kamph* lately, Herr Maple? Or do you just have a screw loose?"

"How about you? Did some bad things happen to you when you were growing up?"

"Bad enough, my friend. More important, I can see what's going on, see it clear."

Stickman paused, decided to go ahead. "You remember talking about soon leaving the Banks' place? I started poking around on my phone and I've learned that there are some huge high school football stadiums, especially in Texas."

"You're fast, but you can't get under the age cap, Mr. Stick."

Stickman ignored him. "Hawaii, Washington State, New Jersey, Utah, they all have big freaking stadiums that hold over ten thousand people."

"And you're thinking we should hit a high school stadium?"

"Exactly. It could be bigger than 9/11. This country would come unglued. High school football ranks right up there with apple pie. The stadium I like at first blush is in San Antonio."

He returned to a website and filled Maple in on Alamo Stadium. Nicknamed "The Rock Pile," it was constructed of limestone. Best of all, it seats 23,000 people.

A lot of the big stadiums, surprisingly, are in rural areas of the West, Stickman continued. Getting away could be a problem in those wide open spaces, but San Antonio is another story, a big city with plenty to do. Hang out for a couple weeks until things returned to normal, then find a remote place to do the fishing routine. The Ozarks would work.

"You do think big, Mr. Stick. Bigger than 9/11 ..."

Nearing Indianapolis, they debated stopping for the night. Fatigue won out and they took rooms at a cheap mom-and-pop motel a mile off the interstate. With the adrenaline rush of the day gone, Maple's mind insisted on replaying the horrific attacks as he struggled to get comfortable on the lumpy mattress. The bodies. Worse, the body parts. The different scents of charred flesh and who knew what, none pleasant. The wailing and the desperate screams. Fires punctuated by explosions. Explosions settling down to become fires. Twisted vehicles. The tour bus torn apart, clothing from suitcases fluttering across the ground as if to flee the terror. Worst of all, the school bus that he fired on even as long dormant emotions filed his eyes with tears. He thought of his own years riding a bus, the horseplay and laughter, a frustrated driver trying to quiet her thirty-plus charges while watching traffic. In an instant the childhood bedlam of his memory was shattered, substituted by a terrible reality of his making.

All those things – and more – moved relentlessly across his mind, his eyes wide open in the near dark. Stark images pressed upon him in hues black and white and gray. After a while some images emerged through a filter with perfectly square alternating spaces, like a chess or checker board. Some squares were opaque, others not, so at times only pieces of images could be seen floating by. Some flashed by while others bounced gently, overlaying the ugly carnage with suggestive teasing. Closing his eyes turned everything vivid, colors bold and dramatic. No pastels. Then the sights of the day came fast forward, the awful sounds of weapons and explosions and screams bouncing through the cavities of his mind at an unbelievable pace, before abruptly slowing to a crawl that emphasized each broken detail. He couldn't tell if the tortured lightshow was a nightmare or his mind remembering, but either way it was overwhelming and horrible. With his hands he covered his ears, then covered his shut eyes and even clamped his hands over his mouth to keep from shouting. His erratic motion fed confusion until the colors were pushed out by black and white and gray copies, and even with his eyes open, even with the ugly images blunted by the checkerboard filter, it all was too gross, to vivid, it hurt too much, and he went to the bathroom and sat on the stool with the lid closed, waiting.

Stickman slept fine.

Chapter 43

Maple's bad night left him shaken, struggling to grasp how the strings of his life put him on an interstate overpass, firing RPGs at unsuspecting victims. He wrestled with whether he was feeling guilt or simply wanted to rid himself of the night's gross images. The maturing cornfields of Indiana rolled by pleasantly, but failed to blot out his dark thoughts and dreadful flashbacks. Stickman offered no distracting conversation, sipping a large coffee as he searched his smartphone.

"These reports say the coppers threw up tons of checkpoints last night. That explains why we haven't seen more activity this morning. Meanwhile, we got a good night's sleep."

Maple wasn't about to reveal his horror show, but needed to talk about more than the news of the day, even if it was about them.

"How you feeling today, Mr. Stick?" he ventured. "Feel like we accomplished anything?"

"Time will tell. What I do know is that things need to change in this country."

"We haven't had that talk in a long time, not really. Maybe not since the al-Qaeda training camp."

Stickman said nothing.

"When I think back I'm not really sure why I got there."

Stickman took a deep sip of the cooling coffee. "I'm surprised. I remember a kid who was very angry at the IRS for screwing over his father and almost as pissed at the lawyers who took pop's money with no intention of helping. There were some other things, too, but I think the worst was how everyone turned on Muslim friends after 9/11. Islamophobia reigned."

"You're right. I was angry, and feeling frustrated and worthless that I couldn't go to college. I felt like my life was stuck on the sidelines. Everything seemed irrelevant. I remember raging how churches were preaching salvation instead of helping kids deal with getting laid, or not."

"That's not what churches do, unfortunately, then or now. Unless you're a priest with a hard-on. I never asked for the asshole to move on me, but I still felt humiliated."

They went silent as the miles slipped by and with them some of Maple's tension. He started to feel better, remembering those earlier years, even if the memories were a mixed bag. His anger as a young man may have been immature, an excuse for not shaking off failures and disappointments. But the anger and disappointment were real. So was his gratitude for the help given by Muslim friends. After the discrimination he had witnessed in the U.S., and keenly felt as a neophyte to Islam, hooking up with their relatives in London was welcome. Sampling a different culture fed a hunger he didn't know he had. He eagerly grabbed the chance to visit Afghanistan.

Stickman must have been entertaining similar memories. "I was angry, too. Angry over my favorite uncle getting screwed by the military. Angry at the cop who rang my bell. Worse than being put down for months was the cops' stonewalling, not giving me any satisfaction. But none of that was near as ugly as what I saw the U.S. do in Afghanistan. The so-called collateral damage from our air raids and the rapes by our troops and contractors and people shot without justification. That wasn't collateral at all. And hardly anyone got arrested."

Stickman talked faster and faster, agitation growing as his perception of his country's sins rolled out. Maple could hear, he was almost certain, an echo of their whispered talks in the al-Qaeda training camp.

"... what made it worse," Stickman rushed on, "was that the wonderful U.S. was there for the most cynical reasons. Protecting our precious living standard by grabbing oil, whatever. Propping up tin-horn regimes. Justifying our grabs by piously insisting we spread democracy. Never mind most people in this sorry world don't have time to give a shit about democracy when they're trying to feed their starving kids. We are fucking Grade A bully! Bully!"

He took a deep breath and Maple gave thanks. Please God, don't let there be a roadblock right now, Maple thought with surprising seriousness. He searched for a way to reclaim the conversation.

Stickman saved him the trouble. "You asked me if we accomplished anything," he said, voice still hard. "I don't know. I just know things are getting worse in this country. This government has to go. Destroy people's sense of security and it will happen."

He hit the radio's power button, sharper than necessary. The commanding voice of a talk-radio host filled the cab.

Al-Qaeda? Islamic State? Homegrown terrorists? Who knows. These killers no doubt have their reasons, reasons that have their total commitment. There could be a huge number of reasons, and you can bet they are mixed with a huge dollop of moral outrage. But make the serving size as big as you can imagine, that still won't change my bottom line: These horrible attacks are senseless. Slaughtering helpless commuters and before that, shoppers enjoying themselves at an iconic mall. I'm here to tell you the people carrying out this mayhem don't know how sick their reasons are or how sick they are.

Chapter 44

Wilbur and Violet Banks had been watching TV most of the day. They flipped channels for a while, but soon everything looked the same, the awful footage losing its shock value even as it mesmerized. Little new information was being released on the first full day after the attacks. Maybe there was little new to release. Names of the dead shooters still hadn't been made public. But it was virtually certain they had been identified, with all the networks quoting law enforcement sources saying the killers had connections in Chicago. The victims were being identified, and some television stations crawled names and photos that seemed never ending. The confirmed death count kept creeping up, like a thermometer on a viciously hot day.

Every so often a network would trot out a photo of the embassy attackers, speculating once again about whether they were the gunmen still at large in the interstate massacre. Each time it happened a mild fight would break out in the Banks' living room.

"Yep, those two could be our renters," Wilbur would say. "They've changed the way they look some, but not enough. They could be the ones."

"Wilbur, those photos are not of Alexander and Demetri. They just aren't."

"Look at the eyes, damn it. You got to look at the eyes. Nothin' else matters."

"I've looked and I've looked. And look as I might I'm able to sleep just fine, thank you. Do you think I'd be sleepin' just fine if mass killers lived on this place? No sir, I would not."

"Well, I'm not sleepin' just fine, I'm tellin' you. Last night I got up to sit in the rockin' chair, my shotgun pointed right at the door. I still couldn't sleep."

"Wilbur, you didn't. Sit in the rockin' chair with your shotgun, I mean."

"Yes, Mother, I did. It's a fact. I'm surprised I didn't wake you up. And I likely will tonight, too."

"Well, don't expect to sleep, sittin' up in a rockin' chair and pointin' a shotgun. I declare."

A bit sullenly, both were again staring at the television when Maple and Stickman's pickup eased up the driveway toward their rented trailer.

"What I oughta do is ring up the Sheriff's Office. They could just pay a little social call on ole Alexander and Demetri. There'd be no harm done if they had nothin' to hide."

"Don't you dare, Mr. Banks. Little social call, my hinny. Can you 'magine the commotion there would be out here if the sheriff thought mass killers were in his county. He'd probably bring National Guard tanks with him!"

Violet's outburst caught Wilbur's attention. Hinny was as profane as she got, pretty much, and calling him Mr. Banks told him to be ready for a battle royal if he ignored her.

"Yes, Mother," he said, resigned for a time.

Stickman and Maple had seen the TV's cheerful flicker as they drove by the turn to the Banks' house. "Wonder what they're watching?" Stickman asked rhetorically. "Yeah, I wonder," answered his partner.

They were surprised to not find Cornell's colorfully painted company van sitting outside his trailer. Usually he was well into a six-pack by now. "Could be he's on call this week," Maple speculated.

He grabbed his small travel bag and was turning up the trailer's short flight of steps when muddy footprints stopped him. "Looks like we had a visitor," he said over his shoulder.

Hearing someone coming up the driveway, they turned to see it was Cornell. "We'd better say hello to the man," Stickman said, moving into the open space between the trailers.

Cornell unwound himself from behind the van's steering wheel and greeted them. "You gents have a good trip?" he probed.

"We did," Stickman replied. "Fishing sucked, but the trip was nice."

"Say Cornell," began Maple. "Did you notice anyone at our place while we were gone? Anyone who went up the steps to the door?"

"No, sure didn't."

"Sure you weren't over here?"

"Me?"

"Whoever was here left muddy footprints that came from boots with a big grid. Like you're wearing, Cornell."

Cornell looked at his feet and glanced toward the steps, wondering how far he could press the lie. "Sorry, slipped my mind. I did come over. Ran out of beer. The way you asked I thought you might be mad. Sorry."

"You feeling all right, Cornell. You're sweating something fierce."

"Really? No. I mean I'm fine. My last job today took me into an attic. It was hot as hell. Haven't been able to stop sweating, I guess."

Lie one admitted. And lie two? Maple mentally replayed Cornell's appearance when he drove in. He wasn't sweating, Maple was almost sure. Now, perspiration dripped from his nose and his shirt had soaked through at the armpits. He was one scared fucker.

Stickman joined the party. "That was some mess near St. Louis, wasn't it? Men, women and children. I can't get how someone could do that. Must be some kind of sick."

The silence was heavy. "Me ether, er, either." Cornell searched for words, not knowing how much anger he could safely vent. "There's a lot wrong in this country," he said quietly, lamely. "People, even okay people, can have their reasons or just, you know, suddenly snap."

"But women and kids?" Stickman spat in a show of disgust. "My God man, women and kids?"

"Maybe whoever did it had lost a woman, kids."

"It wasn't a whoever, Cornell. It was a bunch, a gang, a wrecking crew."

"Maybe they ...," Cornell tried to continue, beset by confusion, just wanting to walk away. "I don't know, no I don't. Just thinking ..."

Thinking too hard, trying too hard to figure us out instead of just rolling with anger. That was Maple's take. Any self-respecting HVAC guy would be outraged, not be a suck-up, trying to figure out what we want him to say. Lies had turned to strikes and now there were three.

Cornell gave a wave of his hands, as if to say he was out of answers. "Well, Cornell, we don't have any beer." Maple made eye contact and Cornell turned quickly, calling over his shoulder as he walked hangdog toward his trailer, "No problem. I'm good. Yep, I'm good. See you guys later."

Two sets of eyes followed him, sensing danger in his every step. Maple looked past him, to the trailer that, unlike his own, didn't have skirting. A dark line caught his eye. Or was it just a shadow? It seemed to go too far under the trailer, was too definitive to be a shadow. It may be something that has been there all along and I've never noticed it, Maple thought. Or not. He tried to follow the line, or shadow, into the lawn, staring hard at the ground between the trailers.

The terrorists didn't speak until Cornell disappeared inside. "I think he's made us," said Stickman.

"Me, too. Just move in front of me, with your back to his trailer like we're talking. I need to try to see ..."

At a couple spots between the two trailers, the ground looked like it may have been disturbed, as if a trough had been cut and the sod then returned. Maple was far from sure. "It's been a tough couple days. Maybe I'm paranoid, but I think there could be a cord or something under his place, hanging down to the ground before coming across the yard. I need to know if it comes all the way to our trailer. I don't think we can just walk over there and look."

"Maybe you are seeing things," Stickman said quietly. "But you're right, we need to know for sure, especially since we think Cornell made us."

"I could go in the trailer and check from the middle window, see if I can see more."

Stickman was thoughtful for a minute. "He might spot you at the window. Listen, if he has wired our place he'll want both of us inside when he blows it ... The truck's pretty dirty. One of us can stay outside, give it a wash. The other gets tools and goes inside to flip on a few lights, then crawl under the trailer to see if we've got a problem. What think?"

"You know how I like tools. If everything goes up, chances are you'll buy it, too."

"I'll try to keep the pickup between us," Stickman said, forcing a grin.

Within a few minutes Maple was taking loose two sheets of siding. He slipped into the dark space beneath the trailer and started toward the opposite side, Cornell's side. God, don't let there be a lot of spiders or a nest of snakes, he said through clenched teeth. Fuck, how they scare me. With late afternoon shadows lengthening, he hoped the flashlight wouldn't cast a glow Cornell could see. Directing the beam behind him, Maple still had enough light to crawl toward the trailer's midpoint. There, he estimated, he would intersect with the cord – or shadow.

He saw a gap in the siding as he approached the opposite side. A sliver of light danced through dust particles. The gap could have been there a long time. He snapped off his flashlight and crawled toward the light, his head brushed something soft. Fuck, a spider web. He hastily reached to brush it off, and found an electrical cord in his hand. Oh my God. Now I wish I'd been wrong about the line, the shadow. Maybe I'm still wrong. Maybe this has been here forever. He followed the cord toward Cornell's side of the trailer, to confirm where it was coming from, before tracking down where it went. A few inches from the siding the electrical cord went down, to ground level. Shit. This is starting to look real.

Maple pulled out heavy electrical pliers and put the teeth to the cord, then paused. Depending on the wiring, if there is a bomb, making this cut could be the last thing I do. He removed the pliers, knowing he must backtrack and learn what, if anything, the electrical cord was wired to. He wiggled the piece of loose siding and was able to move it almost back into place, virtually cutting off the sliver of light. As he did, gray and black checkerboard images of slaughter suddenly played before his eyes. The tour bus and burning cars and the school bus. He shook his head violently but the images fought him, abruptly going to fast forward. Just hallucinating. It will pass. Don't let it turn to color, he said in almost a prayer. The checkerboard started breaking up and he reached for the flashlight. Where was it? It couldn't be gone, you dumb fuck, it just isn't where you thought it was, where you so carefully put it before moving the siding. Fuck, how do I get out of here? The tiny sliver of light beckoned. No, not that way, Cornell will see. Calm down, calm down. He reached to the other side, finding the welcome torch, flipping it on.

Maple stretched out on his back and forced himself to take deep slow breaths, turning the beam nearly full in his face. He ignored the danger of a glow being visible through the siding, basking in the comforting light. Better. That's better. The checkerboard had disappeared entirely. He waited for it to reappear, but it did not. He reversed direction, following the electrical cord back to the center of the trailer, where it split. Oh oh, this is getting more complicated. There may be explosives at two points, perhaps equidistance from the front and rear of the sixty-foot trailer. He chose the branch to the left, toward the back of the trailer. He did not have to go far. His beam played on a package, tucked into the frame of the trailer. Four sticks of dynamite. They sagged beneath the flooring, sloppily roped in place. That's Cornell's kind of job. Maple found himself shaking his head and giggled, feeling less tension. What a loser this guy is.

The wiring appeared straight forward, which should allow him to cut the connections without setting off what he assumed was a second charge on the branch going toward the front of the trailer. But he wasn't sure. He laid back on the cool ground. Clearly, his first priority was checking out the other split. He crawled forward and was not surprised to find another badly tied bundle of dynamite, this one with three sticks. That must have wiped out Cornell's supply. But together, the two bundles would be more than enough to turn the trailer into kindling and aluminum strips, leave little more than DNA samples of anyone inside. Maple crawled into the fading sunlight. "You've got to get back," he told Stickman. "The trailer is wired, three sticks of dynamite at this end, four at the other. I think I can cut them without blowing anything, but I can't be positive."

"We can just run for it."

"If we do Cornell will call us in to claim the rewards."

"So we cut the explosives, then what?"

"We take out the asshole and move on. Where, we'll have to figure out."

"So why not just take out Cornell?"

"Dammit, Stickman, where'd you leave your smarts? If we don't cut the explosives and he sees us coming he'll blow the trailer, trying to get us but mostly to attract attention. Then we've got to kill him and try to get to the Banks before they can call 911. If they don't hear the explosion and call, a neighbor likely will. The wiring looks simple. I don't think it will blow if I cut it. That's not one hundred percent, but that's what I think. Then we take Cornell out and move on. It may be days before the Banks notice we're gone."

Stickman was a bit taken aback by Maple's passion, but didn't argue. He had to agree that if Cornell blew the trailer the yard would soon be crawling with cops. He moved the truck as if to better wash one side, putting a little more precious distance between himself and the trailer.

Maple focused the flashlight on how Cornell had wired the four-stick bundle. Might as well give Stickman a break and start as far away as possible, he thought. Besides, someone would need to wipe out that boney piss ant. Let's get this over with, he declared, positioning the pliers. He shut his eyes tightly, as if that would shield him, and squeezed the handles. Click. He opened his eyes, feeling foolish, but broke into a private, ear-to-ear grin. Eyes wide open in exaggeration and still grinning, he positioned the pliers on the second wire. Click. With a penknife he sawed quickly through the light rope and pulled the dynamite free.

Then he had an idea. Stripping several inches of plastic insulation from one of the wires he had clipped, Maple fed the bare strand through a hole in the trailer's metal frame. He looped the wire through the hole a second and then a third time before tying it off with the second wire. Moving to the front end of the trailer, he quickly disabled the three sticks of dynamite and again stripped one wire of insulation and rewired it into the metal frame.

Maple crawled from beneath the trailer with both packets of dynamite, setting them upright like booty of war on the trailer steps, in the dried print of Cornell's boot. Stickman had remained in easy view of the neighboring trailer, pretty certain Cornell was watching. Now, he walked to the steps.

With a fist bump, Maple declared, "I'm ready to test your theory that Cornell wants both of us in the trailer when he hits the button."

Chapter 45

Cornell, still in a sweat, watched as Maple and Stickman walked to the hydrant. Watched as they talked and drank from the same tin cup that hung on a wire hook. Sitting on his lumpy bed at his bedroom window, Cornell balanced his nearly empty can of beer precariously on a bare pillow. He was angry and getting very nervous. Come on, dammit, quit your yammering and get inside the damn trailer. He grabbed his beer and used the pillow to wipe sweat from his face. Draining the beer, and seeing his neighbors were still talking, he walked to the refrigerator in the kitchen, taking comfort in the loaded, automatic 12-guage shotgun propped against the living room door.

Back at the window he swore at the air-conditioner that couldn't keep up. His impatience grew. Stickman and Maple continued to talk. Their conversation appeared very casual, neither particularly engaged beyond an occasional smile. Sometimes one of them seemed to look his way, as would be expected, but that caused Cornell to lean away from the window, deeper into the shadows. "Hell, you can't see in," he said, disgusted with himself. "Damn you guys!" He shushed himself, watching them closely to make sure he hadn't been overheard. "Don't you know you need to go inside?" he continued in a near-whisper. "I have important freakin' work going on here. Don't you know I am remaking history here?"

The two men began moving toward their trailer, still chatting as they slowly did a two-step shuffle. Cornell took heart. "I'll drink to that, I'll drink to that, I'll drink to that," he chanted softly as they finally neared the corner of the trailer, shooing them on with his hands, slopping beer from the can. "I'll drink to that." Then they were out of sight and Cornell was smiling. Now we're cooking. But long minutes passed as he watched intently for a light to come on or go off. Anything to let him know they were inside. Now the waiting was worse than when he could see them, when he knew what they were doing. "They have to be inside. Don't they? I mean, where else can they be? That's the only resolution you can draw."

Cornell thought about going over to see them. Opening the refrigerator for another beer, he could see himself on their front steps, where his muddy shoes had left tracks. They were suspicious, true. That was not good. But he would explain about being out of beer and even though they didn't drink much he was just wondering if maybe they had a six-pack. Even if they didn't he could confirm that both were inside. That would be all he needed to go back to his place and blow them to hell. Then their treatment of him, their suspicion when he returned from work roared back at him. How he had broken out in a cold sweat as he was caught lying, how he always said the wrong thing, how they had looked at him. That was all too scary. No. I can't go over there. "If I don't see some activity within exactly two minutes I'm going to blow that trailer to hell," he said decisively. The confident sound of his voice made him feel in command, even with sweat running in his eyes. An igniter with a toggle switch was wired to a heavy duty 12-volt battery. Attached to the battery was an electrical cord that disappeared through a hole Cornell had drilled in the bedroom floor. The same electrical cord made its roughly buried way purposely across the lawn.

The igniter shook slightly in Cornell's hand as he silently counted down the time with each tick of the second hand on his watch. Thirty seconds. Fifteen. At five seconds he started counting aloud. Four, three, two, one. His thumb froze on the switch. He couldn't move it. He stared in disgust. No excuse came to mind. "Come on, you son of a bitch. It's time to show what you're made of, that you've got grift. Just like in the John Wayne movie. Now, Cornell, count from ten." He got to "one," sucked in a deep breath, and his thumb worked. The toggle switch clicked. He stared at the trailer. Nothing. No explosion. No siding and metal and lumber flying. No fire. Silence stared back. Cornell madly flipped the switch, over and over. He grabbed the electrical cord, shaking it to ensure the connection to the battery was tight. It was. He slumped back, exhausted from strain. What to do?

Waiting at the corner of their trailer, Maple and Stickman heard sparking sounds coming from under the trailer, from where bare wires were laced through holes in the metal frame. The sparks sent the two men sprinting toward Cornell's trailer just as he glanced out the window. "Oh shit!" he shrieked as they disappeared from sight, hell-bent for his front door. Dropping the igniter he lunged toward the living room, his right foot catching on the cord between the battery and the hole in the floor. He sprawled full length. Desperately leaping to his feet, Cornell dashed for the shotgun. The unlocked door burst open and the 12-guage bounced off a straight-back chair. A load of No. 2 shot ripped past Cornell's face and into the ceiling. Cornell didn't miss a step, charging Maple in the doorway, but took an abrupt dive as a Glock slammed across the side of his face. Maple pulled a dazed Cornell to his feet so Stickman could close the door. He too held a Glock, in his left hand. "You are a foolish man."

Cornell tried to shake off the light show dancing in his eyes, tried to speak quickly. "Guys, we need to talk. Hurting me will be a bad thing." Stickman casually stepped forward as Cornell continued his plea, "The rent money ..." He went silent as the pick entered his heart. Maple let him slide to the floor, flat on his back.

"He won't bleed out much," said Stickman.

In the trailer they found travel brochures on a desk. Several were for safaris in Africa, one for three weeks with the price circled and a scrawled note, "5g premum for late reservatshun."

"Cornell was going to go first class from the price on our heads," Stickman said.

"How should we get rid of him?"

"I don't like the idea of driving in and out after dark to one of our river spots. How about we haul him out back and bury him?"

"Sounds good to me."

Wilbur watched them leave the trailer. "Huh, didn't see them go in. Maybe they and Cornell shared a brew."

That didn't sound right even as he said it. He didn't know of Alexander or Demetri ever drinking or visiting Cornell. He returned to the television and one of the never ending reports on the interstate terrorist attacks. No more had he settled in his chair than the photos, speculative of course, of the killers wanted in the months-ago attack on the Russian Embassy filled the screen.

Banks stared hard. Damn them eyes, he told himself, thinking of a popular torch song. But when Violet joined him, he said nothing. Being told he was wrong was getting tiresome.

Maple planted himself in a lounge chair in the shadows at the corner of Cornell's trailer. He watched as the lights went off in the Banks' house, leaving a glow that soon disappeared, too. He walked back to get the sleeping Stickman. Wrapping Cornell in a canvas tarp, and using an aluminum cot as a stretcher, they carried his body through the small clearing where Maple had killed April. Another fifty yards into the woods, Maple started digging while Stickman returned to the yard as a lookout. They switched jobs once before covering Cornell and returning to the trailer.

"He really was one dumb fuck, wasn't he?"

"Dumb and blind with greed," answered Stickman, pouring hot tea.

"Okay, what's next."

Stickman was quiet for a long time. "So we believe Cornell made us. If he had been blabbing to his barfly buddies, the sheriff would have been out here already. No one else around here would have a clue to us except maybe the Banks. So far, no reason to think they're on to us. We can sit tight for a while or we can move on. Let's sleep on it."

Stickman did, but Maple battled another sleepless night, revisiting over and over the interstate mayhem and his role in it. Role? That's a funny word for killing people, even as a soldier. Whether he closed his eyes or looked into the darkness, it was all there, black and white or in color, vivid or in that crazy checkerboard pattern. The children in silhouette as he fired and then the burning school bus, the flames, the smoke. The silhouettes went away, leaving just the husk of the bus and the flames and the smoke. My God, everything is playing in greater detail now. There should be less detail as time passes. He wondered how long a person could live without sleep, how much longer he would be able to be a soldier. His horror show was so tiring. There had been no fatigue after attacking the embassy. He had watched that carnage on television and it didn't mess up his mind. That must be the difference, it being on television and not seeing everything up close, in real time like he had the interstate attack. Everything was getting more confusing, too, seeing the killing grounds and dodging the law and worrying about who might suspect them. Everything ran together, making it harder to understand what he had done or why or what he needed to do now. Maple felt unhinged, knowing most of all that he was terribly weary, that his mind was dysfunctional. Finally, the dawn brought some relief, invading the darkness of his mind and mercifully pushing back the never-ending replay of the slaughter. Pushing it back or into a corner, but not pushing it out. Out, totally out, apparently was not an option. He groaned as he swung out of bed, padded barefoot to the living room to see what new offerings television had.

Chapter 46

They talked over breakfast. More accurately, Stickman talked. The strain of carrying out the interstate massacre and two long nights without sleep had left Maple's mind fuzzy, struggling to engage. When Stickman said they should stay put for at least a few days, Maple agreed readily, welcoming the time to take a long run in hopes of a strenuous workout restoring clarity.

The day passed slowly. Stickman read and watched television, flipping the channels in search of information. TV and reading could not hold Maple's attention. He could not sleep or even close his eyes without again being visited by troubling images. In the afternoon he took his much-needed run.

Noodling all that had happened with Cornell, Stickman felt uneasy, gnawed by a sense of something gone missing. He thought about Maple's discovery of the explosives, their mad run to Cornell's trailer, his futile resistance. Something doesn't fit, Stickman told himself. Doesn't fit or is missing. Cornell had said something ... something about "the rent." What a strange thing to say as he faced death. Then it hit – Wilbur and Violet expect his rent to be paid. If it's not, someone will come to collect. So what? Get rid of the van and say you don't know where Cornell went. But maybe he meant something more, that something might happen if the rent was not paid. He had fingered us, of that we're confident. What if he shared his suspicions, told the

Banks? Maybe told them to call the cops if he didn't show up with the rent? Maybe that's what he started to say. Should have heard him out. If that's where he was going, it must be dealt with. Ignoring that possibility is too risky. Stickman forced himself to slow down, to walk through things again. He desperately tried to remember when Cornell moved in. Had to be right after the trip to New Jersey because they were covering up Maple being shot by claiming he was too sick to meet Cornell. The New Jersey trip was early in the month, like now, so Cornell's rent is due or shortly will be. It can't just be put in the Banks' mailbox. If Cornell wanted insurance, no doubt he promised to come by. No choice, Stickman thought with cold detachment, we have to get rid of the old farts. And they know too many people to not be missed soon. That means we have to run, too, and soon.

When Maple returned, Stickman had already loaded most of the remaining munitions into the pickup. Still in the trailer were a rocket launcher and the remaining rounds, attack rifles and handguns – a potent arsenal should it be needed before they got out.

After recounting Cornell's last words, Stickman added his interpretation. "Could be," agreed Maple. "Can't think of a better way to look at it."

"It's going to take an hour, probably more to finish packing. We should park the pickup down by the creek as an escape hatch. That's an easy run for us if something happens here."

Maple nodded.

"There's something else," Stickman said. "We have to get rid of Wilbur and Violet."

Maple inhaled sharply. "Why?"

"Why? So they can't call the law, of course, and to buy us more time. We can leave them in Cornell's van. Until he's found, he'll be blamed for the Banks."

Reluctantly, Maple nodded again. Any value from his run was gone. Already he was fearful of being assaulted by yet another round of haunting images.

Wilbur watched the pickup pull slowly out the driveway, followed by Cornell's van. It looked like just one person in each vehicle, but he wasn't sure. Never seen them leave together before, he thought.

Yet another TV story about the interstate attacks came on, complete with photos of the embassy and mall suspects. Wilbur peered at them intently, his mouth clamped shut. I've waited long enough, he told himself, turning down the volume and reaching for the phone. Violet was in the kitchen. This may be my only chance for a while. I really think she would grab the phone from me, or try.

"Hi, Wilbur," he said when Sheriff Martin came on the line.

"Hello yourself, Wilbur."

"How's your vacuuming going?"

"It's going fine," the sheriff kindly told his friend of more than forty years.

Wilbur Martin had come to the county as a young man. He convinced the sheriff to make him a deputy and quickly moved up to detective sergeant. In fact, that made him the only detective on the small force. Over the years he came to know more intimate details about more people in the county than probably anyone. Every time tragedy visited or someone became a crime victim, the investigation fell to Wilbur Martin. He handled that knowledge with the discretion he would appreciate were roles reversed. Those involved came to trust him as they might a priest. They shared their opinion of Wilbur with friends. When his boss decided to retire, he ran for sheriff and won easily–as he had now for nearly three decades.

"Wilbur, I think we may have a situation out here," said the older man, fighting to stay calm.

"Really? Tell me."

Banks listened for Violet, heard her moving about in the kitchen, then hurried on. "There are two young guys, I'd say in their thirties, rentin' one of our trailers, the one farthest from the house. They seem nice enough, I want to make that clear, but I think they look like the suspects from the attack on Russia's embassy, the ones who are back on the TV all the time since all those people were killed up near St. Louis." He heard Martin draw in his breath, his big feet drop from his desktop to the floor.

"My God. That's a hell of a thing to say, Wilbur."

"It's what I think, Wilbur. So does Cornell, the renter who lives in the other trailer."

"My God. What does Violet think?"

"She thinks I'm wrong, but that's not unusual."

There was a long pause and Wilbur knew what the sheriff was thinking–Violet is sharp as a tack and I'm, well, losing it a little. Maybe more than a little. He left the silence alone.

"Wilbur, is there anything else?"

"Yes, there is, Wilbur. As I said, the guy livin' in the trailer nearest us thinks the same as me. He told us to call you if he didn't pay his rent on time and it's due today. I know the day's not over, and I'm not worried about the money, but he hasn't been by. There's somethin' else. I saw Alexander and Demetri come out of Cornell's trailer last evening and a little bit ago their pickup and Cornell's van left together. At least at the same time. Never seen either of those things happen before. As far as I know, Cornell's not close with those boys.

" ...Hey, Cornell's van is pullin' back in the drive. I don't see the pickup. It looks like two people are in the van. When they left I thought I saw one in the van and one in the pickup. Cornell should be at work, far as I know. Something's wrong here."

Violet, your husband and this Cornell fellow have you outvoted, the sheriff muttered to himself. "Wilbur, do you know the last names of your renters, Alexander and Demetri, right?"

"Right. No, not off the top of my head. I could get them from the book, but it's in the kitchen and Violet would catch me."

"Okay, Wilbur. I want you to do two things. Put Violet on the phone, and lock your doors. Wait, a third thing – load your old 12-guage. If anyone breaks in before I get there, shoot 'em. Got it?"

"Okay, Wilbur, but Violet is gonna be mad as hell ... Violet! Come in here, please. Wilbur's on the phone for you."

Wilbur watched the van drive to the trailers, then completely out of sight beyond the far one. Strange, haven't seen that before, either. As he handed Violet the phone he wished he could get out of sight, too.

Stickman and Maple went inside to quickly finish packing. They needed to take everything they didn't mind leaving behind. That meant opening hiding spaces to retrieve IDs and their considerable cash. "Let's grab the fishing tackle, Mr. Stick. That's been a good cover."

Ready to run, they locked the trailer and headed for the Banks' house. Stickman felt the pick tucked into the back of his trousers as he quietly tried the door. It was locked. He knocked. No answer. Inside, Wilbur had seen the doorknob turn. He was on one knee behind a sofa, aiming the heavy 12-gauge double-barrell at the door. Violet was in the hallway, watching Wilbur with frightened pride from her perch on the edge of a straight-back chair. She, too, had seen the doorknob turn before someone knocked.

With growing alarm she saw her husband's arms begin to shake from holding the firing position too long. "Call Wilbur," he said quietly, voice trembling. "Tell him we have unwanted visitors."

Violet was repeatedly dialing the sheriff's number and had only to push the talk button. "He says he's almost here, to start talkin' to them if you can."

Stickman pounded again, heard a voice inside say, "Who is it?"

"Demetri and Alexander. Your renters from the far trailer."

"You'll have to give us a few minutes. We aren't ...ah ...presentable."

"Neither of you?"

"Nope. Neither one," Wilbur answered, concerned that he sounded too close to the front door. "I need to go back to get in my clothes."

Stickman turned with a grin. "We must have interrupted a little geriatric amour. Who would have thought?"

Believing he had bought time, Wilbur rested the 12-guage on the back of the sofa and stood up, his gnarled finger still in the trigger guard. Lordy, that feels good. Minutes passed.

"Hey, Mr. Banks. Can you let us get ahead on the rent? We want to take care of you so we can take a little road trip."

Really don't want us taken care of, Wilbur thought, painfully lowering himself to a knee and again bringing the shotgun to bear. Then aloud, "'Preciate it, fellas. Be there in just a couple minutes."

"Violet," Wilbur said as his right knee suddenly began shaking, "where the fuck is Wilbur?"

"Don't use such language, Wilbur," she angrily whispered back. "How the fuck would ...how would I know?"

"Isn't he on the line?"

"Well, he may be ... Wilbur, are you on the fu ...are you on the line?"

"Yes, Violet, we're about to turn in at your place."

"What think?" Stickman asked. "Want to kick it in?"

Before Maple could answer he heard an engine and tires on gravel and turned to see a black sedan pulling in the driveway. It stopped, waited, as if the driver was uncertain of the address. Seconds passed and the car didn't move.

"I don't know what's going on here," Stickman said, "but I'd feel better pulling back to let things settle down."

"Okay."

"Sorry to have bothered you, Mr. Banks. We'll catch you later."

They were nearly back to the trailer when the sedan finally moved. The driver gave a friendly wave as he turned toward the Banks' house. Maple waved back.

"More shit going on around here than we've had in months. I don't like it." They got out as the sedan pulled from sight.

When the sheriff and his long-time detective sergeant, Henry Lewis, both in plain clothes, climbed from the car, Wilbur threw open the front door.

"Hello Violet, Wilbur. You're coming with us. And get shoes on, Wilbur," the sheriff said with mock exasperation. "Were you going to shoot someone in your stocking feet?"

"Wilbur Martin, I just can't believe you and Wilbur," fumed Violet. "Callin' in the cavalry on the say-so of my poor husband and a guy hungry for a reward."

"Give it up, Mother. Did you see him try to open the door before he knocked? They were up to no good."

"Hurry now, Violet. It's done, and it's not just me and my boys. I talked to the FBI field office in Pittsburgh and they're on their way out here. I'm concerned about them sending helicopters that get too close, tip these guys off, if they are terrorists. That new special agent in charge is way too young. Come on now, I want to get you two out of here."

The officers walked Wilbur and Violet to the unmarked sedan, the sheriff's personal car. It eased into view for Stickman and Maple, standing near the water hydrant. "Can't be positive but I think someone is in the back seat."

"Me, too," said Stickman. "Let's give them a bit and then swing by the house on our way out just to make sure. And to take care of business if we're wrong."

The house was locked and this time no one answered Stickman's knock. "That was no social call," Stickman scowled. "Gone way too fast."

Maple was relieved.

As they turned right onto the road, toward the creek, they saw a patrol car perhaps a quarter-mile away. Three officers stood outside. Maple stopped the van. In the rearview mirror he saw another patrol car and several more officers.

"Shit. This van couldn't outrun Violet," said Maple. "Let's get back to the trailer."

Driving slowly up the lane, Maple thought he heard the steady mechanical thumping of a helicopter. "Hear that?"

"What?"

"A helicopter, maybe. If it is, the sheriff has already called in the state police, or maybe the FBI."

Stickman started to again say he didn't hear anything when a helicopter cleared the forested horizon to the west, moving slowly toward them. "You're right."

They were nearly back to the trailer when the two patrol cars pulled into the driveway and stopped. Officers armed with assault rifles piled out, now wearing SWAT team helmets and protective vests. Covering for each other, they worked their way up the lane as far as the turnoff to the Banks' house. There they spread out, taking defensive positions behind the mature oaks and maples. The helicopter began a slow circle of the Banks' property, staying at what the pilot considered a safe distance.

"They don't seem to be in any hurry," said Stickman. "Haven't even told us to surrender."

"I imagine they're waiting for reinforcements."

"Likely. The helicopter's probably out of Pittsburgh with backup half an hour or so behind. By then it may be dusk. Maybe we can slip out of here."

They went to the trailer, Maple for the rocket launcher and four remaining rounds, Stickman for two assault rifles and ammunition. To his belt he added his beloved ice pick in a snap-on sheath. Maple angled the van back toward the trailer from one corner of the water hydrant, creating a good visual but porous defense. Far more substantial was the four-by-four-foot concrete base holding the water hydrant. The concrete stood more than a foot high – enough to give good cover to a prone man.

Stickman and Maple waited tensely as the sun inched down, all too slowly.

Chapter 47

Junior Weems, the FBI's special agent in charge of the Pittsburgh office, had emphatically ordered the pilot of the forward helicopter to stay far enough from the Banks' property to avoid detection. The pilot, one Wilson Smart, was monitoring radio traffic for the operation as he approached by way of the valley to the northwest. When the sheriff's men moved into position, Smart decided to join the action in case the suspected terrorists ran.

Weems was furious. It was one thing for the sheriff's deputies to move in. They had, after all, been revealed when the terrorists started to leave. But the helicopter's appearance signaled a much bigger operation. The operation was, in fact, potentially huge. As Weems flew to the site, he made radio contact with his superiors and joined the debate over mobilizing enough National Guardsmen to create a virtually escape-proof perimeter. Apprehending the ringleaders of the three worst attacks on American soil since 9/11 was easy justification for throwing such an overwhelming force against only two men. But the uncertainty over whether these were indeed the terrorists sought nationwide gave the bureaucrats pause. Identifying the terrorists turned on the beliefs of an old man suffering from Alzheimer's and a hard drinker who had dropped out of sight. If wrong, the federal officials' misjudgment would be the butt of cartoons and late night comedy for weeks, a national embarrassment of the first order. Avoiding blame was a cardinal rule for any good bureaucrat.

Already, about one hundred SWAT officers were being helicoptered to the scene. They included sniper teams that could attack from aloft or drop into ground positions. Weems also had called for half a dozen officers expert with rocket launchers, seeing delicious payback in killing the terrorists with an RPG.

The special agent stifled his anger as his helicopter and others carrying SWAT teams came within sight of the trailers. No reason for stealth now. The men the sheriff had identified only as Alexander and Demetri no longer had any doubt they were facing an overwhelming force. Even so, the helicopters settled on the road leading to the property, well out of range and sight of Stickman and Maple. SWAT teams ran in a low crouch up the lane to bolster positions of the sheriff's men north and east of the trailer and expand the east perimeter south of the Banks' house. By now, other teams had been dropped in clearings about a half-mile away. They would move in through the woods, blocking escape to the west and south. But, thought Weems, with darkness approaching, finding their way across unfamiliar, rough terrain will take time, perhaps too much time. He worried about the terrorists slipping away in the gloaming, through woods they have had time to know well.

That exact scenario was foremost in Stickman's mind, too, when Weems decided there was nothing to lose by demanding surrender.

"You men, this is Special Agent Weems of the FBI. You have been identified as suspects in acts of terrorism against the United States. You are surrounded by an overwhelming force. Put down your weapons and surrender. You will not be harmed. If innocent, you will be released."

Sweat popped out on Stickman's forehead. He had always known things could come to this, but had never methodically outlined how he would react. Until now, his response always had been to attack or run. Now, if the FBI agent was believable, the option of attack was gone. That left running, and he could see no clear path. He wondered if the

FBI agent was overplaying his hand. He had not heard or seen any activity to the south – the direction of the pickup – or to the west.

"What think, Maple?" he asked from the end of the van nearest the trailer.

"Not yet," came Maple's response from near the water hydrant. "They'd spot us trying to slip out for sure. I think we'll have a better chance when it's dark, even if they've had time to move in. Maybe in half an hour..."

"Have you heard anyone to the south or west?"

"No. That FBI guy could be bluffing. Maybe his troops haven't got here yet."

"I don't think they have. That's why the ones out there now are sitting tight. They're waiting for the rest. But we have to wait until it's darker."

Even with adrenaline pumping, Maple felt surprisingly detached. He wondered if that was another sign of exhaustion, then wondered anew why the hell he was playing doctor at a time like this. The rocket launcher in his hands fed a growing appetite. It gave him comfort, a sense of strength. But stronger was his wish for something to happen. His urge to fire on the government – sheriff's deputies, feds, he didn't care – was so intense he had lost his fear. "I want, really want that fucking helicopter to close in and hover," he said, almost pleading.

Stickman cast an uneasy glance. "That's fine, my friend, but more important is getting out of here. Ten minutes and we could be at the pickup, then get to the interstate and slip into traffic."

Maple's priorities were shifting. He shook his head stubbornly. "I want these fuckers to suffer. I need to use these rounds, and I don't think I can make the run with the launcher. It would slow me down too much."

"Leave it, don't matter if you knock out another pig or two." Stickman was surprised at his words. He was not a child of the Sixties. Mostly, he worried that Maple was starting to come unglued. "Who cares if all the rounds get used?"

"It matters to me," said Maple. He closed his eyes for just a second to gather himself and immediately was beset by the horrific images, images that now could haunt him in the blink of an eye. They were almost always stark, seldom filtered. The gray and black ones tormented him enough, but then cruelly gave way to vivid Technicolor.

Still not a shot fired. The FBI was clearly waiting for greater advantage, the upside being that the noose had yet to fully tighten. Stickman willed the dusk to darken faster.

A bullhorn broke into Maple's ricocheting thoughts, adding the disjointed observation that bullhorns must still be the amplifier of choice in police standoffs. But hasn't technology ...

"You men, Alexander and Demetri. This is Special Agent Weems again. Your situation is hopeless. You know that. There is no reason for bloodshed. I urge you to surrender. You have my word that you will not be harmed."

As Weems' voice crackled eerily, Maple peeked over the concrete slab and spotted motion. Three, no four crouched officers, cautiously moving up, from one tree to the next. "Not be harmed, my ass. I'm going to up the fucking body count."

"Wait Maple, just wait," he heard Stickman say. "Firing now could set off a shit storm. Settle down, man, it's almost dark enough to get out of here."

Maple paused briefly, but the advancing men won him over. He sighted in at a center point of the four lawmen and was surprised when the one in the lead rose from his crouch and sauntered forward, apparently believing he was protected by a huge red oak. Following his lead the other three men stood upright, too. "Here we go, Mr. Stick."

"Wait, Maple. I think we can lea ..."

The rocket's roar drowned out Stickman. The SWAT officers flew from sight, maybe dead, maybe just momentarily lost in the dust and debris of the exploding RPG. But Stickman was right. A shit storm came at them with a vengeance, some SWAT officers firing with abandon as those better trained laid down cover for others scooting forward. Maple dropped to a fetal position behind the water hydrant's protective base. He forced his eyes to stay open even as the hail of bullets sent chips of concrete spitting from the slab, opening superficial wounds on his face and arms. Stickman fared better, if only because most of the return gunfire zeroed in on the location of the rocket launcher, at Maple. Even so, shattered glass from the van's windows also hailed on Stickman as he hugged a depression in the ground. Bullets riddled the van's tires.

As the return fire subsided, Stickman eased around the van's bumper to see two men moving forward from Cornell's trailer. Bringing his assault rifle to bear, he fired once. One man went down and the second retreated. He scooted to the opposite end of the van, drawing fire.

"You okay, Maple?"

"I'm hit, man, bad. You get the hell out of here."

"Still too light. Do sunsets always take this freaking long?"

In the eerie silence, the helicopter piloted by Wilson Smart, hovering out of range, could be heard revving up, moving closer. Suddenly it was above the northwest tree line. Maple, ignoring the wounds he had exaggerated, took aim, but did not fire. The shot was too long. He was startled when a rocket was launched from the copter and, as if to make his point, landed harmlessly short. But it had acted as a range finder and Smart, emboldened by that information, moved in as his shooter reloaded. Smart moved too fast, before his shooter was ready, and it was Maple who squeezed off the next round, uncertain he had waited long enough. He had – and the helicopter exploded in a ball of fire before making an ungainly, tumbling descent to the ground, blades churning.

Retaliation was intense. Within seconds the darkening sky was alive with copters, a sure sign they had made their drops to the south and west – perhaps some time ago. SWAT teams could be within minutes of having the Banks' property surrounded.

The copters hung at the fringe of what pilots perceived to be Maple's accurate range. Then, on command, one would sweep over at high altitude, sharpshooters seeking targets. Exposed at the corner of the van, Stickman quickly crawled beneath the trailer. There he was only a random target, hidden somewhere within the trailer's large outline. In its deepening shadow he had a better vantage point for spotting SWAT officers on the ground. As another helicopter swept overhead, he saw movement at the far corner of Cornell's trailer and fired a burst. No more movement, at least for the moment.

At the same time, Maple was scrambling around the concrete slab, corner to corner in a dance choreographed by the next helicopter's line of attack. The air game was at an impasse, helicopters too high for Maple to risk wasting a shot, also too high for their snipers to be effective. But, he realized soberly, it was only a matter of time – likely not much time – until Special Agent Weems put another rocket launcher in therotation.

A pilot, seeking better advantage for his sharpshooters, dropped suddenly in altitude. Waiting hopefully for that to happen, Maple was ready, rising to his knees as the helicopter nearly slowed to a hover. He fired quickly. The rocket found its target, again creating a fireball and this time crumbling in pieces, two of them looking like flaming bodies. Maple quickly dropped behind his concrete sanctuary as ground fire raked the hydrant's base, more chips adding to his stinging wounds.

"Mr. Stick," he called softly, "I'm hit again. You get out of here now. It's plenty dark."

"No. I'll give you cover and you get over here. We'll go together."

"Can't make it, man. You go now."

"No! We're running together, mon, or we're not running."

Maple reloaded. His last rocket, this one anti-tank. He heard Stickman firing steadily behind him as he watched for another helicopter to make a run. There was a pause as Stickman slapped in a fresh clip, or switched to his other assault rifle, then the deadly bursts resumed. Maple could see shapes moving swiftly in the dim light, bursts of gunfire as more SWAT officers found the protection of Cornell's trailer, Stickman answering their fire. Maple put down his launcher and grabbed an assault rifle, triggering a long burst until return fire had him again hugging the slab. Another thought swept by: We should have wired fucking loser's trailer to greet the feds, using Cornell's explosives, of course. The chatter of Stickman's assault rifle intruded on his weird musing, hurried him back to the firefight. Shadows moved toward him from Cornell's trailer, accompanied by lighted bursts of gunfire, punctuating the near-dark. Stickman opened fire and Maple rose to create an M-16 duet. The chatter was lovely, deadly. The advancing bursts went silent, and Maple was startled to hear he alone was firing. A funereal sensation swept over him.

A flare and then a second and a third draped a shadowy blue-gray light all around him. Another helicopter began its run from the northwest, coming in just above the tree line. Maple waited as it foolishly came at him full speed, the sharpshooters losing any chance of a clear shot. Maple rose to his knees, weighing whether to unleash the antitank rocket, his last, on a target moving so fast. He tried to gather the copter in his sights. There was a blast from near a maple tree along the lane. In the fading light of the flares, the RPG, like many he had fired with devastating effect, ripped into the side of his chest and exploded.

Epilogue

By dawn the FBI had organized a search for Cornell. It took less than an hour to find his shallow grave. His rent money was in a shirt pocket.

A few days later, human remains were found on a bank of the Youghiogheny River, a few miles downstream from the Banks' property. The medical examiner determined the body was that of a woman. Remnants of trash bags were roped around her. Much of her head was gone, perhaps from being battered by floating trees or other river flotsam. Pieces of dental work were recovered and eventually linked inconclusively to that of an April Spring, whose last known address was one of the Banks' rental trailers. Several feet of frayed rope tied around her waist suggested her body may have been weighted down and dumped in the Youghiogheny. There was little sign of the body being preyed upon by birds or mammals, suggesting it had floated from its watery grave only recently.

Violet and Wilbur Banks had their fifteen minutes of fame. Violet hated the press conference and resisted going on subsequent talk shows. Wilbur, who loved the limelight, implored her to join him. "This is a bigger deal than even the Hoover Dam award I got from President Roosevelt." She finally relented. Talk show hosts loved the elderly couple's honesty, especially when she admitted to swearing in frustration at Wilbur and when the sheriff and Wilbur admitted they hated to anger Violet. Wilbur offered to show some interviewers his pin collection, but no one was interested. Sean Hannity had a totally baffled look when Wilbur asked him, "How's your vacuuming going?"

The terrorists' trailer was dismantled, literally piece by piece. Found in a furnace vent was a key to a safe-deposit box in a Rockville, Maryland bank. The key was the only personal item of consequence in the trailer, causing investigators to wonder if it had been left behind purposely. When FBI agents opened the box they found irrefutable evidence of the numerous acts of terrorism Stickman and Maple had committed before their assault on the Russian Embassy. To underscore the need for the showdown on the Banks' property, and the importance of apprehending the homegrown terrorists, the evidence was released to the public immediately. The interstate, mall and embassy attacks had already thrown the news, entertainment and book industries into high gear. Interest soared to an absolute frenzy when the contents of the safe-deposit box were released.

Forensics officials spent most of two days, sometimes using broom rakes and sifters and vacuum cleaners, gathering scattered human remains found near the trailer. To definitively tie Maple and Stickman's DNA to that of Harrison Willford and Mitchell Applebaum – America's Public Enemy No. 1 – the remains and other DNA samples were sent to the FBI Laboratory at Marine Corps Base Quantico in Virginia. The other DNA samples included those collected inside the trailer and various vehicles, among them a Ford F-150 pickup parked about a half-mile south of the Banks' property.

A positive match was made between Willford's DNA and the body parts. Positive matches also were made between DNA samples collected from the trailer and vehicles and those collected from crime scenes, including a motel room where the nude body of a grandmother was found wrapped in a shower curtain.

All of the body parts collected near the trailer shared the same DNA. Not a trace of Applebaum's DNA was found among those body parts. Stickman was missing.

Not Necessarily The End

Acknowledgments

Sincere thanks to friends and family for contributions that substantially improved *Blending In.* I am indebted for editorial guidance to good friends Al Leeds, former president and editorial director, Los Angeles Times-Washington Post News Service, and Judith Austin, former automotive editor, USA Today; my brother Joe Brewer of West Plains, Mo., coach and teacher at Koshkonong High School; and world-class spouse Judy and sons Matthew, of Coralville, Iowa, and David, of Portland, Ore. The cover design by Ann Youm Oh, a former colleague at the Transportation Security Administration, is terrific. The staff of Draft2Digital professionally demystified the self-publishing process. Thanks again to all.

About the Author

Norman Brewer is an award-winning reporter and editor who worked for The Des Moines Register and Tribune and for Gannett News Service in Washington, D.C. He was also Director of Employee Communications at the Transportation Security Administration in the U.S. Department of Homeland Security. He and Judy are retired in Bethesda, Md., a Washington suburb.

Don't miss out!

button below and you can sign up to receive emails whenev- orman Brewer publishes a new book. There's no charge and no obligation.

https://books2read.com/r/B-A-AVLE-GWWN

BOOKS 2 READ

Connecting independent readers to independent writers.